Charles Kennedy Scott is
This is his first novel.

[illegible] is twenty-five and lives in London.
This is [illegible] novel.

Low Alcohol

Charles Kennedy Scott

First published in 1997
by HEADLINE BOOK PUBLISHING

First published in paperback in 1997
by HEADLINE BOOK PUBLISHING

A REVIEW paperback

10 9 8 7 6 5 4 3 2 1

All characters in this publication are fictitious and any resemblance to real persons, living or dead, is purely coincidental.

ISBN 0 7472 5656 X

Typeset by
Letterpart Limited, Reigate, Surrey

Printed and bound in Great Britain by
Cox & Wyman Ltd, Reading, Berks

HEADLINE BOOK PUBLISHING
A division of Hodder Headline PLC
338 Euston Road
London NW1 3BH

For Emma

Part One

One

'You bastard,' said a voice.

Here we go, I thought.

I turned, I did my best to look angry, I attempted to look offensive, I tried to look frightening. But I failed, I always do. I just haven't got the face for it.

'You bastard,' said the girl. Then she walked into the shoe shop. The tiny dog followed her in.

I waited for a few seconds. This had all happened before. And it will happen again, and continue happening until she decides to stop calling me a bastard, until she decides to stop trailing me around London. Or until somebody else decides that she should stop.

I waited. My waiting had an expectant rhythm. This rhythm had its own passing of time, a time closely related to heartbeats – and my heartbeats are all over the place and out of sync, like some palpitating metronome.

There was a scream (the girl). There was a shout (the manager). And then, out she came. Limbs twisting, the tiny dog behind her, on its back, sliding. Out she came, thrown out. Out she came: the late-twenties girl, the girl with crepuscular makeover, the girl with dying eyes, those eyes – those *eyes*. The tiny dog rolled off its back, it sat, the fur purled back over its face, the eyes opened, the head clocked mechanically to one side. The dog was *tiny*.

'You bastard,' she said for the third time. 'Look what you've done to her! Poor little mite.' The tiny dog slumped on its tiny hind legs and glanced up. The girl looked at me. Those eyes stared. I couldn't stare back.

'You bastard.'

'*All right*! You've made your point. Why? Just tell me why.'

'Ooh, you *bastard*.'

'Fuck off,' I said, and walked away. She muttered after me, but I was gone. Her words were lost in space and time. And I never guessed what she might have said. She would never tell me.

I'm in a state these days – a suspended state. I'm sort of hovering expectantly. Expectant of what? I'm not really sure. But I think it might be something to do with the millennium. Something to do with the way time seems to slow up as we get closer to it. Yeah, that might be it: that big M at the top of the clock.

But, Jesus, I'm bored with the millennium. And we haven't got to it yet. Anyway, who knows, I might not even make it. That's a possibility with the way my time has decided to become more laborious, my time might just stop . . . And, as well as my problems with time, there is also the girl who keeps calling me a bastard: she might stop calling me a bastard and try to kill me. Or she might want to marry me, and *then* try to kill me.

Maybe I'll get run over by a bus: extremely possible, because my shoes keep failing and tripping me up in the vicinity of buses – I'm not sure yet, I haven't worked it out.

It's either London buses or my collapsing shoes that want me dead . . .

In the Smell of Leather I had addressed them with a new (for me) customer form: aggression. 'This is the last fucking time,' I started, and then, realizing that my voice was lost in the dark inner ears of eager shoes, I finished, 'that I take a bus.' Noticing that the shoe-server was laughing and clenching the sides of his leather waistcoat, I reaffirmed my delivery by saying, 'This is the last time that I will be coming here and therefore the last time I will ever trip on the bus steps because *these* –' I pointed at my failing footwear – 'fucking shoes keep falling to pieces.'

'Sir?'

'Yes.'

'Do you work with any solvents?'

'No.'

'Any hot liquids?'

'No.'

'In any hardware trade?'

'Excuse me? No.'

'Fair enough. We will exchange your shoes for another pair.'

'*No*.'

'Sorry?'

'I *want* –' I looked around the room for the sturdiest pair of shoes – 'THEM.'

'Yes, sir, you could have that pair –' he hesitated – 'if you pay the difference.'

'A straight swap.'

'But they're twice the price.'

'Good,' I agreed. 'They should last twice as long . . . *Two* weeks if I'm lucky!'

'Um . . . Er. You can have *my* shoes if you like.'

'MANAGER!' I said loudly.

The manager appeared from a heavily disguised orifice and strode towards me. Now here was a man who clearly had shoes on his mind. A man who had laces and toecaps and sizes dancing in his dreams – a man who knew shoes. Just shoes. Our eyes met with confrontation. As always.

'Mr Down,' he said. 'Hello.'

'Hi.'

'More problems?'

'Yes, I'm afraid so. The sole's coming off again. The left one this time.' I raised my foot and flicked it. The sole snapped against the remaining shoe like a crocodile. Bits of decayed leather fell to the floor. He flinched.

'An exchange?'

'I've already had six pairs in six weeks. No exchange. Not this time. I'll be taking that pair. And I won't be coming back.'

'Very well, Mr Down.'

I left the shoe shop in a vent of its leather breath. Outside I inhaled a gagging sample of a air – a mouthful of the air that gulps and pants around the city. Then I lit my last cigarette, my last *ever* cigarette. After this one, that's it. I'll have given up. I'll be in lung-recovery and withdrawal. My twenty-five-year-old lungs formulated a cough; they forced me to exhale. The smoke came back out, arranged itself in the air and then sank. It went at the pavement, drifting under the weight of all the other pollutants that quietly vie for London's airspace and TV news time.

And then, as I stood there, smoking my last cigarette, the girl with dying eyes called me a bastard – as she has to do every time she sees me. I have no idea why she does it . . .

And it's hardly fair, I'm not a bastard. At least, I don't think I am.

But hey, what do I care? Why should being called a bastard bother me? I've just got a new pair of shoes – boots. New footwear to replace the old – the *one* week old – and the failed.

And what trouble I've had with my shoes. I can't believe it, they're only *shoes* after all, but the trouble they've caused me. In the last six weeks I've had six pairs of shoes, that's a new pair every week. On Monday they're new, on Tuesday they're giving me blisters, on Wednesday I'm starting to break them in, on Thursday they break, on Friday I'm walking like a tramp, on Saturday I try to stay in, and on Sunday I'm planning a trip to the Smell of Leather.

So each week it's a new pair of shoes because one of them has broken. *One* of them. Never both. Never neither. Always one. If, say, it was always the left shoe, I'd think that maybe it was my fault, I'd think that I was lopsided or something. But it's not, it's both, and in no particular order.

And it's not just the pain and the inconvenience that I have to suffer. There's something way out and on top of that: embarrassment. With shoes on my feet that at any moment might shed a sole or split down the heel I feel that I am a prime target for embarrassment.

There I was, five weeks ago, with my second pair of shoes from the Smell of Leather, setting off on a midweek date. There was suggestion of a pub, mention of a meal, hint of a film, possibly a show. But first I had to meet her. No problem.

I'm walking the pavement, a blister or two causing a wobble and lilt in my stride, but nothing serious, nothing I can't cope with. I turn a corner and see her standing under the well-lit awning of the wedding-dress shop she works in.

'Come in, Doug,' she said. 'I'll get my bag and we can go. I hope you've got something exciting planned for us.'

And what happens then? I follow her into the shop and the sole of my right shoe lets go, helpfully ripped off by some metal grate in the doorway. Bang! I fall flat on my face.

My date stares at me with a look that makes it clear that she is trying to pretend she doesn't know me. And a large bride-to-be turns away from a seemingly too small mirror she is admiring herself in and laughs at me.

And then, with such urgency that I didn't even get a chance to ask for some Sellotape to stick my sole back on, my date led me out into the street and asked if I was drunk.

I told her that I did not drink. This appeared to be the wrong answer. She suggested that if I had been drunk it would have been acceptable for me to fall face-down in a wedding-dress shop. But, seeing as I was sober, there was no reason other than my sheer incompetence.

After I blamed my shoes she agreed to continue with the evening. So, trying to put it all behind me, I walked as normally as I could with a missing sole and a big toe that kept peeping from the prow of my failed shoe.

We'd more or less got over the bad start when I trod on a smouldering cigarette butt. I screamed and kind of crumpled on the pavement beside her.

'NOW WHAT?' she shouted.

'Jesus! I trod on a cigarette.'

'So?'

'It was still alight.'

'Well, why don't you look where you're going?'

I guess she was right. I guess one should always be on the lookout for smouldering cigarette butts, so I said, 'Oh, fuck off. I'm going home.'

'Yeah, you run along now.'

So I hopped home. And that was embarrassing too. People were staring at me as I hopped. Mothers were pointing me out to their children so that the kids could put their small hands over their small mouths and snigger at me.

And now as I stand here my feet ache slightly as they mould into the shapes and contours of these new boots. My feet, I think, would prefer to be in old slippers, or to be naked. My feet would prefer to put their feet up, to lie down, to stop carrying me around town. But still, my feet hold me up as I lean against the sun-defined shape of a beautiful model. My face nestles closely to her model breasts. She is advertising Natra Tan and she is a poster in the bus stop, her tanned skin shielded from the elements by the graffiti-soiled Perspex. A famous model, they must have paid her a rock star's sum to expose herself near-naked in this rusting shelter. They must have given her some of the money that favours the best-looking. They must have taken a close look at what she had to offer and decided she was worth it. Decided she was among the best-looking.

I'm not looking my best these days: glimpsing paranoid reflections of myself in shop windows, or as I eat, or love, or whatever. My psychotherapist, my *terrible* psychotherapist, Dr Edmund Spritzer, wants to do a case study of me; or rather, he *is* doing a case study of me. Rendering, he hopes, my psyche into a character for his psycho novel. Something, he tells me, that languishes in my past, and it could be especially dreadful (he talks of assault, he talks of worse; I hope he's wrong, and I'm pretty sure he is), is going to make his story live or die.

Down on the long Uxbridge Road the cars were juddering past. With every other streetful of traffic a heavily tinted or low-slung car bounced along with a bass beat shaking it apart and sending an erotic resonance through the coruscated shelter. Then over the hill and into the irascible commuter traffic came the faded red flab that was the bus – a measured negotiator in primetime travel, where size means brawn, or complacency, or both. Where size *does* matter.

The bus journey to the tube was a short one and still cost pence rather than pounds. My fellow passengers (the old, the young, the unemployed, the undernourished student) appeared to be brimming with pence but to be somewhat short on pounds, and the stash of copper and nickel glinted in the driver's eyes in a way that notes would never have the chance to.

I gave the remainder of my change to a ticket man in the tube station, and rode the escalator down into the Freudian dreamscape of phallic imagery. I concentrated on what the moving stair stood for – all I could think of was *going down*. So, going down, my new footwear and I missed the transition from aided to unaided movement and fell helplessly. I cursed my shoes as I went at the floor, swearing at them out loud to inform others of their menace.

In the dry air of the hollow platform I waited with the demographic. Down here the Walkman-wearers are the would-be bass bomb car drivers of the streets above and the kids that balance on the platform edge are the dispatch cyclists that make the best progress over short and difficult distances. Behind me was the same Natra Tan poster model. This time a sprayed-on yellow penis that lacked the power of invagination had ejaculated in yellow daubs across her face. Poor Cynthia Lambour. With her dark computer-enhanced eyes.

The train pushed a fart of underground air from the tunnel

and then burst out like some huge unwanted suppository. One by one the kids of the edge pulled back, and the ten-year-old black kid was the last to reel in and won the test of courage. An aged couple next to me who fell into a cheap car-insurance bracket looked on with a life's accumulation of disapproval. They tutted quietly to each other and felt glad to be old, glad no longer having to compete.

The train stopped and something happened that doesn't happen very often. It used to once, but not now. An old lady leaving her carriage halted on the step. Unexpectedly she handed me her handbag. Well, well, I thought, easy money, I'd make a great mugger – without even having to threaten or assault my victims. But, before I had a chance to get away, she squeaked, 'Here,' and put her hand out for me. She placed her stick on the platform and all her (inconsiderable) body-weight into my handgrip, lowered herself on to the concrete, retrieved her bag, said thank you, informed me that I was a 'dear' and hobbled away. Jesus, I just performed a good deed at this end of the millennium. One of the last. One of my last – certainly.

She went. I watched in shock. And all around squeezed by me into the vertical confines of the carriage. Some grabbed, some hung, others sat, but we all fastened ourselves for this underground roller-coaster ride – like a roller-coaster, only accompanied by the proximate smell of claustrophobia . . . Not the smell of fear: acrid, ephemeral, disappearing in the undulations.

Being called a bastard in the mixed light of the street has some kind of effect on me. When it happens – as it does now with almost appalling regularity – I stop worrying about my usual problems. I no longer agonize over what to have for tea, money worries cease to trouble me, and I lose concern for size and proportions. As my problems hide away, I begin operating in a retrospective fantasy. That is, instead of looking back and wishing I'd said that line, made a move or lied more convincingly, I go right ahead and do it there and then.

So while the carriage was busy with its props – newspapers, books, watches, cellular phones, lap-tops, train timetables and friends – I was busy trying to catch the eye of a girl sat diagonally opposite me. She was familiar, I must have seen her before on my random travels. Her prop was a magazine, a fashion one, its pages limp and dull with waiting-room wear. If I didn't make an advance now I would regret it later – I always regret it with girls like her. So I mouthed the words, Will you marry me? I think she ignored me, or didn't see me. I tried again: Will you marry me? There was no response. Then I saw something awful: I saw the reflection of a face in the glass behind the girl. The awful reflection opened its mouth and the answer came back: Yes. The face belonged to an androgenous creature a few seats to my left. Into the glass I lipped, Not you. *Her*. The reflection said, *Me?* And something else that I couldn't understand. Then the girl's eye caught mine. She looked left, looked right, she looked at these two people talking to the glass behind her. The train slowed, she stood up. 'You creeps,' she growled.

I followed her off the train. She swivelled, faced me and said, 'Don't even think about following me!'

'I'm sorry,' I said. 'It all went wrong.'

'Get back on the fucking train.'

'Oi. This is my stop.'

'OK. Just don't follow me.'

'I won't,' I promised.

So I tried not to follow her. But she was going the same way as I was. Now, as I *was* following her, I tried to pretend I wasn't. I hid behind people, I read all the posters, I stopped and gave money to buskers, I walked close to walls, I stopped and bought a packet of cigarettes. But then I remembered that I had given up smoking, so I tried giving them away. You'd think that it would be easy to give cigarettes away in a tube station; after all, most cigarettes are given away, or asked for, in tube stations. But no, nobody wanted them. One flustered old man said, 'It's a bomb, isn't it?'

'No, it's not a bomb.'

'Well, if it's not a bomb, what is it?'

'It's a packet of cigarettes.'

'I still think it's a bomb,' he said, closing his eyes tightly shut and putting his hands over his ears. So I threw them into a busker's violin case and left the old man, who was now crouching, to wait for the explosion.

The girl whom I was trying not to follow was caught in a people-jam up ahead. She looked over her shoulder and stared at me. I shrugged an apology. She pointed a finger and then shook it reproachfully. I shrugged again. Finally, outside, she sidestepped into a shop. I went on by. Further up the pavement I stopped and scanned behind to see if she was now following me. She wasn't. I walked on in the evening mist.

So where am I going? Yes, you may well ask: Where am I going? And, if you see me walking the streets with my aimless face, my off-centre hairstyle, my worn clothes and my shiny new boots, you may well wonder: Where is he going? Most probably not. But someone once must have looked at me, turned to their companion and said, Check out *this* geezer. Where's he off to looking like that?

I'm on route, zigzagging my way, underground, overground, etc. To Andrew Cipolin's townhouse flat. One-time defeated drugs dealer, now simply a drugs taker. Also insolvent, and a friend. A friend with a beautiful girlfriend. A girlfriend called Annis.

Annis causes Andy all kinds of trouble. She causes him all this trouble because she is too good-looking. This presents Andy with a challenge. The challenge is for him to be unfaithful to her. He *has* to be unfaithful to her. He has to be unfaithful – not because she's ugly, but because she's everything he ever dreamed of. He can't see how Annis will ever stay with him for the rest of his life – after all, dreams never do. So in the meantime he has to be unfaithful.

In addition to causing Andy all kinds of trouble, she also causes *me* all kinds of trouble. She causes me all this trouble because she's the kind of girl I've always dreamed of too. In fact I've had lots of dreams about her: epics, soaps, tearjerkers, tragedies, comedies, reruns . . . Of course, it doesn't help that Andy is so unfaithful to her. If he was faithful, or much less *un*faithful, I'd find it easier to think of her as a mate's girlfriend, to think of her as somebody else's. But he's not. So I guess Andy causes me all kinds of trouble as well.

Here's a secret. Despite the trouble, I've got a good feeling about me and Annis.

Andy is an actor. What kind? Film, TV, stage, method, character . . . bit part? No. Out of work, an out of work actor without even a local radio ad to append to his curriculum vitae.

I met him three years ago when I was falling for this actress: a stage-school alumna from his sect. She was marginally more successful: a two-month London TV run in an advert for Capital Carpets and a barmaid in a lager-saga ad – they gave her a padded bra for that one – yeah, er, titillating. She's an escort or a hostess or a wife, or some such thing nowadays. No, a croupier, that's it, she's a croupier these days – dealt out of my life in some money gamble. He had lots, I had none.

So what do out of work actors do? They deviate, or stray, from their chosen profession. But not far if they can help it. They may well try producing or writing, modelling or designing. Aspiring and denying. Then, on their way down: try their hand at selling, maybe insurance or mortgages. Then, when the booze takes over and the despair kicks in: toilet cleaning and sweeping – sweeping up after the populace, their audience – if only. Oh, and let's not forget waiting. That's what they really do on the dole: they wait. On people mainly – in restaurants and bars.

Logically enough, Andy is attempting a different career and tangentially has chosen comedy. His latest then: a comedian, of the stand-up variety, in the smoke-choked clubs of fast laughter and faster stage mortality.

And comedy, apparently, takes over when everything else has worn itself out: with a gun pointed at your crotch when you've given up pleading, and cried away all your tears, what can you do but escape into comedy and laugh at the crisis? Just laugh at the end and its humour.

So having fisted many avenues of fiscal gain and having slept with the unpopular office jobs – car insurance for the over-forty-fives rating as one of his worst lays he'd ever had – Andy found himself at a dead end, at the comical end, at the end end: where comedy muscles in and drowns the past. This is what he told me. This is what he attested to in the GoodBye pub after another unfulfilling day at the office. This is why he drank on that day and this is why he wanted comedy. Comedy, on the other hand, wanted his pain and his fury. Comedy wanted him to be funny, and funny was one thing Andy truly hoped he could be.

For now he is busy being out of work. For now he is busy as he applies himself to the serious task of developing something that is perhaps comical, something that is vaguely humorous. And soon he will be on stage doing something that might just be comedy.

The top of the sky was black now, black with night, but the air above me was stained with visible radiation, stained for a mile or so with shopping fluorescence, with neon lacework, and rotating with halogen maintained within the orbicular of London traffic.

I trod the streets though late winter, through the cool damp of tumbling darkness, through the settled quiet of the converted street. The street was converted for dark: day shops were closed with the day, night stalls were out with the night and food fumes were being emitted as the night food industry fired up. I grabbed a slick potato and an acidic apple juice from Millennium Meals. A snack pre-priced for year 2000.

The rusting motorcycle stood in its debris, in its oil and fallen-off parts of rusted machine. It stood within a backfire's distance (if Andy ever got it going) from a discarded skip, a skip that was itself now rubbish. A skip that someone would need to find a way to dispose of one day.

The multi-tenanted townhouse was distanced from the road only by garbage – more rubbish in the rubbish front garden. It was in the odd-numbered terrace, and, along with the even one opposite, made up the neighbourhood watch conspiracy, where the neighbourhood watched you leave and then walked calmly round to burgle you.

So this is the road that Andy Cipolin lives in: Rings End

Road. And the odd-numbered house: no. 69. And the floor he lives on: the fourth floor. This is the top floor – the fittest floor – the *filth*iest floor. Either dirt rises like hot air or it falls from the sky, a result of the *what goes up must come down* syndrome. Fuck me, there must be a lot of shit up there. Up there in the sky there is a lot of shit. Don't look up.

'She was a heavy titter,' announced Andy. 'A mega-heavy titter.'

'Yeah? Where did you meet her, this heavily titted girl?'

'In the club, man.'

'The clubman?'

'That's right.'

'You met her in your Mini Clubman? Where?'

'No! I met her in the club called MAN. You know, *MAN*, man!'

'Oh, Man.'

'I got a job behind the bar for—'

'Hold on,' I interrupted, 'you can't call a club Man. Are you working in a gay club?'

'No, man. MAN stands for Musical Art Night.'

'Right. It's acronymous.'

'No way, it's real friendly. And full of babe-sweat.' At this point Andy took a deep breath and held it . . . For a second or two his eyes and his mind skated away. When he came back he said, 'Here,' and offered me a cigarette. 'No.' Then he said, 'Here,' again, and offered me a can of beer. 'No.'

'Man!' he said. '*What?*' And he threw his arms up: an elaborate question mark in the air. 'Why?'

'I'm giving it up,' I answered dolorously. 'Dr Spritzer advised me to, even if it's only temporary. You know – to give me a clear head – to get to the root of my problem.'

'Uhm, whatever *that* may be.'

'Well, it's worth a try—'

'Quack-crap. It's all quack-crap.'

'Tell me,' I tried, 'about the large-breasted women.'

'Sure.' He cupped his hands and placed them six inches in front of his chest. 'This big. The biggest pair of loons I've ever seen – except in the pictures. She came up to the bar, it's a high bar, and she rests them on the counter and asks us for two Campari and sodas. I'd done some Billy last night to get through and was feeling a bit cheeky, so when I'd filled the glasses I placed them on her, you know, one on each tit. They stood there solid, they might as well have been placed on two bags of concrete. Then I asked her if I could take a photo. "Go on then, if you want to," she said. I said, "Keep still," found the camera and took a shot of them. I promised her a copy and asked for her name and number, which she gave me. Then she disappeared back into the club.'

'Good try,' I said.

'Well, you know how much I like tits – I am a *tit* man through and through. So I went and forced another gram of whiz up my nose, went up to her and suggested that if she wait around till the end of the night I'd take her somewhere nice.' He paused and pulled a long drink off his beer. 'So at the end I rescued her from the bouncers who were trying to throw her out, finished clearing the bar and then told her I was ready to leave. But she said she wanted to take *me* somewhere nice. "Where?" I asked her.'

'Where?' I asked him.

'Her apartment.'

'Well done.'

'Right, so we get back to hers and she disappears again. This time I hear a bath running and a little later she calls me.

So I followed the sound of her voice and found her naked and glistening wet in a huge frothing bath, "Jump in," she said.'

'You bastard.'

'So I got my stuff off and slipped in and sat there staring at these massive life-saving lungs that were bobbing up and down in the water. Then she slid over to me and whispered, "Do it to me," in my ear.'

'Sounds like a porno.'

'It felt like one. Trouble was I couldn't get a hard-on cos of the speed. I must've tried for nearly an hour but we were getting cold and our skin was going all crinkly. I had to leave. I must admit I was kind of embarrassed.'

'Did you tell her it was all caused by the speed?'

'No, she thought it was her. She thought it was her fault, and now she doesn't want to see me again.'

Andy stood up, ambled over to the window and looked into the city darkness – out there light still hung in the air. It was still light out there, but it was as dark now as it was ever likely to be. He said, 'Join me in a smoke.'

'No thanks.'

'Come on. Shit! Where are my fucking Rizlas?' I pointed at the orange packet. It lay there on the floor. A lost jigsaw piece with its ripped gaps and irregular teeth. 'Forget Spritzer's quack-crap,' he said, 'and smoke some shit.'

'Soon,' I said hopefully. 'Soon.'

'I don't know why they turned me down for that last TV ad, I was made for the part. "Forget Spritzer's quack-crap and smoke some shit." ' He said it in ordered TV cadence and repeated it three times, speeding up as he spoke. Finally blurting out, ' "Don't delay. Order today," ' as the money ran out in his budget advert.

He rolled a cone, lit it and sat back down – smoking and

drinking with alternate arms. When he spoke again the sweet smoke accompanied the words from his mouth, the words were: 'Do you think I'm funny?'

'What kind of funny?' I asked.

'Comedy-funny.'

'I don't know.'

'Well, you'll get a chance to find out how funny I am when I do a slot at the Miser. I'll be being funny in there in a couple of weeks time, hopefully.'

'I'll look forward to it.'

'Yeah,' he said, making full use of his comedy wit, 'me too . . . Oh, Annis will be back soon. Don't mention tits!'

Andy then started giggling and quickly fell off his chair.

Then Annis did come back, and nobody mentioned tits. I sat there trying to think of something good to say to her, but I didn't get a chance; Andy was doing all the talking. He was talking about comedy, and he was not being funny. He was being very serious – about comedy.

And, surprisingly, what with Andy doing all of the talking, when I went home to dream about Annis and the secretive wink she had given me, still no one had mentioned tits. Though, if I'm honest, I did think about them. But with a name like Doug Down, whose initials are double D, what can you expect? It's not my fault, I didn't ask to have a name that people could make breast-size-measurement jokes about. And everybody seems to forget that DD is also an abbreviation for Doctor of Divinity. Maybe I just don't remind them of that sort of thing.

Two

Last week another rock star went and killed himself. He left a note that said *sorry*. All it said was *sorry*. He did it with a sawn-off shotgun. In the mouth, back of the head came off. Blood bespattered the note, the note that was on the front page of every newspaper.

Who was the last British rock star to top himself? Perhaps this, like every other trend, has made its transatlantic trip.

His record sales are up. Copycat suicides among the bereaved fans are just starting. The first was two days later, a seventeen-year-old girl, blonde, impressionable, etc. On the inside cover of every paper this time.

The easy way out. I've thought about it. Have you? The *easy* way out?

I don't remember what I am supposed to have forgotten. There is, however, something I can't quite remember – It's repressed, apparently.

So I find myself pouring out life's minutiae into the ear of Dr Edmund Spritzer. Young Spritz just sits there nodding and softly encouraging me to open up. My therapy tends to go something like this:

'Do you think that perhaps the root of your psychotic

paranoia lies in a history of abuse?'

'Perhaps,' I say.

'Or indeed that you may have sexually abused the old or the young?'

'I certainly don't remember, but I suppose it's possible.'

'Yes, quite possible,' he says emphatically.

'Of course, I don't really like the old, you know.'

'Exactly, that's why you did it.'

'Did what?' I ask.

'Well, we'll have to find out, won't we?'

He really is, I think, a terrible psychotherapist.

Concerning his book, his psycho thriller, his block-busting mind exposé: it unfurls daily. I do ask, really I do. But he says, 'I'm keeping it close to my chest.' He's keeping it within a professional distance. Nevertheless, I have found out the following: the plot is flexible and not yet decided, I have more influence than I realize and something to do with *gestalts*. Also, he is angry with a recently published novel that used cosmological values as a form of juxtaposing cosmic and human imagery, angry because he planned the same and is now unable to do so because of the novel's prominence. He says he is considering an anthropological equivalent.

One other thing: Spritz is bisexual. He falls into one of the 'newer' sexual groups. He is confused. He says he became a psychotherapist for this very reason.

In my street, my mean street, there is a hard dark movement that grades the shadows on the tight concrete and chalk brick façade. It is the movement of stealth and crime. It is the movement of rape. It is the movement of change.

Among it all the grey-haired still polish their cars on Sundays (their cars are burnt-out wrecks). The young learn their sex as they wait up late into the night and admire couples as they make love intently, or violently, in cars, vans, front rooms or over the faded white in the centre of the road. The young admire the movement of change.

Sometimes the children play a game called tipcat where they tip a cat in the air with a sharp stick. They misunderstand the rules slightly: they are not supposed to use a real cat. And now as I peer through my window I can see the RSPCA van pull over and the children fronting up around it – the dead cat already disposed of in some OAP's garden. The van is rocked gently from side to side as the children push and pull at it. The van sways like some helpless tin beetle with twenty legs.

One of them is jumping up and down on the bonnet, shouting, 'Fuck off, Prevention!' It turns into a chant, but they allow the van to crawl between them as they kick at the royal signatory on the doors. Once clear, it speeds off and breaks a trail through the dust that was the ground-up decay of modern housing.

Back to the cat. You know that old adage, It's a dog's life? Forget it. Dogs have got it great. Dogs are loving it. It's a cat's life now. If you're in the shit, then you're having a cat's life. A cat's life. One of nine.

I find it harder and harder to get out of bed these days. This morning rating as one of the hardest. It would be nice to say that it's because I'm all junked and blasted from booze and drugs the night before. It would be fitting as I wade out of my quarter-life crisis. It would work well. Unfortunately it would be a lie.

The truth is the opposite. The truth is that I find myself in some deep, deep sleep brought on by the lack of drugs and drink, brought on by the sheer vacuum of having no hangover. No hangover to pull me out of bed and into the toilet. And now no promise of a cigarette whose early morning *up* would have helped me rise. No drugs to look forward to. No champagne breakfast. Nothing, just nothing.

The truth then is that I find myself in what Spritz describes as a compound sleep. Self-induced non-narcotic sleep. A cathartic and libidinous sleep.

In compound sleep I muddle through a daunting array of dreams – give me dream-therapy. Give me therapy from my dreams. Take the other night, or rather, the other morning: I was dreaming my way around the body of this sex-girl I used to know when I woke up. Naturally I was upset. Right, so I got out of bed, got ready for work and went to work. But it was strange this work, it was hard work. This work turned into a nightmare, at which point I woke up again – it had all been a dream. Now I had to go to work for real. By this time I was exhausted and the last thing I needed was reality, even if reality was a part-time job at the Frenetic Phone Company. What I needed was sleep.

So you see I'm drug-free and I find it hard to get out of bed. I sleep a lot. Is there a connection?

Around noon I sat in a corner-shop café, in the cast-over interior of the tea-stained walls. Five years ago this place had the yellow warmth of Van Gough's *Café Terrace at Night*. Now it has served too much tea, seen too many people and has worn its way into a darker analogy of modern life.

I spread the *Job Advertiser* in front of me. If you are looking for a job, then this is the best place to start. If you are looking for something to buy or sell, then this is where you will look. If you are looking for a hermaphrodite on Tuesdays or a lesbian who specializes in tribadism, this is the place they will be advertising. If you are looking for a job, don't look in here because it is all too easy to be distracted.

I seriously considered getting in contact with the two girls, nineteen and twenty-one, blonde, brunette, seeking solvent male for fun and friendship, age unimportant. But there was that word, that personal word: solvent. And of course there was my abstinence: my Spritz-advised sexual temperance. Teetotal. Don't smoke. Celibate.

I noted the address of the shoe shop that was looking for a salesperson. I've decided that the only way I'm going to get a pair of shoes that won't fail is to work in a shoe shop. And I need a different job anyway: the Frenetic Phone Company is killing me. I called for another pot. The weary waitress placed it on the scrobiculated table-top and scribbled illegibly in her pad, then padded away like a lone cat unaware and oblivious of what the future had in mind for her. And the future has a particularly twisted mind, with all its scowls and jabs at the past and its pejorative prescience.

I pushed my way out of the café, heaving the weight of the door on its rusted hinges, the door papered under years of flyers: the names of lost bands and forgotten politicians, even the face of an assassinated Third World leader. Out into this barren cityscape that would one day feature proudly as the set of some retro sci-fi film. Outside in the air, the dense air of asthma and allergy, I felt trouble come at me with its familiar stomach punch.

There she was: the girl with the dying eyes. Her squinted stare in my direction, the tiny dog looking on, scoring the transient attention of another human. She brought me trouble; she always does.

'You bastard,' she said predictably.

'One day I'll wake up and you won't be here any more, you'll be gone. That'll be the best day of my life.'

'Oh, Doug.'

'You look like death. Clean yourself up.'

'You bastard.'

'Yeah, yeah . . .'

I turned the corner. She called me a bastard again. I hurried away down the street.

At the far end of the street I went into a newsagent and bought a lottery ticket. Then I left the shop, crossed the road and nearly got run over by a bus. It would have flattened me but one of my blisters attacked me and pulled me up inches from the terrified driver's face. Excellent! *I nearly got run over by a bus*. That's the same as *nearly* winning the lottery. That's like getting five numbers and a bonus ball, like winning around one hundred thousand pounds. Yes, this is going to be my week. This week I'm going to nearly win the lottery.

With my lucky lottery ticket safe in my pocket I sat down in the therapy chair and Dr Spritzer asked, 'Your last drink?'

'Two months ago.'

'Your last cigarette?'

'One week ago.'

'Good, good.' Spritz rubbed his hands together, slapped them down on his knees and asked, 'What is your deepest fear?'

'Driving,' I considered. 'Yes, driving is my deepest fear.'

Then, with a tell-me-all-about-it expression on his face, he said, 'Tell me all about it – this fear of driving.'

'There's not much to say really. I just think that my biggest fear is driving. That's all.'

'And how long have you had this fear?'

'Well, I was fine when I started, passed my test first time and used to make my way around town in my little Fiesta.'

'How long ago was this?'

'Five years ago.'

'When did you last drive?'

'Two years ago.'

'Why did you stop?'

'It all became too much for me: the hooting and the swearing and everyone rushing around in their cars and vans and lorries.'

'So you just decided to pack it in? Because you couldn't cope with it?'

'Uhm . . . You see, it was taking such a long time to get about that sooner or later I would have got in the car, started it up, put it in gear and been unable to go anywhere. I would have remained stationary.'

'Because of the heavy traffic?'

'No,' I said, 'because I found that the only way to cope with it all was to drive slower and slower and in the year I stopped driving I was cutting my speed down by maybe one or two miles per hour every month. And seeing as I never really got above twenty-five miles per hour in the first place, I was going nowhere very slowly . . . Some buses hit fifty, you know. It's much quicker.'

'Do you want to drive again?'

'Certainly. I want to conquer all my fears.'

'In time maybe.'

'I'm stronger now. Much stronger.'

'Maybe. But I don't think you're ready to go back on the road.'

'I think I am.'

'It's your worst fears. Claustrophobia, paranoia, panic

attacks and the rest, all rolled into one.' He paused, pointed his finger at me and inquired, 'Have you seen that girl again, the one with the unhealthy eyes?'

'Yes, I have. She doesn't like me, does she?'

'No.'

'Why?'

'Only you can answer that question.' After half an hour of trying to answer that question, he looked at his watch and said, '*Right*, that's it, your time's up. We're no longer patient and therapist, we're friends now. Let me take you for a drink, a cola or a juice, down at the GoodBye Bar.' He removed his tweed jacket and replaced it with a slightly more modern shiny version – but he still looked just as terrible.

'OK,' I sighed, 'I've time for a couple of waters, I guess.'

Friends. Friends? In some abstract form of friendship perhaps. Our rapport is, I suspect, dedicated to the study of subject by author, as he assesses my character for its consumer appeal and tell-tale flaws that may weaken his plot or, worse still, give it away.

With an expression that was not his own – he must have copied it from a famous author's face on television, and assumed it would help him write a novel – he said, 'All I can tell you is that the character will be mildly schizophrenic, amnesic, and will suffer from delusions . . .' Spritz finished his cocktail and looked over his glass at an attractive young couple. 'As for *orientation*,' he continued, 'I am, er, as yet undecided.'

Dr Spritzer looked back at me. Confusion now covered his face, covered it like a layer of fire-twisted plastic. That confusion denied his words: It's no big deal being bisexual, it just means you get the best of both worlds.

But it is a big deal when you're Spritz, who is indecisive at the best of times, and especially so when confronted by twice the usual number of partners. Her? Him? Him and her? Him, her and er . . . him? Or her? No Spritz, take it easy: *her*. You and her.

Her. He lost her and then asked those questions, those terrible questions. Those terrible questions about everything whose answers can only be more terrible questions.

The sexually based terrible questions: If I do that to a girl, then could I just as easily do it to a man? I mean, physically it would be the same. Wouldn't it? And with my eyes closed would I ever know the difference? This morning she was squealing under the body of her 'other' boyfriend and here I am a couple of hours later licking away the remains – why not cut out the middle man, or rather the middle women, and do it straight to the man himself?

These were some of the terrible questions that Spritz found himself asking after he lost her.

A lot of people ask these questions, or would like to. Spritz did, found the answers, tried them out, found he quite liked them and decided that he was bisexual. He says he's more in touch with himself now than he was before. If you ask me he looks more confused than ever.

He ordered another cocktail from the GoodBye waitress, who had great teeth and sat there looking doubtfully at the fruit that bobbed in the bibulous glass like colourful toys in a baby's bath – he appeared as though he might have wanted to eat it. But he was half-way through another unsuccessful diet . . . His plump body swallowed up the sharp architecture of the bar as he leant against it. Nowadays he drank too much, ate too much and slept around too much. All since she left him, his wife of two years and lover for fractionally more.

The poor guy's hair had turned a shade lighter, hit grey and then started releasing itself into its surroundings: basins, baths, people's mouths, curries, even into his terrible roll-up cigarettes, where strands would burn fiercely like an arsonist's fuse.

He thanked the waitress, complimented her on her great teeth and asked if she had any problems. What kinds of problems? No she didn't have any of those kinds of problems. The only kinds of problems she had were sexually inept men telling her how lovely her teeth were and then coming on to her with their pathetic crap.

A shimmer of heat ran across Spritz's face. Once settled, the face had taken on a new graphic: one less of confusion and more of embarrassment, the blood-red embarrassment of bottle-necked words.

For five minutes he was unable to speak and was energetically massaging his throat. At last, he said, 'Jesus. Fuck you all. I'm going to see Terry.' He felt his way through the office-based drinkers and opened the door into the damp of one of London's kinder streets.

I asked for drink.

'Half a water, please.'

'Half a water?'

'Yes. Half a water.'

'What is it with you people? *Half a water?*'

Later I rejoined London and fell into the casual occlusion of early-evening pedestrianization.

So two years ago I sold my green Fiesta and spent the five hundred pounds on drink and drugs and girls. I had a great time. I was drunk, high and satisfied, and managed – with a combination of uppers and alcohol – to persuade a fat and a thin girl into a threesome. For a few days back then I lived the life I had always planned. It ended abruptly. The money ran out.

By the time I reckoned I had spent most of the five hundred I checked my bank account, expecting to find twenty or thirty pounds. Instead the cash machine informed me of my debt, retained my card and ordered me to the bank for an explanation.

Mr Down, they said, you have seriously violated your borrowing privileges and we are suspending your account immediately.

'It's only sixty pounds in the red,' I argued. 'Surely we can come to some arrangement.'

'These are hard times, Mr Down.'

'How am I supposed to get to work?'

'You should have thought of that before you spent all our money.'

'Fuck you,' I shouted. 'Last year I was overdrawn by three pounds and you charged me twenty-five. Now whose money was that?'

'Administration charges.'

'You know what, Adrian Peeler!' I said, grabbing his lapel badge. 'I'm gonna get someone to do something very nasty to you.' His hand went down and pressed the button all while I was leaving.

I hid in an alley and started crying. Yeah, I cried. And I wouldn't cry again, not like that.

I was penniless and up for a further hundred and fifty court fine imposed on me for threatening behaviour. It would have been more but the magistrate implied that he too had had all his money taken away by a bank, so he understood. He understood the provocation.

Unwittingly or irresponsibly I had commissioned my own vicious circle. With no money I would be unable to get to work and with no work I would have no money to rise through debt.

So I sold my guitar (a Fender replica which I couldn't play) to Andy (who couldn't play either), and I sold my vice (an antique wood vice) to an old boy down the road who wondered why I had it in the first place – I didn't know, I seemed to have acquired it in line with life's extraneous materialism.

That weekend Andy and I went out in search of two rich older women who might take us in as toy boys. We looked to charity.

And the things we said. The lies we told. Suddenly he was a successful West End actor and I was a holiday rep with ten exclusive places to give away on a new luxury tour of the United States . . . Did the gold embroidery of this middle-aged single woman fit the bill? She had to be able to afford a holiday costing at least five thousand: not because she had to pay for this one, but because that was the kind of client we were aiming for. Was she a home-owner with no mortgage? Most of our holiday-makers would be.

We hit a problem. We hit deception – the modern fraud of pseudo-wealth. In those basement singles clubs, those sunken railway carriages, we encountered the signatures of wealth, the signs that said money: the gold and silver, the silk and solid hair, the large notes . . . But it was a double-cross; if these people were rich, then they were rich here, and only here, down here. Up there, beyond the portals, in the traffic-tangled streets they had no more cash than anyone else. Up there they were the same.

Sugar Mums we aspired to never made it to these places. They were banked long before they got this far. They accrued interest in the places that we didn't go. The places we couldn't go. At least, not yet.

On that Monday I caught the bus to work and got there faster than by car. I took my Monday-morning stance in my section of the department store and waited. Nothing happened. All day nothing happened.

The next day two supervisors visited me. I expected promotion to the shoe department. Instead they fired me.

Yeah, Mrs Peeler didn't like what I'd said to her son.

'OK. You too,' I told her.

Sober and stuck – stuck human traffic – I waited tensely for the pedestrian lights to beckon me across the road. I waited in a queue. On the road, the cars were squatting nose-to-tail, like strange dogs greeting. Everybody was jammed. London was in gridlock.

Easing myself out of the queue, I indicated that I was turning right and plotted a different route home up Foxhall Road and through the park – the only park in London that still had green grass, and that was only because the head gardener had sprayed green in the hope of winning a Best Park prize . . .

The speed gradient of darkness was slower now than it had been last month, or the month before. But still it was quick enough and would happily catch a cyclist without lights. At this time of year darkness somehow came from within vision. You found you could see less and less until all you could make out was latent light. In early summer, darkness seems to come from the objects themselves. They appear at first to reflect less light and then become hazy around the edges, the definition defined as an artist's hue. And above you the sky will still be as high as ever and will not encroach as it does in March. As it did when I walked through the park.

But I like it, this darkening time. It brings in your horizons. Your ambitions become closer. Ambitions are within reach. And the ambitious are said to work especially well at night. Night is an ambitious time.

In the fading light of late March I sat on a park bench. Look around, Spritz tells me, there's so much to see. Try looking around in this modern life. It's hard work looking around, but worth it, he says. I don't know, look what it did to him.

I tried looking around. I managed maybe two feet. Stuffed into the slats of the bench was a rolled pamphlet or booklet. I pulled it out. It was entitled *Cooperage in the Late Twentieth Century*.

Cooperage, I find, is the manufacture of wooden casks: hogsheads, barrels, kilderkins, firkins and pins.

Cooperage, the introduction states, is a dying art. *Bring back cooperage.*

Right. OK so far.

Cooperage in the Late Twentieth Century turns out to be a film script. A short one. It's a film script and it's nothing to do with coopery save its setting: a pub. A pub, a pub setting.

What is it?

Horror. Short. Love . . . Pornographic?

I'll read it. I'll read it.

In a cubicle nearby the sound I could hear was the excited suppression of sex. The mellifluous murmur of closed-mouth moans. The amused acknowledgement of what two people were doing: the sound of two men having sex in a public toilet. In the smell of urine and disinfectant and stale cigarettes. In the smell that, no doubt, encouraged instant hard-on. Hard-on association. Carnal perfume, remembered.

All this doesn't bother me. It has its meaning. It still slots into the fragility of modern morals. Morals that have done their bit, got us this far. Now perhaps is a time for unobtrusive immorality . . . Anyway I don't care about two gays doing their gay-thing in this public toilet, I only mind when it worsens my constipation and I sit there groaning without amusement, and I mind even more when there's a knock on my door and a voice says, 'I can see the bag, gentlemen. Please leave the toilet or I will call the police.'

So I pulled myself together, picked up the supermarket bag of shopping and went out to face the bog boy. 'The bag,' I said. 'Carrots, potatoes and eggs.'

'Sorry, sir.' He left. The arsehole. I washed my hands.

In the mirror I saw the gay cubicle door open. A male face looked into the white ceramic light, pulled the door open some more and led his companion out. A woman. Ahh! Prostitution, I hadn't thought of that. She kissed him. She loved him, she said so. An affair? No, they had to go and pick the children up from the crèche.

Is it immoral for a couple with children to have sex in a public toilet? Probably not.

Back on the streets I was still making my way home. The traffic had freed up. Or was beginning to give up for the day and maybe try again when the prospects would be better.

Cooperage in the Late Twentieth Century was jutting from my frayed pocket and my supermarket goods were swaying in the bag as they measured my stride, like an uncoordinated pedometer.

There had been an incident as I was leaving the supermarket. It took place under the efficient light of Customer Services. I saw it start: a woman went rushing up to the desk.

She was clutching a bulb of garlic. The garlic: not smelly enough? Incorrect ripeness? Counterfeit?

'What's the problem with your garlic, madam?' they asked.

'It's not mine.'

'Whose is it?'

'Well, it should be mine, but I didn't pay for it!'

'You stole it?'

'No.'

'How did you come by it?'

'I think it was hidden behind my purse in the trolley. I must have overlooked it and not put it on the belt at the checkout.' She opened the purse (the accomplice). 'I feel so guilty. How much do I owe you?'

The manager walked on to the scene. In all his life he'd never seen anything like it. He would call the media and her honesty would be congratulated by the local community. He imagined that it would become known as the Garlic Incident. The papers would do something clever with the word *garlic* (he could think of nothing himself). Have the garlic for free, he insisted. No! She caused a commotion. The honest garlic woman demanded to pay the weight price. Sorrowfully the manager accepted her money: twenty-three pence. Quietly the crowd dispersed. Clearly shocked at what they had seen.

The car showroom was closed but the lights were still burning glossy windows into the paintwork of new cars. These new cars were at the front of the showroom. At the back of the showroom sat the revitalized motors: their minor rust had been removed, their joints had been seen to, the rattles no longer rattled and they all started first time, most of the time. These were quality cars and had been pronounced fit for sale.

These were the cars at the back of the showroom . . .

Outside the showroom, and to one side of its glass structure, was a car park full of part-exchange cars. Signs said things like: JUST IN: BUY NOW AT LOW PRICE. The part-exchange cars were traded in for the cars at the back of the showroom. Of course, the cars at the back of the showroom were part exchange too – for the new cars at the front of the showroom. Naturally they were not described that way, their description was one of quality: quality used cars. Quality. The cars outside did not enjoy the same quality; they were, regrettably, part exchange. Consequently any faults – missing hubcaps, cracked grille, no engine, etc. – could be placed at the door of the owner, whose name and address were on the documentation.

On the other side of No Name Motors' electric fence, but part of the same operation, were the second-hand cars. These were the fuck-ups at the bottom of the part-exchange cycle. These were not admirable motors.

The fuck-up I found myself looking at was lit not by spotlight but by the faltering blink from the sodium street-lamp across the road. I gave it the 'once over'. I liked its rust-proof brown paintwork (similar to a lot of other cars in the yard). I liked its six months' tax. And I liked its price.

I liked most of all the private attack on the timid driver within me. My singular dread of four wheels was beginning to be broken down. 'Yes, Spritz,' I'll say, 'I'm still terrified of driving,' as I look out of the window at the brown Fiat parked up the street.

Oh dear, I've decided to buy a car. I've decided to buy a little brown Fiat.

I resumed my walk home and thought about the prospects of

mobility. The *double entendres* of car ownership: the pulling power and the grunt, the body, its lines, and the sheer being inside.

In advertising the world seems to have personified the motorcar. A car will give you a step up in life, it will take you where you want to go. It will never say no and it will marry itself to your needs.

Graffiti has done the same. Cars kill. Cars suck. Cars are communists. Cars are aliens. BAN CARS!

Apparently, and I like this one, apparently, *Cars are insane.*

I went on home and turned into my mean street. The police were there again, sizing up the hole in the corner-shop window, a hole whose shape bore resemblance to a five-year-old's drawing of the Star of Bethlehem. I used to buy beer in there. I will again someday. Today I walked past and trod the concrete up to my flat.

I put the key in the lock and turned it through the gates and chocks. The purple door to flat 17, The Manors, slowly opened on its painted hinges. I bent to pick the post from the green doormat, flicked the light on, the white light, and went through into the kitchen. I say the kitchen; in fact I went past a couple of chairs to a recess where a cooker happened to be. This recess is painted in fluorescent green. The walls through the rest of the flat vary in colour, but not in brightness. They are bright yellow, bright red, bright blue, bright pink. The ceiling is not coloured, it's bright white. The floor, the hard floor, has a lurid orange carpet stretching to the fuchsia skirting-boards. This is a doll's house. This is playschool. This place is disgusting. 'Don't worry,' my landlord told me when I moved in, 'I will redecorate it for you.' He never did. Everyone refused to come in the place. Their eyesight was more important than the job.

The reason for the bright colours: the elderly couple living here before were suffering from failing vision and this colour scheme helped them coordinate their movement. Fuck, it was probably the colours that blinded them in the first place.

Three letters. The first I didn't open, I knew what it was, it was stamped by the City Treasury: tax. The second: a card congratulating me, Mr Downe, on a cash prize I had won. It could well be thousands. To obtain it all I had to do was purchase the latest in stay-warm winter wear: a pair of electro-thermo-reactor socks. And the third: I opened the envelope and pulled out a photograph. Posed naked with black strips across her eyes and mouth was a girl straddling a beer barrel. On the back it said in child's handwriting: 'You're going down, Down!'

Is this harassment? Am I finally receiving harassment mail after all these years? Is some naked woman going to come flying through my window astride her trusty barrel and take me out? Oh, no! It's Barrel Woman. Only Beer Monster can save us now! No, this is a prank, a friend playing a game: a humour-gauged reaction test. Nice-looking girl though. Pretty good for what looked like a reader's wife photo. A photo that would appear in a magazine with a car's name.

I went back to the kitchen and made my tea. My student tea: food, including beans – always . . . I was going to be a student once, I wanted to do the student thing. But I wanted to take advantage, I wanted to get myself a place somewhere, hopefully London, go there and spend all my grant in the pub. Go somewhere else and do the same again. Carrying on with this ploy for as long as I could get away with it. I failed my exams so I never had a chance, a chance to try the student thing. I don't really know what it's like to be a student, but I met one in a library when I was looking for some banned art photography, and he led me over to a computer. 'This is what it's like,' he told me. 'I once made a typing error on this word processor – you see the B and the N keys are next to each other? I was writing my details on top of a dissertation and instead of "student" I typed "studebt". Stu*debt* is what being a student is all about. That's how it feels.'

Maybe I'll have another go one day. If I can afford it.

I sat down and ate my tea. Then I remembered *Cooperage in the Late Twentieth Century* and stopped eating. I thought, What's all this barrel business?

'Yes, that's right, a brown one.'

'You want to buy a brown car?' asked Andy, his incredulous tone modulated by the limited frequency of the phone line, its peaks and troughs levelled in transmission. 'Why brown?'

'Well, it won't rust, will it?' was my rhetorical response.

'Yes, it will. It will rust.'

'Invisibly . . .'

'A Fiat you say, how much?'

'Two hundred.'

'Uhm . . .'

'Listen, Andy, all I want you to do is check it over, give me some advice. A second opinion. I don't want to buy a fucked-up car, do I?'

'No. No, you don't.' I sensed sarcasm.

'Tomorrow then. After lunch, in the mall.'

'OK. See you then.'

'Hold on,' I said, 'before you go, have you sent me anything in the post recently?'

'No, why?'

'Not important. See you tomorrow.' The line clicked. I replaced the receiver. I picked it up again and dialled 1471 for the most recent incoming call (I had called Andy). No. No number was stored. Only the apology, the mysterious message: Sorry, no number is stored. No help, it could have been yesterday or just before I walked in today. No number. No clue.

With the TV switched on I stared at the screen as it came to life. From the darkness a newsreader stared back at me. She glared into my eyes as she gravely told me about the escalating war in the European Bloc. She did her death story and death never came through her vision. Jesus, how do their lovers look into their eyes (their TV-trained eyes), and tell them they love them? When she could happily gaze back at her lover and say, I love you too, thank you and goodnight. It's that *and* that does it: that topples the impact of the statement. An and.

As I get older I need to be more and more dedicated to sit down and find something interesting to watch on the TV with its single hand-count of channels. I must be less receptive. Unchildlike. And stumbling into my second quarter-century.

I found nothing.

Instead I pulled out *Cooperage in the Late Twentieth Century* and looked around its pages. A film script: the title, a little more about cooperage and then the script. There is no author's name, no suggestion of a reason for its existence. Its origin remains shrouded.

The directions state that the film is based mainly on the experiences of lead character Chattaway. They go on to say that a God's-eye view would be useful when the action takes place through the other characters. It's not long, about forty pages. Probably aimed at art house and filmed in black and white.

I flicked the pages. The words I saw suggested alcohol. They suggested drugs. They suggested sex and violence. Critically, they suggested that if the film was ever made I would most likely enjoy it. If it was already made I felt that I was missing something.

From what I've read, it starts in a pub. Chattaway in the corner saying nothing. The landlord behind the bar, coveted by barmaid Bella. Chattaway, still silent, is watching them from the corner . . .

Nothing so far to do with barrels.

I went to the kitchen and did the easy-wash thing with the washing up: cover with water, hot, and leave for a day or so. Then rinse.

I went next to the bathroom. The tiny turquoise-tiled bathroom. Too small to even contain a *bath* – there's a shower that I crouch under. I looked in the mirror. A whisper of grey in my black hair was quietly telling me something, urging me to consider the concept of ageing. And asking me to do so well before time. My face had less to say, at least to me. It was still growing and shaping for a wiser version later in life. That teenage thing had left me sometime ago, that acne heartache, but its successor was slow in coming: my facial hair still has trouble making the date. Out there in London is Andy with scorched stubble on his face and Spritz with his silk goatee beard. And in the mirror there's me with my slim-line skin and a suggestion of juvenile down on my upper lip. But Velcroed to my chest is a winter harvest of hair. What's going on with this body of mine, this body I own? I'm a slave to it: my only possession. My fucked-up body.

In the Day-Glo interior of the main room, the *studio*, I took another look at the photo. Somehow it wasn't quite pornography, it had the personal lilt. And pornography never had your name on it. It had to be anonymous.

The photo could be my sister. I couldn't tell.

I could think of no good reason not to, so I ripped the edge off the Treasury letter. It was council tax. The two hundred pounds arrears, pay within ten days or prepare for further action. So here I had a threat. A council threat. A legal threat.

The two hundred was available. I could buy a stamp, an envelope, send them a postal order and be down by that sum plus a few pence for postage; or I could keep the money and spend it on something more exciting, the car for instance . . . It was two hundred pounds, two hundred pounds that I discovered had already aimed itself at a car. The money was gone, it was spent.

I find it incredible the way these decisions get made. Scarcely has the thought crossed the mind when it creeps up on you, takes on form, and before you know it you're right up there with the article. Right now I'm in my little brown Fiat, racing away from the bailiffs who've come to collect on me. Suddenly I'm a car-owner and there seems to be no going back. I'm a car-owner and I haven't owned a car in two years.

I was still up there in my head when the bird-scaring sound of the phone made its connection. The phone is ringing. Hey! The phone is shrieking. I picked it up and it said, 'Doug?'

'Spritz.'

'Listen, I'm sorry about this afternoon. Leaving like that, I was offside. Please accept my apology.'

'Don't be so obsequious,' I told him.

'Ah, a word you learned from me.'

I hadn't. I'd seen it in graffiti on the social security office. On the wall it had said OBSEQUIOUS TOSSERS. I said, 'Sure, no apology needed.'

'It's important that I see you in the next few days. I have a subject I need to discuss with you with regard to my novel. When are you free?'

'Depends. When are you going to let me into the plot?'

'Soon, I promise. First, I need to be sure of it myself. Artist's prerogative.'

'Yeah, but you're a scientist not an artist.'

'No, I simply have a scientific approach to art. The two are not mutually exclusive, Doug.' There was a silence, I said nothing. A pulse later he asked, 'So when are you free? Next couple of days?' We arranged a time. 'Anyway, must go,' he said. 'Someone's waiting.'

'Who?'

Silence.

'Terry?'

'No.'

'Who?'

'His friend.'

'Be careful,' I said (Hey, what am I? His mother?). 'Oi, have you sent me anything through the post in the last couple of days?'

'No, I don't think so. Bye.'

I pushed down the receiver button and waited for the dialling-tone hum. Then pressed 1471. This time there was a number. A London number; but not Spritz's.

I made a note of it. For paranoid reference.

I needed a wash. No, strike that, my *feet* needed a wash, or a soak. They needed a hot steeping in steeping-hot water. My boots are holding up well. Showing no signs of decay. One week under my weight in the scuffle of modern pedestrianism and they're still absorbing the concrete shock – the footwear's fine. The feet, on the other hand, are partially fucked; in a nanosecond or so of cosmological time they will be whittled away to the size of neutrinos. Which, Spritz tells me, are subatomic particles, smaller than electrons. One hundred billion of them pass through your body every second at around the speed of light – I guess they have to be going that fast for us not to notice them.

I have massive reserves of water down there on my feet. Breast-sized blisters ready for the desert. And the heel sores. Boy, are my heels sore.

So the footwear came off and I thought, Forget sneezing, shoe removal has got to rank up there with orgasmic potential. Or orgasmic fraction.

Clean. Fresher. Slightly damp, I sat with my feet smarting in the water. I did nothing else. Nothing: something I'm getting better at as I get older. Nothing is what I'm good at. Nothing is my forte. There's nothing I'd rather do than nothing these days.

Outside I could hear the rain. Inside I could hear the rain. The sound of the rain was being smuggled into my flat. It was gentle rain, steady rain – the hiss and interference of an untuned radio by the window. And I seemed to get this every night, this radio rain. The rain is drowning us with its precontract for March. The rain, unlike the sun, is far too reliable.

I was busy doing nothing. I was having a whale of a time doing nothing when I realized the phone was ringing again. Up I stood, trod a cartoon print over to the sound and lifted the receiver. What was the call? Nothing. There was absolutely nothing on the phone. I did the stored-number thing. Sorry, no number was stored. No number. Nothing.

So I started doing nothing all over again.

The phone didn't wake me. The door did. The knocking came through my sleep like a reversed echo: it got louder. Some arsehole was knocking on my door. Some arsehole wanted to come in.

'Jesus!' I said at the door. 'What do you want?'

'Nothing.'

'Well, fuck off then!'

'OK.'

She started to leave. Then she made her play: she burst into the flat. The girl with dying eyes pushed past me and into the room. Hopefully, I thought, the colours will blind her and I'll be able to chuck her out of the window.

She stood there in the centre of the room, twirling. 'Nice colour scheme,' she scowled. 'Just what I'd expect from someone like you. You bastard!'

'You look so ill,' I said. 'Go to hospital.'

'Oh, Doug. I can't believe I ever loved you.'

'*Loved* me?' This was news to me.

'I used to.'

'What is it? Drugs? Alcohol? Money? Or do you simply suffer from good old delusions? Is that it? Are you just insane?'

'Look what you've done to me.'

'You did that.'

She stared wordlessly. A full frontal assault from those eyes. I looked away, but there was nowhere to look: the colours were blinding. She stood there. She was the focus, with her damp clothes and frayed hair and those dying eyes. Christ! Any moment now I'm going to suffer from psychosomatic blindness.

'Would you like to go out for a drink?' she asked. 'For old times' sake?'

'No. There are no old times.'

'*Doug . . .*' she toned sycophantically.

'Go away. Go home.'

'First,' she said, pulling something from her purse, 'this.' She ran over to the window and pointed something at it. The sound was of a firework launching into the sodden sky. Obscurely she was spraying the glass pink with a high-powered aerosol.

As she left, I asked, 'What's your name?'

'Lucia de Londres.'

'No, it's not.'

'You're right. It's not. Goodbye for now.'

Three

It's two o'clock now. I'm sitting in a coffee shop, a coffee shop in the mall; and all around me is the pastel of pink and green, the maze of mirrors taking the colours great distances and out into the street where they meet grey, where all colours meet and make grey. Where grey (for now) is the only colour.

I've just finished writing a job application letter to a shoe shop called the Shoe Shop and now I'm reading a newspaper. Second-page news: suicide among the young is up. Suicide is becoming popular. Suicide must be curbed. It looks bad, says the government, stop committing suicide now! Don't commit suicide. Commit crime, then you can be punished. Commit crime: become accountable.

My favourite drug of the moment is caffeine. It's what I do. Caffeine is my crime. And I am accountable for my heart palpitations as they rocket through my torso. Thankfully caffeine is an easy fix to get hold of in a coffee shop. I order some more and wait for the hit. Here comes a waitress . . .

'Yes, Andy, I am scared of driving – Coffee?'

'Cheers.'

'Could we order a large pot, please? But I'm gonna get over it.'

'By buying a brown Fiat?'

'That's right, a brown Fiat.'

'Can't you stretch to something a little more stylish? A *red* Fiat even?'

'You pay fifty quid extra for red,' I argued. 'No, I'm happy with brown. And anyway, Andy, what do you know about style with that rusting motorcycle of yours outside your house? That's not stylish.'

'It's a motorbike, therefore it is stylish.'

'But it's rusty!'

'Rust gives it a special style. A lot of people have asked me to flog it to them, you know. *They* like its style.'

'Well, I like the Fiat's style.'

'I don't think you understand my point.'

'Which is?'

'Basically that brown Fiats have no style.'

'Right, you're paying for the coffee.'

'I was about to offer.'

'Forget style. Just have a look at it and make sure it's OK. Make sure nothing is about to fall off or explode.'

'Sure,' he agreed. 'Hey, this is good coffee!'

'What colour is it?'

'Fuck off.'

I spiralled in the long-life and drank the roast-timber-resonant coffee. I looked around the mall. England was changing. It was trying out a new style, and the style came from America.

Accepting the sufferance, Andy pronounced that he had to buy Annis a birthday present. Three days' time. He was late last year.

This year he had plenty of time, time was patiently waiting

for him. Yet he was suffering from gift-giver's block: he had no idea what to buy her. Underwear sprang to my mind. And I told him. Unsurprised, he imagined that many men had pictured Annis in only her skimpiest frillies (he had once). He also imagined that these same mental voyeurs had pictured her without any underwear at all. Right again, Andy. I'm one of those imaginative men . . . All this imagination is finally unnecessary as the svelte Annis wears her clothes so well – and knows it. She does it for the boys. She likes the attention. Thank you, Annis.

However, Andy wasn't keen on underwear. He felt that it came at certain stages of a relationship: earlier and later on. And this was not a late enough stage. The stage now was one of settling for the future. He almost said the word *love*. I saw the tip of his tongue press against the insides of his white upper teeth, the lips poised, ready for the declaration. But it never came, the tongue came down and the face fell in ruins about it.

'How about this?' I asked, pointing at a book entitled *All You Ever Wanted to Know About Car Insurance*.

'She'd leave me!'

'Yeah, she probably would.' Annis hated car insurance. She had worked in it too long. Andy hated car insurance too: Annis kept moaning about it all the time.

Her hobbies were from the same family as Andy's: music, drugs and sex. With Annis they remained hobbies, with Andy they had more resolution. All three slightly difficult to buy her as a gift. After all, a CD meant nothing these days. Her favourite, cocaine, was too expensive and over too fast. And sex could only be fractionally better because it was her birthday, it could not substitute as a gift. Andy rejected all my other suggestions. They were too obvious. Annis did not like the obvious.

He led me around this dark segment of London. His actor's mind fighting with its comedy. Ultimately, I sensed comedy led him to his choice. He, however, was humourless. He bought her a motorcycle helmet, some gloves, some boots and a set of L plates. To complement this he put her name down for a full set of training that would get her out and on to the road. On to London blacktop.

I have my doubts. We'll just have to wait and see if the adorable Annis is as excited as Andy Cipolin.

We spluttered and coughed our way to the car yard. Great explosions from the Mini's engine left a trail of smoke bursts in varying shades of grey or black or blue. The more violent bang gave the darker emission and the more general knocks and barks were accompanied by whiter, denser clouds. At one stage we waited longer and stiller than before and saw each other disappear as stinging smoke gusted around the interior like in some car-suicide pact.

The first thing the car salesman said was, '*No way, mate*. I don't want it!'

'It's not for sale,' said Andy.

'Thank fuck for that!' exclaimed the salesman, the relief clear on his face as his forehead lost its ploughed field and went smooth again.

'No, I'm interested in the brown Fiat,' I said.

'You're not!'

'I am.'

'Right then, my friend. Follow me.'

I looked at the car and the film in my head started rolling again. This time I was on a day trip to France. A little ambitious possibly. But the little Fiat didn't seem to mind. It was set in the future and the boot was loaded with duty-free, the back of the car squatting in the road – like the mind-obliterated smuggler's car with half a ton of hash under the tie-dyed blanket.

'I got to admit she certainly is a sound motor. Got a lot of miles left in her yet. Here. I'll start her up.'

He turned the key. The sound was of an excited dog meeting its master. When the engine eventually got it together and started, the crashing and banging sounded like an entire school of children knocking pencils and rulers on desk-tops.

'Shit! Tappets!' shouted Andy above the percussion.

'Is that bad?' I asked.

'Yeah. Usually,' he answered.

'No way, lads. We'll sort it for you.'

'For free?'

'No problem. I'll get Traffic on to it.'

'Traffic?'

'My mechanic.'

Andy went round the car and wiggled parts of it. From the rear he shouted, 'Rusted subframe,' and from the front he shouted, 'Dodgy wheel bearing.'

'Is that bad?' I asked again.

'Expensive.'

'No problem, lads.'

'Traffic'll sort it?'

'Sure. Absolutely.'

Out on the road Andy was in the driving seat and I was the passenger trying to coax some recognizable sounds from the stereo, or should that be from the *mono*. Our salesman stayed at the yard, he had punters to attend to. Besides, it was probably in his interests not to chaperon us: if we stole the car he'd get more insurance money than he would by selling it. But no one would steal this brown car. It wouldn't be worth 'ringing' and any joyrider who suggested stealing it would (presumably) be beaten up by his fellow joyriders.

Out there on the dull metal the little Fiat was doing well, soaking up the lorry tracks and summer ripples . . . Looking through the shaded corrosion (a watercolour rust-wash) of the rear-view mirrors, there were no long plumes of engine smoke, no treasure trail of unnecessary components and no wake of scornful pedestrians. The problem was the orchestra of drums under the bonnet, but that Traffic was going to sort for us. No problem.

So the stereo didn't work too well. In fact smoke had just started coming from the surrounding console and now it didn't work at all, never mind. The lights lit. The indicators indicated. The brakes broke speed. Speed: we vibrated all the way up to fifty and nothing went nuclear. 'Offer him a hundred,' suggested Andy, 'and you'll get it for one-twenty-five to one-fifty.'

So I offered him the hundred. No way, mate! He had to get Traffic to see it. Labour's expensive. The lowest he'd go was a hundred and eighty. I sniped it at one-seventy-five. Pick up noon, Friday.

I was now the courageous owner of a little brown Fiat. Almost. Andy simply said, It's your money. And waited in the Mini.

In his car we talked about Andy's comedy. He told me there was comedy in his head, a joke shop holed up in there. There was comedy in his head that made him laugh, or chuckle quietly to himself, when the punch-line would wake him from sleep. And in his dreams he laughed madly in the court of laughs, only to forget it all as the dream slipped back into the night and the day came for him.

Tell me a joke, Andy.

No.

The comedy was not – not *executable.* He wasn't prepared to sit there driving the car and driving me into hysterics. All he would do was discuss the sketches that occasionally dashed through his head, scratching at his memory on their way.

Tell me a sketch, Andy.

'OK,' he said, as we entered another congestion-stalled street.

'I thought of this one the other day when I was having a shit. I don't think many people will find it funny, it's kinda surreal. It's stupid. Stupid, that's why I like it.' He started laughing, already. 'It's set in a unisex hairdresser's. It starts with this bloke with his head back in a sink while a girl washes his hair. After washing it she asks him to go over to the chair where she will cut it. All this done very seriously, no smiling or anything, dead serious. The bloke gets off the chair, but instead of walking he gets on a children's tricycle and pedals furiously over to the other chair. She then shaves off all his hair. He thanks her and pedals off to a lorry. Saddam Hussein opens the door for him, he gets in it and then drives away.'

He looked at me.

'Yeah,' I said. 'Surreal.'

'My stand-up stuff's much better. It's not like that at all.'

I changed the subject. 'You know, Andy, I might take up exercise.'

'Exercise? Like running, or cycling?'

'No. Nothing as strenuous as that.' I couldn't see myself getting out of breath; besides, running and cycling were considered, *urban*ly, dangerous nowadays. 'I was thinking of going to the gym or doing a couple of laps of a pool now and again.'

'The gym? Like body-building?'

'No! Just a little exercise to get fitter. When I've got my car I'll be able to drive there.'

'Don't you feel healthy enough already? Now that you've gone all square and don't drink or smoke?'

'I don't feel much different. To be honest I feel mostly lost, if anything.'

'So how long are you going to keep it up, this boring health shit?'

'We'll see.'

'I've got a bit of speed, do you want some?'

'Yeah, but I'll say no for now.'

'*Shit*,' shouted Andy. 'Fuck!'

'Relax, Andy, I'll do some soon.'

'No. Not that. I'm meant to be meeting Annis down at the GoodBye.'

'When?'

'Now!' We looked out of the car. Two lanes of stationary traffic stood on either side of us. Were these cars parked, double-parked or part of the traffic? It was hard to tell from the vague hominids they contained with their newspapers and props. You couldn't tell. 'Can you meet her for me?' he asked.

'It's a little difficult,' I lied.

'I'll owe you one.'

'All right, mate. I'll do it.'

'Cheers, Doug. You're kickin'.'

'See you soon.'

'Yeah. I'll park.'

The GoodBye Bar was a few blocks away and would maybe take five minutes on foot. I put my feet out on the cold macadam and stood up. Gravity fell through my body, through my boots and into the ground, where it bounced back and spiked at my blisters. Gravity had come through the clouds; it had filtered through the cumulonimbus that was heaping up high above me like an ever-growing pile of road-stained snow. There was light at the top; the base was dark. Soon the radio rain would be tuned in and falling on London.

On the way the best thing I saw was in another world. This other world consisted of sun, heat and sand. Ah, these travel operators can really find their way out of late winter when all around are suffering from some strain of seasonal disorder: damp depression or night toxicity. My last holiday, four years ago: a Canary island with Lucinda. So bring back that sun and sea, cheap beer and cigarettes (not much use to me right now). We both went topless and no one looked, not even at the foliage on my pruned pectorals, it was normal, very few had very much on. Try and imagine that out here in London in this late winter with a great heap of cloud looking on.

Lucinda had been so drunk when I first met her that in the morning she couldn't remember my name. Here was a girl I was going to get on with. I told her: *Doug*. Then she forgot it again. It was two weeks before she stopped forgetting. Soon after, we went on the holiday. When we got back I could take no more: she had unleashed the paranoid within me. And before I had a chance to tell her, she told me to fuck off because I forgot her birthday – the bitch. We never even suggested that we should remain friends. It was a clean break. A loveless gash bleeding soon after my twenty-first birthday, when things might have changed direction.

Up ahead of me there was some kind of city commotion. Usually it would be a crazed drunk or a psychosing smack-head. Becoming more common was abduction, or attempted abduction. Of course, there was also violence, murder and rape. Today I saw the commotion coming at me open-mouthed with its teeth brighter than the light suggested possible. I watched it pass, people trembled in its wake. Today it was a cockeyed dog on a delirious supermarket-sweep. The Prevention were screaming after it in their van. So was the dog-catcher. Who would get to it first? The dog turned a corner and ran head-on into the road.

An RTA with a police car.

No more city dog.

In the GoodBye, Annis was sat up against the bar. She was performing to the pub light, a two-degree tilt of her head and a side glance in the bar mirror. That's good. Annis liked the light. And the light liked Annis, its wavelengths neatly showing her off. The pub liked Annis too. Or at least the pub males liked her, her new hairstyle – shorter and blonder – causing much hopeful speculation and beery gazumping among them. Then she saw me.

'Doug. Darling!'

And the light shifted. And lit me up.

'Annis.' I kissed her. 'How are you?'

'Very happy. And you? How are you? You look so well.'

'I'm good. Do I?'

'You do! Would you like a drink? No, you're not drinking. That's a shame – would you like a soft drink?'

'A Coke. Cheers.'

The waitress with great teeth was looking on and listening. 'A Coke?' she asked.

'Please.'

'Your hair,' I told her, 'it's you. It's great.'

'Thank you, Doug, I'm glad you like it. Where's Andrew?'

'Parking the car, the traffic's incredible.'

'I know,' she agreed. 'But what can we do about it?'

'Well, various proposals have been put forward, for instance—'

'Doug. Your hair is all over the place. Let me fix it for you.' I looked in the bar mirror; insanity stared back at me with its jowl-eyed smile. 'Jesus. It's hot,' I said suddenly, pulling my cheeks down with callipered index finger and thumb. 'Where's that Coke?' Annis started playing with my hair. Fixing my hair. The hair tensed at its roots.

'It's so fine, this hair. You need to put some body in it.'

'Do I?'

'Try Body Blow In after you wash it. You're hot?'

'A little. I think it's just coming in from the cold.'

'I hear you're buying a car.'

'Yes. A little Fiat.'

'How nice. What colour?'

'Dark tan.'

'Brown?'

'Yes.'

'You'll have to take me out for a drive sometime. I'm sick of choking to death in the Mini. It can't be good for me, all those fumes.' She lit a cigarette, giggled with the irony, and held the packet to me.

'I will. No thanks.'

'There's nothing wrong with you, Doug. You don't need a therapist. You've always struck me as perfectly normal. Special even.'

'Special?'

'You know what I mean.' I didn't, but have always found it easiest to agree with such comments: I nodded once. The head came down, eyelids lowered. It did the trick. She smiled: her teeth were on show. It was between her and the GoodBye waitress – this tooth showdown. And in the Good-Bye the ultraviolet cherished great teeth and chastised, say, the sub-brilliance of grey hair.

'Guess what it is in three days' time,' she told me.

It was Friday and it was also her birthday. I had a choice. I said, 'Friday?'

'No. It's my birthday.'

'Really?'

'Yes. I'll be twenty-one . . . plus a few years.'

'So what are you doing for it? You and Andy?'

'Hasn't he said anything? I bet he's forgotten again. We're all meeting here and then going on somewhere. You're invited, obviously.'

'I'll be here. Do you know what he's buying you?'

'No idea. Depends on whether he remembers. Maybe nothing.'

'What would you like?'

She went through a muddled and unprepared list. She would like this. No. In fact she wouldn't. There was this great band she wanted to see, but she'd see them soon anyway. Nothing obvious; no lingerie. She didn't know. She wasn't sure. Then she said, 'Wine!' surprising herself, her mouth shaped with erotic possibilities as she described a claret she drank once, and only once – sadly.

An expensive bottle of this claret wine I decided would be my gift to Annis. Somehow I had to persuade her to drink it with me. Not with Andy.

Now, there's all that trouble that sometimes occurs between me and my best friend's girlfriends. I've never seen it documented and I've never told Spritz about it. I don't know whether it's just me. It might be common. Expected even. Could be common in love. I don't know. Your best friend introduces you to his new girlfriend. Quickly you assess her, the usual: would you or wouldn't you? This assessment is really the only sexual notion that should be entertained. After, you expect to have no more such thoughts, she's your best mate's girl and you don't tread on his toes, predatorial etiquette and so on . . .

No doubt similar appraisals go through her mind too, but the bias is different: presumably she has less to lose.

So there you are with his new girlfriend, and because there's no pressure on you trying to find a way to get her into bed, you find it possible to strike up a platonic friendship. That's fine. As far as I know that's where it stops with most people.

With me, and here's my problem, I find that due to the lack of pressure I have got to know the girl much quicker and much better than if I'd actually been trying to get her into bed all along. At this point I take a look at her and realize that I actually want to fuck her.

So, I long to say, Annis, I want to fuck you. Unfortunately it's a difficult line to deal when I'm always sober. If I had a drink I'd be in the clear. I could say it and then blame alcohol when she accused me of ruining our special friendship. I looked at her. She was mumbling and moaning about car insurance.

Do you want to fuck me, Annis? No, probably not.

Car insurance! She put her hand on my knee and asked, 'Is your car insured?'

'I wasn't going to bother.'

'You must. I'll arrange it for you. Ring me at work with all the details.'

'Would you?'

'I'd love to.'

'Would you like to f—'

'*Andrew!*'

Andy came over to us, the radio rain dripping in electrical pools around him. 'Fuck the weather. Fuck England.'

'You're absolutely drenched,' cooed Annis. 'I'll call a taxi.'

They offered me a ride home. I refused, I had to go next door to collect something.

Outside the weather was a rock concert pumping out a billion watts of thunder and producing a massive stage show of lightning.

Oh, this radio weather is so out of tune. Some pirate station. And way, way off the dial.

Four

Today I finished work at noon. That's over four hours . . . Man, do I hate these early starts. And what a morning, with its capricious callers: boiled-up bachelors and harrowed housewives – sorry, dogged domestic engineers; these calls, the lines were jammed.

The job description described a part-time customer services position in one of the new phone companies. Straightforward, Doug, all you do is phone our customers and go through the questions on the screen. The computer will do the rest. It's easy, as simple as that . . . No problem, I told them, I can do that.

True to form, the job description was not the job. The Frenetic Phone Company had got it wrong, or had misled me. The Frenetic Phone Company is so truly dire that for nearly four hours I sit there connected to the phone, the computer and the mains, listening to the coil of complaints that come whizzing up the wire: rehearsed polemic and futile follow-ups growled into my earpiece.

Sometime earlier (I was getting ready to switch my phone off in preparation for my break, when I would purchase another wild delicacy from the Frenetic cafeteria), one of my colleagues buzzed through and said, 'All right, Doug, I've got a Mr Grottish on the line. He wants to talk to you.'

'Who?'

'Mr Tom Grottish.'

'What kind of a name is that?' I asked. 'People can't go around with names like *Grottish*!'

'I agree. It's a crap name. But he says he wants to talk to you. Apparently you set his phone up for him last week.'

'Well, he's wrong. I'd remember dealing with someone called Grottish.'

'I'm putting him through. Be patient with him, Doug. He sounds as though he's talking with a bag of chips in his mouth.'

Mr Grottish began the conversation with the words: 'Um mach hoppy.' Or something like that.

'Hello, Mr Grottish. This is Doug. What can I do for you?'

With increased volume Mr Grottish said, 'It's Grottish. Not Grottish!'

'Yes – Mr *Tom Grottish*.'

'Grottish!'

'Yes, sir. What's the problem?'

Mr Grottish explained the problem. But I couldn't understand a word he was saying. So I said, 'Mr Grottish, don't think me rude, but I can't quite understand what you're saying. Are you eating?'

'NO! CHRIST!' I think that's what he said.

'Mr Grottish, I'm sorry but I don't seem to be able to find you on the computer. Are you sure that you are one of our customers?'

'MY NAME'S GROTTISH!' he carried on shouting for a while and then started swearing (I knew he was swearing because swearing is a universal language and because it was what you came to expect from Frenetic's customers: they all swore sooner or later).

'OK, sir. Spell your name.'

'MR—'

'Yes.'

'*T . . . I . . . M.*'

'Uh huh.'

'*G . . . R . . . I . . . F . . . F . . . I . . . T . . . H . . . S!*'

'Ah!' I said. 'Mr Tim Griffiths. Right. I think I've found you. If you could just confirm your address.'

After a few (angry) attempts, he gave me his address. And, yes, he was right, I had set his phone up last week. But Mr Griffiths had not been pulverizing potato last week. So, eager to get this thing cleared up, I asked once again, 'What is the problem, sir?'

Speaking very slowly and very loudly – he appeared to have decided that the only way I was going to understand him was if he treated me like a deaf foreigner – he said, 'NO . . . ONE . . . CAN . . . UN-DER-STAND . . . ME . . . WHEN . . . I . . . CALL . . . THEM . . . ON . . . THIS . . . FUCKING . . . PHONE!'

'Right, sir. I'm very sorry. I expect it's broken. Don't worry. We'll send you a replacement. Just send the old one back to us.'

After giving me a little more deaf-foreigner treatment, Mr Griffiths said goodbye and went away happy with my promise that he would receive a fully functioning Frenetic phone within three working days. Which of course was a lie. *None* of the Frenetic phones are fully functional.

I've said sorry so many times that my facial muscles have been sculpted into a slavish aspect, one of bewilderment, eager to apologize. As I finish work and shut my computer down, I sit there and see this sorry face of mine staring back at me from the dead screen. My sad look, a speechless semblance shared with the blank computer face.

Happily, when I get out of the building, my composure climbs back into shape as the cold air plays in my crevices and my face is no longer barren like the moon, more the swirling gas of Jupiter, and this is the graphic that I wear to the social security office every fortnight: Wednesday, one-thirty, when I sign on. Here I come up against what may well be the real world. Everyone's represented. Everyone, the whole bang. Last week the guy over there had a Porsche and a house. Not now. Now his business is smashed and he's on the state. The well-spoken lady in the corner clearly had a better life once. Everything about her says, Of course, I wasn't always in this predicament, it's only *temporary*. And here they are mixing with the drunks, the junkies and the homeless. Where else would this happen? Where else would they let it? The whole bang all stuffed together signing their name and asking for money.

And don't forget the criminals. Criminals love the social. Hey, it's easy money, not to be passed up, no way, mate. They cannot resist it.

Neither can I, but I haven't got crime to fall back on. Or is this crime?

'Any work in the last two weeks, Mr Down?'

'No. None.'

'Please sign here.' I pass the paper back.

'Thank you.'

'No. Thank you.'

In two weeks' time I'll do the same, commit an identical crime. Meantime I hope the Dole Abusers Squad doesn't swoop on Frenetic and haul off the cash-in-handers.

Walking down the street, and into the caliginous clime of Bridlington street, you look up through the cold shadow to your left and see the offices that block out the afternoon sun. You wouldn't think that a psychotherapist worked up there. You wouldn't imagine that professional mind-tweaking took place behind those pockled walls. A satanic cult quite possibly. But not the control that comes by the hour, rather than the pledge . . . The grey building with its porous concrete set up there in three levels. The first three steps to the troposphere. Spritz works from the second and loves the metaphor: up or down, it's up to you.

It wasn't busy around here. Bridlington Street remains overlooked, permanently forgotten with its empty parking. There was a long slot further up where I planned to park the little brown Fiat. It wouldn't mind, it would fit well in this street where brown is more intensely interesting than grey.

Then the female face-off.

Let's face this one head-on, I thought.

Head-on. Here she comes again: the girl with dying eyes. Leaving that building, that professional building. Here comes Lucia de Londres.

She came towards me, the tiny dog bouncing around in front of her with its happy yap and quivering tail. What I really wanted to say was, Hello. You must be Death. Is it time? Instead I asked, 'Are you following me?'

'From where, Doug? Where would I be following you *from*?' she remonstrated. 'I come out of the building and here you are. *Are you following me*?'

'Why the fuck would I want to follow you?'

'Because you want to apologize.'

'For what?'

'You know!'

'I don't.' The tiny dog was jumping at me. I stroked it. It seemed pleased.

'Lancelot,' said the girl.

'What?'

'She's called Lancelot.'

'*She's* called Lancelot. Why?'

'I'm interested in Arthurian legend. That's all. Now, are you going to apologize?'

'Where have you just come from?'

'Why do you want to know?'

'Just tell me.'

'No harm in that, I guess. I've been to see my friend Edmund.'

'What? Spritz?'

'Edmund Spritzer. Yes, you and he know each other, don't you?'

'Why?'

'Why what?'

'WHY HAVE YOU BEEN TO SEE HIM?'

'He helps me. I've not been well – as you know. You are to blame after all. Yes, for the last few months I've seen a lot of Edmund. He's a great help and I feel much better these days.' She paused to assess how much better she felt. 'He's told me all about you, of course, and the awful things you do to people. I hoped I was the only one. I feel so sorry for the others. You bastard.' She came at me, slapped me and ran off.

'Fuck off,' I shouted after her. 'You're totally insane!' The tiny dog scrabbled behind her as she did her maniac run down the street. I held my cheek and started the steps.

'OK, Spritz,' I said calmly. 'What the fuck is going on?'

'Whatever do you mean?'

'That girl, the one with the unhealthy eyes, what was she doing here?'

'She's a patient.'

'And?'

'What more can I tell you?'

'*What more*? How about explaining what you told her about me?'

'Doug, the girl is suffering from extreme delusions. She believes in entirely fictitious events. Much the same as you when you first started therapy.'

'I was never as bad as that.'

'You were,' he argued. 'Now let's change the subject.'

'Is she in your book?'

'That's not important.'

'Tell me. Or I'll walk out.'

'Don't be silly, Doug.'

'Right. See you around.'

'No. Wait. Yes, she is in the book.'

'So we both are?'

'In a way. Now, I asked you here—'

'What do you mean, *in a way*?'

'It's not *you* and *her*. It is two characters mildly – very mildly – based on the two of you.'

'So you need me then. I'm important to you. And so is she. We are your *material*.'

'You are of some importance,' he admitted. 'However, I am able to finish writing without you.'

'Tell me this,' I started. His face became attentive and his ears twitched; his ears twitched because he was one of the few people I know who can wilfully twitch their ears. 'Why does she hate me?'

'She hates everyone,' answered Spritz. 'Now let's talk about you.'

'How does she know where I live?'

'What makes you think she does?'

'She came round and terrorized me the other night, telling me she used to love me and being generally mad.'

'She might have followed you.'

'I'll call the police then.'

'Don't do that, Doug, she's not a danger to you. I'll talk to her, calm her down, ask her to leave you alone . . . She'll do it for me. I have quite a lot of influence over her,' he said proudly. 'Now then, I asked you here for a reason, not to talk about my other patients. There is a test I want to do on you.'

So he set out his test. Man! I never thought he'd go so low. I thought he had more professional integrity, billing himself as a modern scientist in the art of mental therapy.

That old picture test. 'What does this remind you of?'

'It's a shit.'

'This?'

'A cock.'

'This?'

'A cunt. Come on, Spritz,' I said, 'this is pornography.'

'And this?'

'Albumen.'

'That's better,' he said. 'Now we're getting somewhere. This one?'

'A heavily pigmented nub of skin.'

'Good, good. And this?'

'It's disgusting. I can't look.'

'Part of your problem lies in sexual association. You see things sexually and it frustrates you. It creates a negative energy within and there can be no release for someone like you. Your sexual entropy is in disequilibrium.' His eyes asked for a response. I said nothing. 'You are unbalanced and that is bad for your mind. If we can disassociate the objects of sex themselves, we will be able to give you a more realistic grasp on everyday life. Are you sexually frustrated?'

'A little.' (Frustrated, yes. Sexually, no.)

'What's this?'

'A curve.'

'This?'

'A limb.'

'And this?'

'The landing strip.'

'Doug!'

'Sorry.'

'I'll get there in the end with you.' He sighed.

'Maybe.'

'You need my help.'

'When you phoned me and asked me to come along today you said it had something to do with your novel. Was that test it?'

'Part of it, yes. Do you remember when we first met, you believed you had committed an abhorrent act?'

'As I remember it was you who believed that.'

'No. No, Doug. You were not very well, you've obviously forgotten. We came to the conclusion that you had assaulted someone, a girl. Mentally. And possibly sexually.'

'Did we?'

'Yes. And you had put it from your mind, blanked it out. As you appear to have done once again, I'm afraid.

'It is a little familiar.'

'Well, now is the time for me to let you into part of the novel. The character, which as I say is based loosely on you, has committed a similar act at the beginning. The story is about how he comes to terms with it. That's where you come in, in a sense you are a case study. I am watching and helping to see how *you* deal with the guilt of assault. The character,

Simon Sole, also has a psychotherapist who steers him through. The best novels reflect real life. I hope mine will be one of the best!'

'Simon Sole! Doug Down! It is me. I never hurt anyone!'

'Calm down, Doug, it's only a story.'

'So what about *that girl*? How does she fit into the story?'

'Merely a secondary character who is a friend of the psychotherapist. A past lover.'

'Do you love Lucia de Dying Eyes?'

'Of course not. Don't be so asinine, she's a patient!'

'What, then, was the significance of the test?'

'Simply to assess your sexual reaction. Not really anything to do with my novel. You are my patient after all and you're not well. You may be a rapist for all we know.'

'Don't be so fucking ridiculous!'

'I dislike being this hard on you, but you must be prepared for the worst. One day when you recall the diabolical event you will need to be ready for it . . . How do you feel?'

'Angry.'

'Good. What else?'

'Like ripping your fucking head off.'

'*Excellent*.'

'What do you mean, *excellent*?'

'Oh, sorry. You've given me another idea for the character . . . Doug, what do you plan for your immediate prosopography?'

'My *what*?'

'What do you plan to do with your life in the next few weeks?'

'Not a lot really. I might buy a car.'

'No. Don't do that. Don't buy a car. You won't, will you?'

'No. Probably not,' I lied once again. It's all I can do with

Spritz these days. He sits there pocketed into the corners of his big chair, asking me these questions and proposing insane scenarios. Me a rapist? Gimme a break. OK, no might not always mean *no*, but I'm pretty clear when it does. I've stepped over no body boundaries so far in this supposedly lewd life of mine. I asked him a question. 'Tell me about the psychotherapist in the novel, what's he like?'

'I had little choice in his development, having to pander to consumer appeal. He's a red-blooded, heterosexual, handsome male. The girls adore him.'

'I expect you adore him too.'

'I prefer women, you know that.'

'Does Terry know you prefer women?'

'Terry's gone. I'm not interested in that sort of thing any more, I'm too busy with my novel.'

'Have you got any of this novel that I can read?'

'I'd rather not let you see it.'

'I'd rather you did. I feel as though I have a right.'

'Perhaps. Maybe in a couple of weeks I'll allow you to see the first chapter. I quite like it.'

We ended our session there. Another patient was due. I asked whether I knew this one too, whether this patient was in the novel. 'No,' he assured me.

I passed the patient on the tropospheric steps, a stooped octogenarian surely too late for psychotherapy. But still, this is modern life. Modern life where his concepts are less welcome. Less welcome in this world of constant invention; every day someone invents a new atrocity, a new form of mind control, even a new word. Every day the media reports such events and gets credit for their coverage of laser murder in the Middle East. The psychos that did it are of course sick. The journos highly skilled to find and report such tragedy.

And the photos are so vivid. The modern reel. Is this why the octogenarian needs therapy?

Spritz says he's worried about Dead-eyed de Londres. He made me promise to phone if I see her. He didn't imagine for a moment that I would; but if I did, phone him.

If the dice roll in my favour I will not set eyes on her. I hope I don't see her, she aggravates me. Also I have my suspicions that she is a raging feminist and I can't deal with that. Hey, she's so fucked up she might even be an ardent misogynist – and I couldn't deal with that either.

Spritz is aiming at a two hundred thousand word novel. Phew, I said, how many pages is that? Nearly six hundred in paperback, the format I'm aiming for. Nearly six hundred pages, that's plenty of room for a lot of shit. It could be more, he says, it could be less, depends on how things work out. Don't do anything stupid, Doug, don't upset my apple cart.

Yeah, I am important to him. More so than he will admit.

Today's light has some life left in it yet. So has the sun, five billion years – four, till it goes red (cheers, Spritz). I'm walking again now, back on the concrete and crushed crap, doing my boot side-of-the-foot walk. There's enough light to get home in. There's enough light to save me from damp-night nausea that occasionally comes rearing at me.

A little update, some personal insight, from the heart, from me: I was ill. I wasn't making out well up in my head a few months ago. I was not the full bucket of water, or whatever it is that people say when they're not quite right . . . Whatever – but I wasn't mad. And I'm not mad now. I'm not cruising down insanity alley. I'm perfectly – well, maybe not 100 per cent, but I'm well. Let's leave it at that: I'm well.

Thanks for the concern. Thanks.

I keep meaning to ask a doctor: Do I pop them or leave them? I have assuaged my teenage desire to burst everything. But should I pop these? Would it help if I popped these foot blisters; would I walk better, faster, more – *adroitly*? Should I bleed the fluid from them, from these, my desert blisters? Or do I leave them as balloons? Hey everyone, I'm walking on water. I am . . .

Right now hunger's kicking around in this hollow head of mine. Perhaps that's not true, perhaps hunger is kicking around somewhere else: all around in dark secluded alleys – and in my bass-pan belly. The thought, the eat-option, however, is most definitely up there in my head, the microvolts connecting in my brain. There's an equation to be balanced in the hemispheres and it goes: money, check; food, *please*. It rifles out the answer: a takeaway. So it's decided: a takeaway tonight.

Next option: English, French, Chinese, Indian, Thai, American, Mexican or Millennium? No, not Millennium, the money doesn't balance.

Indian? Yeah, curry.

Last week I had a Phall, with a friend. Forget, if you will, this Vindaloo Vocation of those 'lager ladies'. It's simple: vindaloo's a statement, Phall's a dish, a gastronomic one – the ingredients will be the best the chef has got.

And out they kept coming, my Indian friends, watching my face, watching the hot pools of sweat come draining off me, on to the table, over the floor and menacingly close to the floor-flush electricity socket. My tongue hanging from my pale wet face like a ragged dog as I crammed another mouthful in. 'Fuck,' I said to my (increasingly) alarmed female companion, '*this* is good!'

Smiling, and rubbing their hands together, they urged me on. Urged me to the end, where at last I arrived, drained and exhausted, longing for ice or cocaine numbness. 'Did you like that, Mr Doug?' I nodded, unable to speak. 'Would you like to try the chef's special next time?' My eyes asked for more information. 'It's hotter,' they said. 'Much hotter!' I was passed a mint, I sucked on it and was able to mouth the word 'Maybe'. Maybe.

And you know the rest of the story: the morning story. Seated until noon, and then ready for the dash . . .

But anyway, there you have it. Tonight I'm having a take-away curry, a mild one, without the chilli.

'Without chilli?' replied the incredulous Shadat. 'You go somewhere else, Mr Doug!'

'What's the weakest? I'm not well at the moment.'

'Abdul says you *must* have his special. Now!'

'I will soon, I promise. Not tonight, I need something mild. I – I've got to share it with – with a girl.'

'OH! You should say before. Korma.'

'Korma?'

'Yes. Ten minutes, chicken korma, OK?'

'OK.'

'OK, here's your poppadom.'

I sat on the L-shaped foyer seat and picked up the poppadom, which more or less exploded the moment I touched it and had me crouching and reaching under the furniture to retrieve its spicy shrapnel. Up in the corner of the undernourished foyer was a television, its TV-colours straddling the guts of the room. And up in the other corner: a surveillance camera, choosing shots as it converted all into grainy black and white, and waited, like a burglar alarm, for crime. *Give me crime,* pleaded the camera, as it panned the room for an armed robbery.

The camera loves crime, getting plenty, but wanting more. It is addicted to crime. If the camera had any sense, which of course it doesn't, it would point its Lilliputian lens directly into the TV screen. It would watch and record *CrimeTime*. And what is it with this new channel, is everyone watching it? Except the criminals – who are out on location filming its footage.

I'm learning. If I was going to commit a crime I'd plan it spectacular. If I was doing crime I'd want to get on TV, I'd hope to secure a feature on *CrimeTime*. Is that it? Is that how it works? Is someone out there paying the criminals to commit more televisual crimes? What's the slice on an armed robbery, or the cut on a ram-raid? The public love them: they make great viewing; ram-raiding is so TV-friendly.

'Mr Doug,' said Shadat in an American accent. '*Enjoy*.' I picked up my takeaway and my stomach went concave.

I'm heading home now in this late light to eat. I'm heading home to the korma-coloured carpet in my flat. I'm heading home and out of Spritz's novel for a while. I'm heading home.

Next day I woke up in the morning. I woke up in the morning. Not the afternoon. The phone rang early, the doorbell rang early. I let them both get on with it. The refuse lorry got jammed in the traffic: much shouting, swearing and octane-revving. And every child was awake and killing in the street. The cats were screaming – their lives notched away on the tipcat stick.

My take away awoke me too – with its groans and its stabs. It awoke me angrily.

Glass covered my eyes before I washed. It melted in the basin, the morning glass.

Back in bed I exhumed *Cooperage in the Late Twentieth Century* from a pyramid of bedroom rubbish. It fell open on page five. Page five, where I'd left it: Chattaway still silent in the corner.

The landlord (so titled, he remains anonymous) speaks with barmaid Bella. He is reviling Chattaway, who, it appears, is bad for business: he hardly ever buys a drink, yet he's in my boozer all day taking up valuable pub-space. The landlord is uneasy, Chattaway makes him uneasy. He decides Chattaway must be queer. 'Ugh,' he says, 'it really puts me off my stroke when I'm giving you one in the beer cellar.' He contemplates poisoning him.

Back to Chattaway: the landlord has no idea that he is hated by him. Chattaway has drinks brought over by the landlord – the landlord must fancy Chattaway. Now he thinks the *landlord* is queer. It would devastate the landlord if he knew how much talkative Chattaway hated him. And Bella's clearly falling for Chattaway in a big way; Chattaway loves her.

I know very little about films, about their production, their pans and scans, their close-ups and zoom-ins. Maybe I'm learning, maybe I've learned from *Cooperage in the Late Twentieth Century* that the director has got a real job on his hands. What's he going to do with it? It's all *over* the place.

Page seven: is this it? We're with the landlord this time and he says, 'I had Bella over a barrel last night – *literally* like!' Is this it? Is this the barrel reference?

After having her over a barrel, she turns to him and tells him to do something about that freak Chattaway, she can't stand him. Landlord has a solution, a rather violent solution:

'That's when I decided, if this guy is gonna crop up in our lovemaking, then his presence in this public house is no longer to be tolerated. That's why I've elected to maim him, more specifically to chop his cock off. Since you can't come into a pub if you ain't got a cock, unless you're a bird of course, like big Bella here.' His plan then: to get Chattaway drugged, call his cabby mate, Cabbage, cart him off to the deserted house and do the cutting . . .

Is this the product of a slightly twisted mind? A slightly twisted *female* mind? No, it's film, no explanation necessary.

In a sense we are all scavengers. Searching the city and its streets for answers and something to give us an edge. This is largely something we are aware of, and it is expected of us. I guess it is a state of consciousness.

Outside this known scavenger lies another kind, a less respected one, a less well-appointed one. This scavenger is more interested in the immediate and operates to differing degrees in us all. It spots a packet of sweets on the pavement when you are a toddler, it spies comics in bins a few years later, cigarettes when you start smoking, discarded pornography and, later, drugs lost in clubs. Of course, it always looks for money and always will.

Sometimes the scavenger gets confused and hands you something you weren't expecting; in my case *Cooperage in the Late Twentieth Century* . . . What use is it? Do I really need it? Is my scavenger all fucked up and clean out of its head?

The jouster's battle resumed in my belly, so I got out of bed and did what I could to stop the pain. Then I ate some food. Crisps, chocolate, chewy sweets. High energy, fuel for the day.

Finally I looked out of the window at the day, the pink-impinged day. I did that boring task of adding the word 'scourer' to a shopping list – the pink spray was coming off the glass.

Even through the pink I could see the sky and it was blue. The sky was blue and this was a change, the sky had no right being blue. Something had to be done about this and, as though emitted from a huge and industrially fantastic factory, a blotchy cloud came lolloping on to the scene and pit-stopped in front of the sun. It absorbed the light in all its flab. The sudden change gave London an artificial light, as if a sudden power loss had kicked in the emergency lighting. The grey had returned. I waited up there in my flat for my vision to adjust to this monochrome frame: this old worn photo that I send to friends in far places.

I envisaged spending up to twenty pounds on the bottle of wine, Annis's present. I understand that the price should not come into it, the wine should tell the story. However, being unaware of the complexities of her palate (and not really knowing what a palate was anyway), I needed a reasonable price to back up the wine if the taste didn't buckle her knees. I needed to be able to say, 'But it cost . . .' The twenty-pound price tag having to affirm the quality . . . It was a claret, she was sure about that; a claret that had disarmed her before. Whether this claret cost two pounds or two hundred I had no idea. Clearly I was going to need some vintner's advice and I had the wine shop marked out, the route scribed in red on the street map in my head.

Before I bought the wine – my first alcoholic purchase for two months – I had to phone No Name Motors about the Fiat to get all those details for the insurance company: the breadth and the girth of the power plant and how many seats it had, wheels, gizmos and grinders. I spoke with the salesman. Traffic was about to get busy with his spanners, it was in hand and, Oh yeah, mate, you're lucky that the tappet drive is mechanical not hydraulic. Am I? Most definitely, hydraulic's expensive. We confirmed pick-up time: an exchange at noon, Friday. Cash for the car, no strings.

Armed with the gen, I phoned Annis. Or I tried phoning her. I had the number for her company but these electronic voices kept sending me all over place, redirecting my call through a hierarchy of departments. Eventually I reached her and then didn't recognize her voice; the voice that welcomed me was pitched at the wrong speed, at low battery power that turns the happiest voice into a slow saturnine scroll. It was the voice of repetition and time, a voice that had lost the meaning of the words it spoke. A depressed voice, despondent and career awry, 'Doug?' it said, confusion breaking into her language. 'Doug!' She became mercurial. 'Oh, it's so good to speak to a human being. How are you? You're after a quote? No. Cover for the car?'

'Please.'

'I'm sorry,' she said, 'but I'm going to have to ask you a lot of questions.'

'Go for it, fire away.'

'What's your name, sir?'

'Doug.'

'Yes, of course, sorry, I go on to automatic pilot in this place. Do you have a middle name?'

'No.'

I gave her my address, car details, inside leg measurement, cock size, etc. Then she asked me for the details of any accidents I may have had in the last five years. And there had been an accident: three or four cars had crumpled around me. The drivers all said I'd been driving too slowly, my retarded progress had caused this pile-up. Helpfully the police and insurance companies had seen it differently: no crime had been committed by driving too slowly. No crime. They forgot to mention that it was compulsory in the congestion where car-levitation remained an enigma to all but the highest of drivers (who would later claim in court that they had been piloting a plane at the time of the pile-up that they hadn't caused).

The good news: the crash would not affect my premium.

The bad news: how long was it since I last held insurance? Over two years? My no claims bonus had expired. What? After lapsing for two years it was void, I would have to start again. 'No. Fuck it,' asserted Annis. 'Hopefully no supervisor is monitoring this call, I'll give you sixty-five per cent NCB and let customer services deal with it. Just plead ignorance if they write to you.'

'That'll work, will it?'

'Sure. It's so disorganized. Nobody's got a clue what's going on over there. I could probably charge you ninety-nine pence for a year's insurance and they'd not pick up on it.'

'Go on then.'

'I tell you what I'll do, I'll charge you, er . . . fifty-one pounds. How does that sound?'

'I'll take it.'

She gave me a policy number. I was insured.

I think I like this life with its connections and its hook-ups, its sidesteps into cheap car insurance. Its *who you knows*. So I don't smoke, I'm teetotal, celibate and insured . . . my taxes, car and council, can wait. And I'm claiming income support but I've got a job. What can I say? How correct can I be, how well behaved do I need to be? Really, is there any point being legal when no one else is? I'm sure the woman in the Garlic Incident has her vices, her law-breaking binges: she jumps the lights, parks on double yellows and deigns not to hand in the damp note that her personal scavenger led her to. How law-abiding do I need to be when no one else is?

Outside it was brightening up, the weather-mood improving. As the sun burnt into the obesity of the fat cloud, rays of light filtered through. Actual rays from that spotlight up there eight and a half light-minutes away were picking out and flooding favoured areas of London. And in a layer less than half a light-microsecond away were the frozen jet trails: a Tipp-Ex correction in the mistreated sky.

In my corner shop I asked Gary, an entirely anglicized Indian, whether he recommended Haligum or Clear Chew. Haligum was the bigger seller. 'Most probably due to the TV advertising campaign,' he said. Both are minty breath-freshening gums containing some active ingredient and my breath was tasting actively non-minty. I could taste garlic in my mouth and smell it in my sweat pores. Abdul, in a chef's vengeance, replaced what would have been chilli with garlic. The takeaway tasted good, garlicky, but now my breath must have been of mephitic proportions and I feared the look on people's faces as they pulled back when I spoke, staring sideways with noses round the back of their ears. He recommended the Haligum and I bought two packets, stuffed a couple of slabs into my mouth and started chewing them to the viscosity of hard rubber. How do they work, these sanitizing deodorant gums, is it a chemical reaction? Is some catalyst involved – some enzyme? More to the point, how do we *know* they work? It's commonly accepted that if you have bad breath, you will not be able to smell it. You may get a clue: a discourteous taste, invidious remarks, hospitalization of loved ones; but generally you will be the last to know. Assuming that it does work, you still can't be sure that your guarded breathing is free from fetid air pollution, all you can taste is mint; and mint might just be covering up the smell, a little like spraying deodorant over two-week-old socks or air freshener into a small toilet where someone has recently lost two stone by emptying their bowels.

Haligum might be just that. It might be a late-twentieth-century cover-up. It might not work at all.

With gum working out between my teeth, a newspaper in my outstretched arms and painful scenes inside my boots, I ambled along the pavement – or the sidewalk, as it will soon be called – towards technology. In the newspaper – which was a broadsheet, the quest for nearer truth or less well-endowed stories of well-hung aliens leading me to this format – I read about the latest crisis: a paper shortage. Unlike the lascivious lakes of wine and butter mountain orgies, there was a shortage of paper. It appears that there is no tissue box the size of Nottingham on reserve in Scandinavia and no toilet roll of Channel Tunnel dimensions hanging off the side of Uranus hidden away in order to force up prices. It appears there really is a paper shortage.

A pulp consultant gave readers the lowdown in the large pages with small print. Pulp – the mush they make paper out of – was in short supply. A ton of pulp was going to cost you 50 per cent more than it did a year ago. And all because the bloke who was meant to be growing trees couldn't keep up; some joker kept coming along and chopping them down when he wasn't looking.

Oh dear, Spritz, how much pulp are you going to need for

your 600 pager? How many trees? Can the world afford your 2,000 centuries of words? Oh dear, Spritz, you'll be needing a blue pencil and a long, long ruler.

Tell me about this book business. Are books not redundant yet? There's no technology in them; just words and paper. Can they not be harmonized, digitalized, left to nanotechnology where they can build themselves molecule by molecule. Books have got to catch up; they're lagging behind. Christ, we're nearly in the third millennium and they've been around so long. Come on, books, make an effort, get with the times, you lazy bastards . . . Everyone else has.

With orphaned newspaper sheets ghosting and wrapping themselves around the caged protection of feeble tree trunks, with the print of this dead and dying form suffocating in the air, I walked down Science Street. Here the children cut their teeth on the gritty liquid-crystal-display playground, and skip school to take their parents for modernization and update. Here a thousand cameras will watch from shop-window displays and transport you inside through a computer that takes you apart bit by bit and rebuilds your image byte by byte into colour digital. There I was inside the black box of Marian, the latest on-screen transmutation system, and I fancied, even, that I saw myself in another shop, not my reflection but a hologram, a coherently lit interference pattern of my lifelessness. Once inside all this technology I was in someone else's control, my image lasered to the fiery sun through satellite link-ups.

Here's a question. Does technology frighten you?

Tell me honestly, does it?

Me? I'm terrified.

But I'm ill apparently.

Apparently.

★ ★ ★

I love the thought of wine. I love the *concept* of wine. Someone clearly went to a lot of trouble to open a niche for wine. Then they closed it and wine remained a speciality all of its own. Wine has got a good thing going, it has got a great future, it's untouchable until they find a way of synthesizing it, a way of getting *technology* into it.

I love the concept of wine. Love it. The wine itself I am less enthralled by. I have this gripe with grapes. They say, when it comes to wine, that you either like it or you don't. I guess I fall into the second category: I don't really like it. I drink it though, or used to. I will again soon, with Annis hopefully. I'll have to put up with all that body and acidity and wood and cost. Beer and spirits are my drink . . . They were my drink in the past when I still drank . . . While I may love the idea of wine, it is no more than a romantic notion, I know nothing about it. My first question will have to be something like: What is claret? . . . It's red, yeah. I know *that*.

There was no sun on the area of London where the Wine House did its business. Like me, the sun did not drink, it was far too busy releasing huge quantities of radiation energy from fusion reactions that went on at the surface of its core. And the sun is much better at fusion than earth-bound scientists after nearly five billion years of practice. Perhaps if we had five billion years, which of course we do not, we too could master the process.

There was no sun shining on the Wine House, instead the light effloresced from the building like a white phosphorous grenade. It was light in there, the comparison was light. And outside, despite the sun's efforts, it was dark with the day.

'Could you tell me where the claret is?'

'What?' The bearded man behind the counter looked up at me. 'You eighteen?'

'Twenty-five. How old are you?'

He looked away and started playing his computer game again.

'The claret?'

'Bordeaux's over there.' He pointed with a spare hand, the other fired at a computer creature.

'No,' I said. 'Where's the claret?'

'Bordeaux *is* claret.'

'Over there?'

'That's right.'

Advice would be good, but not from that arsehole.

Hundreds of bottles of claret or Bordeaux, or whatever it's called, stood there in sections shining black in the light; stood there like rockets pointing to the above, with their three hundred and sixty degrees of glass reflecting, watching and noting all that went on around them so that they were ready to launch when no one was looking. There were prices and summaries on each bottle, five pounds upwards, saying things like well oaked, rich, a typical claret, damp dog, Eastern manure and soiled pyjamas.

Apart from the bearded fuck behind the counter, there was one other Wine House employee who was saying goodbye to a customer. I wandered towards her through the thousands of bottles and prepared to ask her advice. I opened my mouth: Hell— 'Hello, dear!' screeched an old woman who had just walked in. 'Do you sell Suicider?' The old woman pulled the sheet-plastic headscarf off her face and scratched her crotch. 'Suicider?'

'Suicider?' asked the girl.

'Yes, dear. Suicider.'

'Do you know what Suicider is, Chuck?' she asked the computer-playing bumboy.

'No, Wendy.'

I knew Suicider. 'Cider,' I said. 'It's strong cider.'

'That's right, dear, it's cider. Do you have any?'

'I don't know,' I told her. 'I don't work here.'

'Don't you, dear?'

'No.'

I knew Suicider. We'd all been drinking it for a while. Strong stuff, ten per cent alcohol, cheap and tasted OK. It's one of those tricky drinks; it gets you drunk, then spins you around and the only cure is to drink some more. Most of us had given up on it now: it was the hangover – some cocktail of additives used to balance and preserve it led to the worst head. Even worse than cheap sherry. A few could take it but for most of us the after-effects made us feel like – like suicide. A campaign had been launched to ban it. Not by mothers, police, worried teachers or religious leaders, but by the drinkers themselves, who were sick of seeing their friends in such suicidal states. The trouble was that no one took any notice of the campaigners because they were always drunk and their protests consisted of staggering around the council offices and slurring, Sluicslider killths, ban Sluislider, you basthadths. Then a local reporter went down to interview them. It can't be that bad, he said. *Try it*, they told him. He did, and became a Suicider, and that was the last publicity it ever had. So the drink remains underground and hard to get hold of. Yet it remains legal.

'So do you have it, dear?'

'No. Sorry,' replied Wendy. 'Have a look over here, we have a selection of ciders. Maybe you'd like one of these. Some are quite strong—'

'No, dear. I only drink Suicider.' The woman, in addition to her plastic headscarf, wore what appeared to be a dressing gown which she had combined with patent-leather pink shoes. It was the dress sense of someone who wore clothes simply because everyone else did. Not because she didn't want to, or did want to, but because it seemed the best thing to do; and even then it wasn't planned. The result was a woman who wore clothes. That's all they were: clothes. Oh, she was scratching again.

Apart, she muddled along in her own world and was now converging on the white wine, the tall Wendy falling in behind her. She looked the wine up and down, from side to side, her eyes an array of drool and desire and drunkenness.

'Ooh,' burst the woman. 'How strong is this one?'

'That's a low-alcohol Chardonnay.'

'Ugh!' said the disgusted woman. She threw the wine back. Wendy winced as the bottle danced, ready for a low-alcohol spillage, but after some ludicrous loops it closed in on its centre of gravity and stopped. Wendy smiled. Chuck, who had been reaching for the mop like a killer going for his gun, also smiled – or stopped looking so sad, and fell back in his chair.

'My husband and me used to drink sweet white wine. Do you have it, dear?'

Wendy pointed.

'I can drink two bottles and still know what I'm doing.'

'That's nice,' said Wendy, 'I wish I had your resolve.'

'My what, dear?'

'I wish I could drink two bottles and still know what I'm doing.'

'I can drink three bottles and still know what I'm doing as well.'

'That's very good,' chuckled Wendy. The woman's short attention span lost interest in the white wines and was now commanded by red wine.

'Don't like red wine. It's too, what's the word? . . . Dry. Too *dry*.'

'I expect you like sherry, don't you? Sweet sherry?'

'Yes, dear. I do.'

'Well, here's the sherry.' Wendy gestured. The woman looked at the fortified wines and read the labels, proclaiming the names like lost friends, mumbling the prices at Wendy and trying desperately to make sense of all the liquor she had stumbled upon. Suddenly her attention was drawn again. This time: 'Champagne! I love champagne.' Her eyes glinted in the thick dark glass of bottles whose bulbous foil tops held within the muzzled anger of highly stressed champagne corks.

'These are sparkling wines,' corrected Wendy. 'Champagne's over there.'

'Brut,' said the woman, ignoring Wendy. 'I love this one. Brut. It's my favourite.'

'Yes, it is very good,' agreed Wendy.

'How much is it, dear? Ooh. That's better.' She stopped scratching.

Wendy told her the price.

'I'll buy the Brut then, dear.'

'We have to sell a minimum of six bottles. It's our licence, I'm afraid.'

'Six bottles of Brut?'

'You can have a mixture if you wish.'

'I can't afford six bottles of Brut, dear. Not till next Tuesday, I get my money on Tuesdays and Thursdays. I'm paying for a wrought-iron coffee table and a stand with lights on it; it's very pretty. I've paid half now and have half left to pay, so I won't be able to buy the Brut for a fortnight. Our friend made it for us. Out of wrought iron.'

Chuck was behind the counter and on the floor, quietly crying himself into a happy madness. Wendy stood there grateful for the blonde hair that partly covered the earnest hysterics that toyed with the graphic on her face, pulling and pushing at her features like a hand behind the mask of a silent rubber puppet. She made no sound.

Until the woman left. When the tears began and the noise came through her mouth and nose and ears. Wendy's model face was in the throes of comedy. And beauty, when it laughs, is even more confusing to watch than beauty itself.

Looking back into the gossamer of light that was draped over the bottles, I picked a wine and rolled it between my hands. Wendy came over, the twists and shrieks beginning to fall from her face. She asked if I needed any help.

'What's this pooliack like?' I asked.

'Pauillac, "poy-yack",' she corrected me. 'A ninety-one Château Lynch-Bages. It is to lay down? Or for immediate drinking?'

'Immediate, the next few days.'

'Ninety-one wasn't a good vintage for claret. How much are you looking to spend per bottle?'

'Twenty.'

'A better wine would be this eight-eight second-growth Margaux, Pavillon Rouge.' I smiled. Even I had heard of Margaux, hopefully Annis had too.

'I'll take it.'

'Unfortunately we have to sell a minimum of six bottles.' So I charmed her, a ruse that is much easier to attempt with beautiful women, though not necessarily more successful.

And somehow she fell for it. Or she wanted to get rid of me and relive the previous scene in her own private laughter. 'Don't tell anybody,' she appealed. I won't. I won't.

Outside, London welcomed me with dark tears in its eyes and boluses lodged in its throat. This, the sad pain of what the capital was, and stood for. A sad pain as it followed the movement of change. And, metaphorically, change was around that quotidian corner: time, the time at the century's end when champagne will be flowing through its bladders and Auld Lang Syne shies away from the next 1,000 years as a new song is ushered in, drunk and flat on its back, in the time of change.

Meanwhile mathematics has a hold on time as it totals up the years. Mathematics is counting time and calling the shots. Mathematics has power to make us all act like this.

Maths. Math. Mathematics. How long is it now?

Minus . . . and counting.

Five

Here it comes again. And again. And again. At last I answered: 'YES? Who is it?'

'Andy.'

'It's fucking nine-thirty, mate. I'm asleep. Go away. Call me later.'

'Wake up, you lazy bastard. Get out of bed and do something.'

'Do what?'

'Look out of the window. It's sunny.'

'No way. Fuck off.' I pulled at the bright green curtains and a ray of sun burst in, lighting the galaxies of dust that orbited and expanded in its path. 'Jesus! The sun.' Through that pink glass came the antidote to my sad seasonal affective disorder. It came in at the speed of time and bounced around the rainbow room in a multicoloured dash as it headed for the centre of the planet. 'It's sunny. Is that why you phoned me? To tell me it's sunny?'

'Doug, you don't like the day, do you?'

'Huh?'

'You don't like the day. You're a night person. Unlike me. I'm day and night, I've no preference.'

'No, Andy. Speed has no preference.' He had heard so

many stories (he'd not read them – he hated reading) about the late, the fallen and falling greats. Some had been visited by their muse while using amphetamines. He said it was creative and efficient – and comedy was going to get faster and faster as the mind reflected the fractioning action-time of its offspring: computers. Andy started saying things like, A laugh waits for no man, A stitch in the belly saves time, There is no line like the present . . . All nonsense. But it kept him happy.

'I called you about tonight, Annis's birthday, we're meeting in the GoodBye at seven-thirty. You'll be there, right?'

'Yeah, I'll drive over.'

'Well, don't park too close because they won't let you in.'

'You've found that, have you? From personal experience? They saw the smoking Mini and didn't let you in?'

'You guessed it.'

'How old is she today?'

'No idea, she won't tell me.'

'Come on, how old?'

'Straight up, Doug, I don't know. She refuses to give out that sort of info. Her parents don't know either. It's bizarre. Kidder reckons I should knock one of her teeth out and take it down the dentist's for dating.'

'Jeez, Kidder's an arsehole.'

'He was joking, Doug. Kidding.'

'Is he out tonight?'

'Who knows? Couldn't get a straight answer out of him. Do you know how many rocks he's doing every day now? . . . Five. Fuck knows where he gets the money.'

'That's bad.'

'Yeah, it's a shame,' agreed Andy. 'But it's got its funny side.'

'Which is?'

'I shagged his girlfriend in an empty carriage on the underground the other week.' He paused. 'Then two weeks later on *CrimeTime* they were playing the "Caught in the Action" section and there she was, bobbing up and down on my dick. All you could see of me was my woolly hat with the bobble bouncing back and forward.'

'Cameras on trains. Wherever next?'

'On the end of your dick, mate. Watch where you put it or you'll end up on DickTime TV.'

'So is Mrs Kidder out tonight?'

'She's confined. Will not show her face, and can you blame her? She can't see the funny side. Lost her sense of humour the minute she shacked up with Kidder.'

I asked who else would be in the GoodBye. He told me. I said goodnight and tried going back to sleep in the morning light.

If the rain comes at London like an untuned radio, then I guess that the sun is its huge carcinogenic battery burning away. If we accept that carbon-based life on earth depends on the sun, we can say that sunlight is important, it elevates us to 'living observers' of the universe. Without it, without that light, we wouldn't be here, there would be no nexus of energy and we wouldn't exist – trouble is, it's too obvious, far too obvious, and, like Annis, most of us shy from the obvious. Paradoxically it is also very complicated. It's just there and in your face and you're not about to argue with it. It just *is*. Only the geniuses and the insane tackle the obvious, because they have the trivial detachment necessary to forget about next-door neighbours, milk prices, road rage and genital girth and . . . Only these people are locked away and given time to contemplate the obvious. And the obvious is the hardest to understand – obviously . . . And that's why it's so fucking complicated.

I'm neither of these people, I'm just confused. Ignore me.

Outside, someone hollered through the mean street, 'Thank Friday it's sunny.'

Inside, the blank TV screen imparted a green warmth from the electrons that the sun had excited.

And on the *side* – of which everything was either *in* or *out*, in this case the window – the glass was glowing gas-pink through the bombardment.

Later, when I waited in the post office queue, I looked around and realized that no one really cared what the sun was up to; as long as it did its job . . . Such is life, says Spritz, remember you're bonkers, remember you're mad. No, Spritz, *you*, I think, are the crazy one.

There was a time when I used to do queues, *do them*. Queues are intended to give everyone a fair chance. But not everyone actually queues. And since queues have no statute or common law they are easy to do. Simply one strolls up to the front and pushes in. Nine times out of ten it goes smoothly. Sure there will be grey-haired witters and children mummying and pointing, but that's usually all. Most people watch, swear silently and hope you won't take too long. If challenged an excuse is required and it's not what you say, more the look on your face and the delivery. As I said, there was a time when I used to do queues. I stopped because of my last – and unsuccessful – attempt: I was in a video store and had opened my mouth, ready to validate my jump, when a seven-foot bouncer appeared from hiding, highballed over, ripped me from the ground and into the air, then threw me into the miniaturized scenery of the latest sci-fi film. After climbing from the wrecked spaceships, laser stations and extraterrestrial toilets, I made the decision to start queuing again, and have queued in English queues ever since.

The post office queue was convergent. You had to queue to get a place. One counter was open and one queue led to it, two queues led into that from either door and whisker queues came off these. Couples were arguing as to which door they should queue through, forgetting that as both branches were the same length it really made no difference and neither presented a quicker way.

So there I was in the left-hand door's queue when another counter opened and the right-hand side went piling up to it: walking sticks, tartan shopping trolleys, dentures, their artillery in this desperate battle to get to the front. Who gave them all this stuff anyway, these weapons of queue war? Surely no one claims that the civilian is not armed when there are these trolleys in circulation. Shore the police up with shopping trolleys and there'll be no more trouble – Trolley Force.

This is one of those new post offices taken from the back streets and old squares, out of the past with its discoloured brick and pigeon-stained stone and appended to a modern site. You'll find this one in the pastel mall, with its strikes of red a tropical flush in the pink and green shadows. This is a minimalist statement of privatization spun from strips of grey and transparent Perspex and alloyed uprights. This is functional, steady functional, without the old cart of fruit and veg backed into a corner. This is the post office that has followed the movement of change and this is where I come every fortnight to cash my Giro, which I am entitled to because I haven't got a job . . .

My plan is to pick the car up at twelve and then drive to work. I start at twelve-fifteen, so there need be no problem, no travel hitch, just a ten-minute motor through London back streets to the Frenetic Phone Company, where I will endure more unwonted customer complaints. And they are getting wilder: two weeks ago a customer had been on his Frenetic phone and was chatting to his mistress (he said wife). He had just started giving her directions when he got a crossed line or a node-transfer. A 747 pilot was asking for guidance from the tower and our customer unwittingly began guiding the plane as he gave his mistress the route to the hotel: 'Follow the ring road,' he was telling her, 'and leave at junction fifteen, go under the flyover and through the tunnel.' 'This is Bravo Uniform Mike 747. Please repeat! Affirm new flight-path.' . . . So far such incidents had been copywritten by spoof film-makers and now Frenetic made it truly possible in real life . . . Last week an old lady's phone electrocuted her cat and she is now suing for the cost of burnt-fur removal and for feline trauma. And this week, who knows? Planetary interfacing, dipole decomposition, cellular clap or maybe someone will phone up and say, 'There's something wrong with my phone.' 'What's that, sir?' 'It's working, you damn fool. It's working!' 'Don't worry. It's only temporary.'

I was stymied in the longest queue, and frankly this is one of the reasons why I started queue-jumping in the first place. I'm one of those people who always picks the longest queue, even if it's the shortest with two people while the other has twenty. There is, of course, an explanation: the pop-haired gent at the perforated glass is holding up the cashier with a bumbling diatribe of the purest boredom which completely misses the point of – well, of fucking everything: Why don't you put the prices on stamps any more? No wonder we're in the state we're in. When *I* was a . . . Yeah yeah yeah, pop-hair.

An hour later I pushed my cheque into the counter's

underpass. She looked it over, it appeared in order. She asked for no ID, violently stamped it, counted out a deck of notes and pushed them through. Now, as I walked out, there was no queue, just a huddle of people patiently waiting. Waiting patiently in the post office to buy stamps for their office post. And it was a calmer and more congenial place now, now that the trolleys had been withdrawn and dentures were off the catch once again. Around London walking sticks hung next to exit doors like rifles ready for the next sortie: bingo, later.

There is irony. Double, triple, quadruple irony. Today's irony was forgery, financial forgery. Counterfeit money falls into two headline categories: the very good and the very bad. The very bad stuff is often so bad (photocopies, potato prints) that it can be weeded out and flushed away; it doesn't get very far, it's short-lived. The good stuff has got to be really good. It's got to be good enough for you not to know it's not real. It's got to be real. Then you can believe in it, put your heft behind it and tab it around town. So my irony is that I was given two forged tens by the post office (a bank), which is meant to check its flow. The forgeries were of the very good variety and you can only tell by direct and detailed comparison. It's all there: the watermarks, ultraviolet, metal, pissed Queen . . . You can back this gear to the hilt and place it in the proffered hand with no guilt-twang. Use it. The point being that if it's good enough for the post office, it's good enough for me.

And the only reason I know about all this is thanks to the exponential properties of hearsay: a keen eye (an apprentice forger) spotted a trait on one of the forged notes (a tiny mark, where the plate must've got nicked) and told his mates. And so it went on, the knowledge mushrooming until finally the expeditious Doug Down overheard the talk. He then tried buying some, unsuccessfully; the result: cranial gash and bullet threats. This was back then in the darker winter of London when the sky was never described by any English teacher as ink black. No way. The sky was Xeroxed, and it was Xeroxed negative: black. And the night was the same, only with a coating of gloss: shinier, stiller and icier.

I trundled down the bus steps and out on to the mosaic pavement as it now lay jigsawed together after years of underground updates and communication rethinks, with all its manhole covers worn to a dull shine like the wires showing through an old bald tyre. I stood there among the aimless movement, my feet decomposing, cadavers in those robust boots of mine.

Surely the sun was mistaken casting this year's clearest and darkest shadows, giving definition to the surroundings: varietal architecture, trees and weeds, twenty-pence-a-shit toilets, virtual reality information booths and, of course, to movement. Movement that appeared freshly energetic as if the shops were now insectaries and the sun stood on as the angle-poise of an entomologist . . . The black grass had picked up the light and started smelling of spring. Surely, then, the sun was wrong with its light and its heat. Surely, then, mistaken: off-beam and out of focus.

Through the shadowed image that now fell on London's streets, through this, the aftermath signature of atomic wipe-out, I did my side-of-the-foot walk (still having not popped my blisters). Counting blocks through the light and dark crossword perpendiculars, I headed for No Name Motors, one hundred and seventy-five pounds counted, folded and stapled into the seat pocket of my casual jeans – my red burgundy jeans. Adaptable, the jeans boy told me, wear 'em to work or wear 'em down the pub, they's adaptable. I asked him if they would need washing should I spill any wine on them. Yes, he told me, cos the wine will leave a stain, you know. White wine's cool, yeah, no stain, it's *colourless*. But . . .

I was ready for the road. It's true when I tell Spritz that my biggest fear is driving, but that only makes it more exciting. Fear's fear and driving's scary. That's good, it's a challenge and I'll feel great afterwards – if I survive.

I was ready for the road. Ready for its hustle and buckle, its hair-tearing and nail-nibbling miles, ready for its indigestion and constipation, its time and its speed. I was ready for road. The slow road that covered one per cent of Britain with grit and grey.

Closing in on No Name Motors, I picked out the salesman among the part-exchangers. He was chatting with a young couple who stressed by their appearance that they were new to the car-buying game, first-time punters, innocent eyes. No Name's foremost employee had one of his big hands spread across the waxed roof of the potential buy, the other harassed the overgrown sideburns that pillared the edges of his big honest face. He gave the couple an urgent stare, cocked his head to one side and slapped the bodywork, as he may do with his wife or favourite lady friend, *this is the car for you*. The other hand briefly touched the sepulchral sculpture of his forehead; this was meant for me. I returned the salute and then crammed my hand back into a pocket. I was still too young to be going round tipping my fictitious hat and saying *how do*. Too young, or in a different time . . . I sidestepped through the puddles and oil-soiled gravel of the fuck-up's yard and kicked away the chocolate lumps of rust that blocked my way. The low sun bounced off the little brown

Fiat's roof. I squinted like the hard man in an old US movie. Here it was: *my* motor. Trickles of fear, or excitement, impearled as sweat on my forehead and driving hands. Once again I was unreeling the road movie in my head: the little brown Fiat, carriage to three Oriental beauties who would take turns within its confines: Bry ne, Lorn-es-qua, Lara tuu, hands up, my pretties, who's next?

'Mr Dawn!' said the big man.

'*Down*. It's Down.'

'You've lost me, Mr Dawn. What's down?'

'I am.'

'I'm sorry to hear that. Been a bad week, has it?'

'No, I'm called Mr Down.'

'That's right, so you are, Mr Down.'

'I've come to pick the car up. Is it ready?'

'Slight problem there, I'm afraid.'

'How slight?'

'Difficulty is we've been unable to do the work. Traffic's been in a smash. The love of his life is no more. He's devastated so I gave him the rest of the week off. Poor kid, she was a beauty.'

'I'm sorry. How long had they been together?'

'Four years.'

'That's awful.'

'Certainly is, he had a driving holiday planned for them next week.'

'So when's the funeral?'

'Reckon he'll take her down the breakers tomorrow and squash her in the press. Get rid of her completely, wipe out the memory, so to speak.'

'A car?'

'A work of art she was.'

'Not his girlfriend or wife?'

'Traffic? Girlfriend? You'd be lucky. No time for birds has Traffic.'

'Right then,' I said. 'When will the Fiat be ready?'

'Tomorrow. Tomorrow afternoon, should be. Traffic's brother, Lights, is filling in. He's a keen hand with the wrench. We'll have her sorted for you, no problem. Tappets, weren't it?'

'Don't ask me. It just rattled a lot.'

'Yeah, tappets. No problem.'

'All right then, I'll see you tomorrow.'

'Give us a ring first. Save you a wasted journey.'

'What's the time,' I asked, 'and where's the nearest bus stop?'

He told me. In nineteen minutes I had to be at Frenetic. Ten by car, now not possible. Thirty on foot with short cuts. And by bus, who knows? The trouble with Frenetic – one of the many troubles with Frenetic – is that they are fanatical time-keepers. When you're late, every minute up to the quarter counts as fifteen. So if you're one minute late you might as well be fifteen, because they'll take as many off your pay. In fact I spend four and a quarter hours there but they only pay me for three hours fifty-five minutes. On our own time, they allot a quarter of an hour break in the middle and a pause of five minutes to take when we feel like a cigarette or pisspull or handjob. I used to smoke in this time. I needed desperately to smoke in this time. Now I sit inside – still needing desperately to smoke – with the non-smokers, who really are a different stock of people. Here discourse frames healthy eating, sensible sex, not smoking and *gardening*, which I know absolutely nothing about. I'm learning though. Get this: last week Thomas (who has never smoked or drunk in his entire life) was telling us about his herbaceous border in a way that would be fascinating only to a fellow gardener. Still with his garden, he was telling us that one morning last autumn he had looked out of his window and was absolutely amazed to see at least twenty naked ladies on his lawn. Suddenly we were all listening, wondering what fucking naked ladies were doing in this tosser's garden. He was absolutely amazed because the naked ladies usually appeared two weeks later and he had put their early appearance down to favourable weather conditions. You lucky bastard, we said, what did you do? Well, he photographed them and sent the snaps off to *Garden*. Why? Because naked ladies were Naked Ladies, and Naked Ladies are a type of crocus. And a crocus is some sort of flower. He then started talking about his old man's beard. I didn't stay around to find out what that really was . . . Apart from meaning I have to deal with green-fingered plant voyeurs and fiercely fit agonists who believe exercise is more rewarding than sex, giving up smoking seems to have alienated me from the people who have not given up smoking. The crowd that warms itself with communal body heat and shared smoke would once give me a full-on, 'Hey, Doug! How's it going?' Now it's no more than an askance 'Hi' from the crowd's edge and a mutter of contempt at non-smokers who used to be non-non-smokers . . .

I don't know what's happening to me these days: I'm not myself. I'm not someone else, but I'm not myself. I'm behaving differently, I'm behaving like I used to. I'm not behaving.

At the bus stop I scanned the times and calculated that the earliest I could arrive at Frenetic, after the changes and reroutes caused by the latest Bus Pact, would be nearly twenty minutes late. That would cost me half an hour's pay and the allied, What time do you call this? And, Over two million people haven't got a job, you know! . . . I couldn't get a tube and I certainly couldn't walk there on my fucked feet; a taxi perhaps . . . From the fallow globes of my thalamus an emergency plan was burgeoning; look around, I told myself, see what you can find. I did this until – and this is why I don't know what is happening to me – until I saw an unlocked bicycle propped up in a landfill alley. There it was, an old butcher's or grocer's bike with its compressed geometry, its static bending moments and dime-sized front wheel. The rack that stretched from the handle bars looked like a lectern, or a bumper; the bike would be suitable for mobile preaching or market-stall ram-raiding. OK, so the triangles and circles were rust and you sensed that if it fell on its side it would leave a perfect rust-pattern of itself in the rubbish. Fuck it, I had decided to steal it. If I didn't, someone else would. Carefully placing the undamaged arches of my feet on the pedals, I rode the machine off the pavement and out of the street where I was in most danger of getting caught.

Three streets later I had my first incident. Up front, traffic was easing for the lights, so I pulled the break levers and waited to lose speed, but the vulcanized break shoes just rasped and shaved rust from the wheel rims. The back of a lorry stopped me. I went flopping into its heavy steel crash bars; there was a sad and pathetic plop as the front tyre exploded. The lorry driver at the wheel of the huge inanimate object noticed nothing; the same can be said of the car drivers, unless they had seen it all before and now ignored, or accepted, it as part of their car culture. I rattled on with a flat tyre which kept trying to throw me off in the corners. Three-quarters of the way to Frenetic I was coasting a roundabout when the rear tyre decided that it too had had enough and sent its rusty air hissing into London. The bike now went sideways on two empty tyres and laid an inappropriate shower of evanescent sparks from metal contacting the super-grip road surface. As the bike went down I stepped off it and continued on the tangent that momentum sent me – then stopped. Next, as a juggernaut came snorting towards the spillage, I ran to the barriers and jumped over. The bike crumpled like an old coat hanger as the big wheels pounded it into the road. Jesus, I thought, look at it now, it's two-dimensional. So I got out of there; I wasn't going to stick around and explain this one. I ducked away from the scene and ran down the back roads on my jelly legs and fucked feet to Frenetic. And you know what? I was one minute late. Sixty fucking seconds. They'd nick two quid off me for that, the arseholes.

I got myself plugged in, synchronized and electrified, and pressed the incoming-calls button. 'Frenetic Phones?' 'Yes, sir.' 'You bunch of *fuckers*. What do you do? Sit there *fucking* your mothers all *fucking* day long? *Motherfuckers*. Where are you? I'm gonna come down there and stick this *fucking* phone up your *fucking* Frenetic arse . . .'

And so it went on.

The time now is five o'clock and I need to decide what to wear this evening. The jeans are out. Apart from rust-staining and crude oil on the hems, I suspect that they have no seductive rating, that they are not cut out for a girl like Annis. I have this suspicion about her, an eroto-belief, and it's that she has more class than she is letting on, that if you trace her parentage there is a strain of sophistication, of class, that is suspended, unrealized. Somewhere lingers this recessive gene. Her mother's got some class and her father hasn't, so maybe that's it: recession. Annis seeks the fashionable, and shuns the mundane that surrounds her; perhaps being a mondaine would suit her. Sometimes when she smokes a cigarette, or drinks a cup of coffee, the fingers stray, they start to point elsewhere, away from the palm of her hand; perhaps at the family aristocrat rendered in oil and framed on the country house drawing-room wall. And the way she arranges her hair: elaborate, purposeful, big; like a gay hairdresser . . . There's a suit hanging like cardboard in my magenta wardrobe and a suite of socks in the cyan drawers. There's a quiver of ties draped over a tie rack and a stolen iron still in its box, its stolen box. I have some possibilities . . .

But first: a haircut. I'd clean forgotten about the dark clumps up there doing their heliotropic dance in today's sun, so I dragged myself down to Cut Cut. Clancey said she could fit me in before closing.

'Haven't seen you for a while, Doug,' she noted, as the scissors made an exploratory probe. 'It is Doug, isn't it?'

'Yeah, I've not had it done for two or three months.'

'It shows.'

She started cutting. Then stopped, and said, 'Look at this.' Clancey held her thumb up and showed it to the mirror. I leant forward for a better view, her thumb travelled backwards but I could see it more closely in the glass – the parallax was reversed and operating in reflected space, space that wasn't really there, space that was in fact home to the plastic, the leather, and the celluloid girls and boys of the sex shop next door. The Cut Cut wall mirror was meant to give the salon more space, but it was trick space belonging to the sex shop, it was sex space . . . There was a red prick in the centre of her thumb. 'I was cutting a gent's hair earlier today and I got a strand of it stuck in my thumb. Bleeding painful.'

'I don't think you'll have that problem with my hair,' I said.

'No, I won't. He had a wig.'

'You had to trim his wig?'

'Stranger things have happened.'

'Like what?' I asked with interest.

'You know. *Things*.'

'Do you sell Body Blow In?'

They did. What kind did I want? Thick hair. Medium hair. Fine hair. Normal hair. Dry, interim dry, dry dry, very dry, very dry dry, parched dry, fragile dry, breaking dry, dead dry. Or dead? I settled for dry dry.

'Would you like a Millennium Metal Rinse?'

'What is it?'

'It's a special treatment we do for the discerning customer. It gives great shine to the hair and relieves the follicles. We do copper, silver, gold, platinum and mercury. Mercury's most popular.'

'Go for it, do the mercury one,' I said, hoping that I didn't end up looking like a thermometer.

Back at the flat, in the fierce colour, I blew in the dry dry Body Blow In and styled the shining strands into a shape I'd never managed before and in the mirror I watched a whole index of colours mixing in the refractive surface of my hair. This was some hairstyle: a wedge of *come and get it!* perched up there on head.

When it finally came to clothes I settled for the cardboard suit and beat it with a broom until it was limp. This I matched with a shirt. Both were dark, unlike the flat . . . The tie I was less sure about. Someone once said, If a tie's not up to much don't wear it, fasten the collar button, or leave it undone, depending on the impression you hope to give. I fastened the button and put one of my ties (none of which were up to much) in a jacket pocket.

The wine (the claret) was standing in the corner of the room looking perfectly out of place on the orange carpet. I had bought a birthday card for Annis and was thinking hard for something witty to write inside. Little couplets toyed loosely with corrupting the Latin *annus* into Annis and taking that to *Annis mirabilis,* which would purport to be Annis's year of wonders, whereas it would actually mean *wonderful Annis*. There were others, all just as hopeless. Ultimately, for a response, they would need to be explained: Oh yes, now I see, how clever! So I gave up and wrote: Happy Birthday, Annis. Your Present's On Its Way. Love DOUG. The wine I had resolved to drive to her and hand over with the proviso that it was for a special occasion. All I needed to do was think of the special occasion that would include only the two of us.

I rode the evening bus down to the GoodBye. It was top-heavy with the usual Friday night fraternity. So I looked different in this tidy new guise, and yes, I was feeling self-conscious; but as Spritz used to say at the beginning of my therapy, They are not looking at you. They do not notice you. They would not recognize you if they saw you in the street. Who's *they*? I had asked, fearful that I was under constant observation. Rather unhelpfully, he answered, They is everybody. I had regressed after that, but it was months and months ago and now I'm learning to be oblivious.

In the drying London night I stood on the square opposite the GoodBye Bar. Here was a change, the air was cleaner and flowing more easily: I was sucking it in without suffering from its customary glottal clots and breathing blocks. The air was fresh even, revitalized by the unexpected sun that had briefly appeared this afternoon. It was free and it was bifurcating in my lungs.

Then I saw the girl. Her dead eyes spied me, high-lining through the stainless air. She was ensnared in the arms of the two greedy GoodBye bouncers; the tiny dog doing a berserk fire dance around them. They succeeded in separating themselves, fat from thin, two from one, and jetted her into the street. 'Fuck off, you stupid bitch,' said the flat-faced bigger bouncer. 'And don't fucking come back,' said the other. With thigh-like arms hanging in by their sides, and with heads back and resting on their thick rings of neck flesh, they assumed their sentinel stances and jeered her away. She followed her dog on to the idle space of the square. Pretending to look at a watch, I steered off to an opposite corner. She was behind me, and in the dark triangular corner of my eye I saw her click the dog and heel in my direction. The problem here was that the bouncers would probably bounce anybody who even looked at her. I tried a little jog but my feet pulled me up with their blister-bitching so I crouched behind the heavy graft of a cock-shaped marble monument and hoped she'd not see me. I waited.

I heard the slick dog-pants and turned to see the tiny and tense Lancelot straining at me. So I growled at her.

'Don't fucking growl at her. You'll upset her.'

'Fuck off,' I growled at Lucia de Death.

'Nice to see you, too.'

'Go away. Just go away.'

'Looking forward to tonight are we? It's her birthday, isn't it? I hope she likes the wine.'

Christ. She's been following me again. I said, 'Stop following me!'

'Pity about your car not being ready. I expect you wanted to fuck her in it. Like you did with me. You bastard!'

'Please go away.'

'I think I still love you, Doug. I know I shouldn't. I know it's bad. I know I'm going to pay for it one day. Take me away, Doug. Take me out of this hateful place. Take me into the streets of love.'

Clearly insane. I tried this: 'You know you're in Spritz's book? You know that you're – you're a cog?'

At last she was silent. I've found a way, I thought.

'Bastard!' she screeched and slapped me. Then she ran off across the road, through the chip-shop air and over the mashed-potato pavement.

'Hold up, soldier,' commanded the flat-faced bouncer. 'She a friend of yours, is she?'

'Who?' I asked.

'That bird you was chatting with.'

'Her? No. She wanted some money for dog food. I gave her some, then she started swearing at me. She's insane, I reckon.'

'In you go then, soldier. Have a good night.'

Including the lovely couple – the comedian and his birthday girlfriend – there was a party of ten or so people standing around two high tables in the criss-crossing conversation of the GoodBye lounge. Annis's friends from her car insurance catastrophe and a few of Andy's drug takers. The others would meet us at the club later, the club called MAN. Andy had not worked there this week, a numb narcotics deal had kept him away. But he could still get us in cheaply, he had a good deal going with the bouncers and regularly bought and sold with them. He would buy the drugs that they had confiscated from clubbers on the door. Often Andy found himself selling these drugs to their original owners. He had recently got into a dispute under the techno light with a punter who discovered he was buying the lump of hash that the bouncers had stripped from him earlier. The same bouncers grabbed the kid and took him out back and beat him up for trying to buy drugs in the club. A violent circle, said Andy.

'*Doug*,' mouthed Annis through the reds, greens and ambers of the GoodBye signal light. 'Over here.' She was dressed short. Short skirt. Short-cut jacket. Recently shortened hair; the blonde filigree pointing at the big eyes. She was laughing with her companions, her face driven and dynamic under the health of its permanent tan.

She kissed me. 'We wondered where you'd got to. We'd almost given up on you.' It was true, I was late. I'd had a last-minute shirt intermix in the nightmare colours of my wardrobe. Dark red or darker red? I chose darkly. I chose the darker one. 'Let me introduce you: Bob, Taz, Suzi, Henrietta and Esfyn . . . This is Doug.' 'Hello, Doug,' they said together, as one, as if they'd practised. I did my quick girl-rating and then looked at Bob, whose heavy frown made him appear *farouche* and intimidated, or guilty of nursing a huge erection he held under the table for one of these girls. I kissed Annis again and covered myself by wishing her happy birthday.

Grabbing my attention mid-sentence, '. . . her strawberry bush – *All right, Doug?* – was quivering as I . . .' Andy was speaking effusively to John and Rhubarb – called Rhubarb because at stage school with Andy he had such bad elocution that they recorded his voice, overlaid and overdubbed it, and used it as background crowd noise. Jon, the other John, without the h, was at the bar with an outstretched note . . . I greeted Andy with a raised flat palm, then pulled Annis's card from my pocket and gave it to her, saying, 'Here's your card. I've got you a present as well, I'll bring it round sometime.' 'Thank you, Doug. That's what it says in the card.' Now she kissed me and followed it up with a congratulation: 'I've never seen you looking so good. I could quite fancy you.' One of the big eyes winked. 'And I see you've taken my advice and bought some Body Blow In. And you've had a Millennium Metal. Silver or mercury?' 'Mercury. You like it?' 'Certainly do, it really works on you. What's my present then?' 'I can't tell you now but I know you'll like it. Hopefully we can share it.' 'Give me a clue.' 'No.' Annis lowered her head, prepared her look and gazed up at me with all the gravity her eyes could generate. 'I'm not telling you.' 'Not even if I—'

'What did Andy buy you?' I asked, even though I already knew.

'Well, he certainly surprised me this year. He gave me a full set of motorbike gear, and some lessons so that I can pass my test. And a video on the art of comedy by Archibald Prescott. He's watched it three times already.'

'So you're going to be a biker then?'

She hesitated. 'I guess so.'

'Don't you want to get out on the road? Feel the wind in your hair? Go camping in muddy fields with Big Bob and his chop and all them?'

'Promise not to tell Andy,' she stated, and without giving me time to promise, finished, 'but it's not really me, is it?'

'Perhaps not . . . Tell me about the video. Is it good? Archibald Prescott's meant to be a very funny man.'

'It is good. It is funny. Maybe it's because he's so ugly he just makes me laugh. Oh, I am cruel . . .'

At the bar I didn't get a chance to order my drink. The waitress with great teeth saw me, raced off, came back with a glass of water, then walked away. I had to call her through the urgent alcohol-requests that the money-waving hands were asking of her and order a complicated cocktail for Annis.

'A *what*?'

'A London Blitz.'

'What's in it?' I checked off the ingredients with my fingers, the long list that was required to give it its zing and ping and ting, and total wipeout. Behind me a wide boy was saying, 'There are no rules in business, love. You shaft the customer and then move into a new line. There are no rules. Make money; that's the only rule. As I have. Like, I started with . . .' He said it not to me, but to a young girl whom I guess he was trying to impress. She stared helplessly, having not yet developed the weapon of telling men to fuck off, or explaining that she didn't talk to ugly men.

I gave Annis the huge brandy glass that contained the cocktail. She removed the intricate paper umbrella that perched on the edge like a lone palm tree on a tiny island. The umbrella had served its cosmetic, or aesthetic, purpose, now it would only get in the way. Annis didn't know that if she pulled the umbrella apart and unravelled the central stem that held the whole thing together she would find that it was made from rolled-up Oriental newspaper. Annis didn't know that dark children hunched over a table with their repetitively injured hands were building these bright and friendly objects, going home all those hours later after the man had loaded the boxes on to the truck and then sent them off to the Western-bound ship that waited in the port . . . On the table the little umbrella melted into the spilt drink and released its dye. Like a bomb, it took much longer to make than it did to be used. Like a bomb, it was quickly scrap.

'All right, lads?' I ventured. 'How are you all?'

In order they replied, 'Good. Sound. Cooh. Kickin.' Cooh means cool and came from Rhubarb. Kickin means Andy is speeding. 'Hey, boys,' he said, 'guess how Doug got here tonight?' 'Taxi? Bird? Tooh?'

'No. All wrong. He came here by brown Fiat. Let me say again, *brown Fiat*.'

'Fuck me,' said John. 'What you playing at?'

'Bad news. I took the bus.'

'I thought you'd be chick-cruising in the Fiat. You should have brought it, man. We could have pissed it into a better colour.'

'It's not ready. They've got some fine-tuning to do. Turbo or something.'

'*Turbo*? You'd be lucky. *Tappets*, I think you'll find.'

'Yeah, tappets. Anyway I'm picking it up tomorrow,' I said. 'I was planning on driving over to see you and Annis in the afternoon.'

'We're off to see her parents unfortunately. Old fuckers.' Andy then asked a question, 'Doug, are you going to drink or do any drugs tonight?'

'Not sure yet. See how I feel. I might have a pint later.'

'If you do decide to come back down to earth, here's what I got planned for us: speed for whoever needs it, hash for the end of the night, some pure MDMA ecstasy and coke's waiting for us in MAN.'

'No peyote then, Andy? Shame.' John, Jon, Rhubarb and Bob – who had either gained some confidence or lost his erection – put their heads together and started planning this drugs issue with the same intensity they might apply to an opening gambit versus a grandmaster of chess. Taking me to one side and for a moment talking in space that was his, that was his private space, Andy said, 'If you do stay straight tonight can you keep an eye on Annis? We all know what I'm like by the end of the evening.'

'I'd love to. It shouldn't be a problem.' Then I gave him a serious look, the kind of look you might expect from a glossy agony aunt who had strayed into a pub and wanted to ask what was *really* going on. I asked, 'How are things between the two of you at the moment? OK?'

Andy shook his head very, very slightly. 'Between you and me. You know. Between you and me . . .'

'Yeah?'

'Let's leave it at that. Between you and me.'

Well, between *you and me,* he didn't always make a lot of sense. Especially when he was speeding and didn't have time to explain.

The GoodBye was a stop-off point, a meeting point, a night starter. It was part of the traffic. It had no up-to-date-and-into-the-future DJ sporting reversed baseball cap and light-fading shades who pumped out the latest sounds at terminal volumes. That DJ came later at different venues in other places. Instead it had the jukebox whose music spanned from the landlord to the underage drinker. A music that the landlord didn't want to be too loud. Loud music encouraged his deaf aid to try and deafen him.

With the promise of an excellent response, I said, 'So all you girls work in car insurance as well?'

Yes, they did.

'Do you enjoy it?'

No, they didn't.

If I had no ambitions concerning Annis I would make a clumsy pass at one of the four. A clumsy sober pass. Invariably unsuccessful and not to be recommended. I guess it makes sense for Annis to have good-looking friends. Not better-looking. Just good-looking. Taz: some thought went into putting her together, she came as an overall package; unlike Henrietta, whose construction appeared to be somewhat confused. There was Suzi: slim, dark, tight; nothing extra, nothing unnecessary. And girls, you know why we like women like Suzi? Simple: they make our cocks look bigger. With girls like Suzi we're all well-hung pornography. And boys, if your mate likes fat women it might be because he's got a horse's cock down there in his boxers. Or it might just be because he likes fat women – as you always thought.

Then there's Esfyn. She would, I feel, be the most likely recipient of a muddled come-on, were I to attempt such a thing.

'I see you're an REM fan?' This was a solid start, Esfyn was wearing a green T-shirt with the three letters contouring her chest. She stopped listening in on Annis and Taz, and answered.

'They're fantastic. I saw them in Cardiff last year.'

'Good gig?'

'Brilliant.'

'So who did you go with? Your boyfriend?'

'No. Some old college friends.' This was looking good, until she continued, 'He couldn't come, he was working.' She held a hand up to parry the spotlight that fought her eyes and asked if I had a girlfriend. I gave her a rough answer and was then persuaded by her innocent face, with its zero aggression, to ask the question, 'Will you marry me?'

She laughed playfully. 'I'm taken, I'm afraid. If it falls

through, though, I might call you.'

OK. Nothing lost. Petite Esfyn took it well. With pride.

The evening continued. As opposed to stopping. By now some form of drug was mapping out the veins of everyone except me. I guess there may have been a trace of nicotine from passive smoking that was plotting a route from my lungs' alveoli, so I goldfished the air that had the most smoke twisted into it and waited for some kind of hit.

I danced with Annis at MAN. Tending to do my duties as promised to Andy. She moved closer. Or drifted towards me through fatigue or excess. On the dance floor in the organ-bursting bass and thick musical air I asked the following three times: Annis, do you want to fuck me?

Well, do you? She didn't answer. She couldn't hear the words. And lip-reading a question that was said with the same prosaic import as *Annis, we need some more washing-up liquid* was open to misinterpretation. You really need to wide-mouth the word *fuck* slowly and expressively for it to be understood by eyes alone. It needed aggressive, or erotic, context. Grab a mirror. Try it. *Fuck*.

At the side, in some dark alcove, she questioned me.

'Did you ask Esfyn to marry you?'

'Yes.'

'Why?'

'Well, I thought if she had nothing else planned she might like to get married. Take her mind off work.'

'Don't be sarcastic, Doug.'

'Sorry, birthday-girl.'

'Would you ever ask me to marry you?'

'Probably. But not tonight.'

'When?'

'I don't know. Sometime in the future. It would help if you were single.'

As requested I gave her a hug and then went for another Coke.

We get on pretty well, me and Annis.

I apologize to the unfaithful comedian.

Oh, and Annis, where did you get your name?

I went home sober and straight. Straight home from the club called MAN that wasn't gay. Unlike the two blonds tonguing in the kebab shop.

These lustful streets were not bigoted and felt no need to discriminate.

Were these the streets Lucia de Despair seeks in everlasting insanity? Are these those streets of love?

Six

Right now I would guess the following is happening: Andy is holding back as he and Annis drink tea with her parents; Spritz is in some unknown man's (or boy's) bed after getting drunk and desperate and cruising a gay bar; Esfyn is discussing marriage with her boyfriend who couldn't make it to Cardiff; Kidder has broken into a warehouse and fenced the electricals for his crack; Lights is under the bonnet of the little brown Fiat and twisting his spanners; someone has just looked at Lucia de Evil Eyes and got out of her way – someone has just had a lucky escape; someone has just told their partner they love them and now they've come and they're not so sure; someone has just told their partner they love them and now they've come and they *are* sure; someone has recently been born and someone has recently died.

And everyone else – them, you – is getting on with their thing to great aplomb, with a delicate poise in their actions.

That only leaves me, Doug Down, in his hole, his rainbow rental room, me, what am I doing – apart from nothing? I'm busy sniffing around and the smell I'm getting is the carry-over from last night. The smell is pub. Pub in my charity piles of clothes, pub in my bed, pub in my hair and pub in the multicoloured air. From pub smoke and pub drink.

The smoke can be explained: I was in pub and club fug last night. As you know, as you saw.

The drink has two explanations. There is the passive pick-up from leaning in and being spilt on: the pervasive qualities of pub drink. The other reason is, last night when I climbed back up here I decided that I deserved a drink. I decided that I deserved the small can of beer that I kept as temptress, that kept me sober for as long as I didn't drink it. So I removed it from the stark light of the fridge and set it down on the vert table and then, in the confined space, squeezed past a chair and reached in the cupboard for a glass. As I did so, one of my blisters reared up at me and sent me grabbing for the table. Slamming a palm on the table catapulted the can into the air and on to the floor, where it bounced from the orange lino and off across the orange carpet. With a glass ready I reached under the bed, pulled the can out, sat down and slowly opened the it. The beer frothed and came all over my hand and into glass. I threw the can away and lifted the glass to my mouth. At this point the under-bed dust attacked my nose. I sneezed. The paroxysm that shivered down my body cleared all but a mouthful from the glass. Before anything else could happen I drank the remains and went to bed and waited for dreams that usually come at me during the night. And this is why I can smell pub up here in this morning light.

Oh, and the other thing I'm doing is looking out of the window – now scoured free of pink spray – at the weather. It's not sunny, it's not dark, it's not wet. You could say – as people do – that the weather isn't doing anything. It isn't up to much. I guess it can't be bothered every day.

Quarter of an hour ago the phone rang. With a voice tired from shouting in the club last night I croaked a baritone,

'Hello?' At the other end a female voice said, 'Is that Catherine?' 'No,' I said. The voice then stated, 'You're not Catherine.' I replied that I was aware of that. She asked if I knew Catherine's number. I dismissed her with swearing. Christ, I thought, does my voice sound as though it belongs to someone called Catherine? 'Is that Bernard?' I should have asked, 'old Bernard?'

So now, having answered the phone and smelt the funk, I plan to wander naked around my flat. If I listened to Spritz he would have me believe that there is some dark significance attached to this *in puris naturalibus*, that it means something. But don't forget that he is a psychotherapist and therefore must be obsessed with such things, he must be obsessed in order to find the answers. Which, as mentioned, come in the form of his terrible questions. He asked himself one of his terrible questions when he sold his old house. It was: Now that I am selling my house, how will I cope with all the stress that this will bring? In order to find the terrible answers he had to submit himself to as many stressful situations as he was able, so that he could assess how well he coped with all the terrible stress. And he didn't cope very well at all. There was far too much terrible stress. He became impossible to live with. Which is why his wife, who thought it quite opportune that he was selling the house anyway, decided to move out and leave him for good. With her gone he addressed the terrible sexual questions. And now look at him: clutching his sore arse (the lube having been lost in some pub toilet fumble or grapple) in another dark road under the early morning birdsong that escorts the embarrassed one-night-standers on their way home.

Walking around naked in my flat really is no big deal; it's not sexual, as Spritz would insist. Just natural and expected.

As it would be of a young child who unknowingly devours worms and cat shit in the sewage sand-pit. Just like my baby sister did. She did that, it means nothing.

I'm getting dressed now. Hastily pulling on a shirt and hitching some whipped jeans around my waist. I'm doing this because the doorbell is ringing. It's the postman, I spied him through the peephole.

'Mr Down,' he said, furiously looking away from the colours, 'could you please sign here?' I scratched my double-D signature into the box and braced myself for the weighty-looking parcel. He lowered it into my arms. 'Oi!' I said. 'It's empty!' 'Not my problem, mate.' On the table I looked for a sender's address and, finding none, ripped away the brown-paper packaging. This revealed a parcel-taped box. I shook it. It rattled. Not totally empty then. Inside I found an inflated black balloon and, pulling it out, discovered that it was the source of the rattle. With a pin that was normally used as a toothpick I burst the balloon. Jesus. Inside the balloon was a pin, a fucking pin. The cinema in my head that usually runs road movies featuring the little brown Fiat switched to a different screen and began showing the start of a black thriller, the hapless victim receiving a pin in the post as the music did its portentous prowl around the auditorium. If someone out there is trying to tell me something they could make a little extra effort, they could be more direct. I mean, what's a fucking pin in a black balloon meant to mean?

Something that detracts from my generally low IQ is the transient intellectual stimulation of a Saturday broadsheet that comes to you like an encyclopedia with its many sections, giving readers like me the suggestion they are bound to learn something. Accordingly, every Saturday I will stretch and yawn my way down to Gary's corner shop for my reserved copy (it has Down scribbled in pencil above the date), give him the week's float of copper coins, pigeonhole the paper under my arm and meander home trying to pass as erudite and affable and wait to be approached for catastrophic advice. Not once, not one single time, has anyone stopped me, proffered that I look like a learned gentleman and proceeded to ask for that advice.

The catch here is that I really don't read a lot of the articles – I don't have the time or the eye stamina – though I do gaze at the war photography and check out the latest share price of my one hundred units in Anglo Ashtrays. Currently worth twenty-six pence each. So as long as there is a brokerage fee they will remain virtually worthless.

After a couple of hours, during which time I have been occupied with other matters – biting my nails, blowing my nose, coughing and thinking of excuses not to tidy up – I will add the folded weight to the cornered pile, retaining only the TV guide for nightly reference.

Today I persuaded myself to read an article entitled 'Suicide: The Ultimate Crime?' It was in response to the growing number of young taking their own lives. Noted by the author as a worrying precedent for future generations. The piece rested the blame on the deceased rock star, dead now two weeks. A 'thoroughly irresponsible act' was the accusation, without concern for family or fans. This was not the government's approach, nor was it the Church's – who, in assuming the high ground, described it as a remarkably sad act, yet nonetheless immoral and against God's will.

A distraught mother advised that the star's estate be split up and divided among the victims' families. The editor in an unusual footnote responded that this debate was sure to gain momentum and asked any *interested* readers to write in with their views. Spritz, I'm sure, will pick up on the piece and take time out from his six-hundred pager to conjure a reply. Spritz, I'm sure, will have a great deal to say. Suicide being a past obsession of his – one of his many terrible questions.

I'm not suicidal. There was a time, a sadder time, when I had a flirtation with this existential get-out clause. A brief and harrowing one, hidden away now by the blindage of time. Time: the greatest healer or cover-up ever. No, I'm not leaving you, I've got living coming my way, there's still some life to fuck and fight away: a couple of quarter-centuries, or more, if I'm lucky.

I laid the paper to rest on its predecessors (the mulching pile in the corner) and washed my hands free of print ink and sweat. This sweat trail-blazing as the prospect of driving moved up a gear and walloped me in the chest with fear, or longing . . . After pressing the seven London digits I held the phone to my ear and waited for someone to answer the No Name Motor's dedicated ringing tone. As it rang on, my arm became less hopeful and tried replacing the receiver. The arm came back, faltered, decided to replace it, moved away. Then: 'Hello, No Name Motors. George.'

'George. Hello. Is the Fiat ready?

'Mr Darn? Hello?'

'Down.'

'Down, yes. Hello, Lights is finishing her off just now. Be about half an hour.'

'I'll be there.'

Off I walked into the weatherless day, thinking about driving procedures: mirror signal manoeuvres, junction policies, roundabout rules. Then I remembered – experience reminded me – after passing the driving test you had to forget all that, and with aggression (a useful commodity, the road has plenty) head for the nearest gap and establish yourself. Importantly, address the horn and pulse the mainbeams. Not how I finished driving two years ago – no aggression, no speed, no distance – but how I started.

Travelling on a London bus, I shared the air with the Saturday shoppers. Some were on their way home now, hauling their wild purchases up and down the steps: shed-sized boxes (that housed the latest stereos) perched on their laps, car body parts, someone had a door, someone had a bonnet, drooping carpet rolls, even a dog kennel up there behind the driver. The bus chugged around and pushed out oily grunts of diesel mist. It stopped and waited with the traffic to move, waited while cyclists, runners and pedestrians – many humpbacked with sporty backpacks or multi-buttocked by bum-bags – hastened past and stopped up ahead to stare at the dead lights of a smashed car. The double-decker crawled on and crawled to a halt at my stop, its mass lilted and settled into the depressions laid in summer heat, the bus with its huge toy shape. Rerunning yesterday, I walked the crumbling pavement and headed off pedestrians in the shadowless streets. My money folded, counted and stapled into my jeans. Green ones this time, labelled as grass resistant – that's if the grass is ever green again.

The little brown Fiat was parked up in the part-exchangers' yard. Recently washed, water was still dripping from the arches and seams – dripping brown with rust and paint gathered in its current. Muddy streams ran in rivulets away from the car and across the concrete court. I made a mental note not to wash the Fiat – water was the last thing it needed, what it needed was rebuilding . . .

George caught my attention with a dog-assembling whistle. From a door of the prefab office he called, 'Mr *Down*.' Emphasis placed on the '*own*' to show that he'd got the name correct. Not Dawn, darn, Don, Dan or Din. He was wearing a boxy pink suit as reference, I presume, to his view of Saturday car buyers, or because he enjoyed looking like a TV game-show host. Cash now rolled and uncurling in my sweaty palm, I followed him through the door. 'Paperwork. A couple of signatures and she's yours.' He handed me the No Name purchasing agreement: no guarantee once off the premises (the Fiat had to break down within ten metres if I hoped to get any money back), no responsibility with the vendor (aforementioned No Name Motors) in regards to any illegality on the part of the car, the documentation, the previous owner or owners. Here was the MOT – three months, not six: the sign was old, he'd been too busy to replace it. Here was the form that the law required me to send to the DVLC. 'Sign here, I'll print you a receipt.' I signed my double-D. Instead of asking me for the cash, George opened his mouth and gave a huge smile that set off his teeth in the No Name filament light. Some teeth black, some yellow, most missing, the bottom row looked like a sparsely rocked desert skyline. His big hand placed the keys in mine, a plastic brown Fiat fob hanging from them. 'There's half a tank of juice in her. Usually we siphon it, but that old car's been standing so long we thought best to leave it.' I suggested that this was very kind of him. He assured me that it was no problem, but now, if there was nothing further, he had to get back to his paperwork, of which he had a mountain to get through.

The Fiat door gave a long and arching groan of desperation. This was despair. The brown door voiced its despair – desperately. Abuse was heading at this car. After months of standing, all that time relaxing, and along I come with my mad grin and sweaty palms, give a roll of cash – that has passed through people via the same routes as sexual disease – to a fat guy in a pink suit and suddenly I become its owner. Status gained. In a matter of seconds. It showed its lamentation: from great reservoirs stale rain and soapy wash-water fell through its tear ducts (which were cracks, jagged holes and pitted rust). Sluicing away, it carried with it a whole flotilla of tiny rafts that were rust flakes and old bits of old car.

Inside, the unpadded and uncomfortable seat reminded me of the gum-splodge and cigarette acne of bench seats in short-hop buses. It smelt the same: stale smoke, worn perfume, baby puke, urine – and sparsity. Sparsity: the smell of bare space devoted to utility. And of course it smelt of plastic. Brittle, brown and fading with design.

I turned the ignition key; a light blinked from one of the dashboard dials. The engine clicked when I turned the key against its spring, then limbered up with a climbing yawn, climaxed, dropped sharply and began to slowly turn over. With a sudden and unexpected burst of energy it sneezed into life and started. I sneezed too as smoke and dust whorled inside. I listened for the rattle. It was gone. Lights had done his job. The windscreen was covered with a gel-like layer of water, which the wipers, no better than a pair of worn and cracked paintbrushes, pushed from side to side in striped arcs, smearing it around like Artex . . . then I stalled it, or it just died. Whichever, the engine went UGHH, stopped, waited for a second and then backfired very loudly. A gunshot would probably be reported in the vicinity of No Name Motors. Giving the key another twist started it, it remained running, I left the forecourt and turned into the road. My first drive for two years.

My plan was confrontation with my road fears: entailing

driving as fast as possible, slamming the brakes on, speeding round a corner and swearing and threatening any drivers I felt like.

Propelling the car along the road, I was soon up to twenty-five miles per hour. I slowed for a left-hander, entered a new street and went in search of some open road in my new projectile. Going through the gears, I was in third, doing maybe twenty, when I heard police sirens all around. Christ, I've only done 200 yards and already the law's on to me. Surely they don't think I've stolen it. In the mirror the big Ford was flashing its headlights and the disco lights on its roof were going round and round and round . . . Like a deadly prowler, it powered past and slithered to a stop up front. A police hand waved from the window: pull in. I pulled in. There was a police pause, then the uniformed officers stepped out and paced towards the Fiat, eyeing it like a suspect, or a naked girl in custody.

'This your car, sir?' asked the moustached one.

'Yes, officer.'

He turned to his companion. 'She's a beauty isn't she, Shooter?' Shooter agreed. Shit! They're going to shoot me.

'Is it *really* yours?' asked Shooter, who didn't have a moustache.

'I've just bought it,' I told them.

'From No Name Motors?'

'Yeah?'

'How much did the little lovely cost you, son? Not more than fifty, surely?'

'A hundred and seventy-five.'

'They saw him coming, didn't they, Shooter?'

Shooter agreed. He suggested they had seen me from a long way off.

'You insured?'

'Yeah.'
'Got a licence?'
'Yeah.'
'Documentation for the car?'
'Yeah.'
'Road tax?'
'Yeah.'
'Where is it?'
'I think the disc has fallen off.'
'Fallen off? Who's he think we are?' Moustache asked Shooter. Shooter didn't know. 'Fallen off? You know you're breaking the law?'
'I'll buy some.'
'This car really is a piece of shit, son. What made you buy it?'
'Impulse.'
'*Impulse*? If I acted on impulse I'd have Shooter here shoot all the criminals.' He looked encouragingly at Shooter. Shooter nodded fiercely. 'Do you have any idea now many people we nick on their way out of No Name?'
I explained that I had no idea whatsoever.
'A large number. A *very* large number.' Looking again at Shooter, he asked what he reckoned they should do with me. They decided.
'Seeing as my wife's recently had a nipper and I'm in a good mood, and because I feel sorry for you owning such a shit car, I'm going to let you go. Bring your docs and your tax down the station within seven days and we'll call it quits. By the way, have you thought about a respray? It really is a disgusting colour.'
Off they went, the big patrol car changing its own gears – speeding. But who's going to stop them? Who stops the police?

So there I am, shaken up, the car pointing at the kerb as if it wants to go further, further across the pavement and into the house of a granny who sits there by the fire twisting wool together with her plastic needles. As if it would like a woollen cover-all blanket to pull up around its arches and oxidized paintwork. As if it longs for the cosy warmth that can only be supplied by the old with their wool and their stories. And I feel a little like that too, waiting around in this brown interior with its flicks of plastic wood that a previous owner taped to the doors. Sometimes I too feel like retreating into the old granny's house and settling down with the huge jumper, the tea and scones, and the big fire that burns for ever and is not affected by technology, and not touched by the melancholy that the cold nurtures in the porous bones of the lonely helpless. And sometimes I even get it. And that's what keeps me going: the warmth and the prospect of more. Now that I'm hopeful for the future I'm warmer too. Much warmer, and stoking the real fire.

By now the curtains and the nets had stopped twitching and the street was back in its armchair, returning to its more pressing problems, the bills: the gas, the electric, the phone. The taxes mounting, the payments marginal. The wait for that day when the cash will finally expire and the inhabitants will pack up their last few possessions and head out into the (suddenly) empty tracts and scapes of London. Their dreams long forgotten and now only a span of life left with nothing but memories, nothing but the past. And what could the future possibly do to save them? The future was going to kill them, that's what they thought, that's what they knew. And that was the only clue the future gave as it sped off and never bothered to look back.

As far as my future is concerned, I don't know. Right now, I know that the engine is whirring its cogs and drives and, apart from another backfire (that set the curtains twitching again), it won't fucking start . . . The mechanical yawning started to get slower and slower, turned into a low growl that wouldn't scare anyone and finally into a reproachful click whenever I twisted the key.

'Need a push, mate?' This was a young kid who had just knocked a gold-ringed fist on my window. Around him was a gang of pre-teenagers smoking and drinking and goosing the girl who hung with them. I nodded and said, Yeah. I remembered how to do this, the bump-start. Turn ignition on, put the car in gear, second or third, push clutch pedal to floor, get car moving and release it with some throttle. They started pushing. Inside, with the car moving without engine noise, I could hear all the clunks and rumble of broken components echo around like distant thunder. '*Come on, mate.* NOW!' shouted an exhausted voice. Clutch out and the engine popped into life – resurrected in this city street with its kids junked up on hooch and the nineties.

I was heading for a dual carriageway and planned to bury the throttle in its dirty pool of rusty water. I planned to come barrelling down the slip road and fight for maximum speed.

Now lolloping along a busy peopled street, occasionally hitting five miles per hour and then slowing to leave space for the pedestrians to squeeze through. And through they kept squeezing like urban belly-dancers. One ran to the car, jumped over the bonnet and over the rails into the subway, his black brothers with sticks chasing after him. Their dog howling on its lead, eager for blood having tasted it before. Drugs, women, porn, snitching? A broken leg and he'd not be doing it again. The way of the street: its violence, hate, love, all mingling together with explosive synergy.

Once away from this snap of metropolitan subculture the route veered into a road that carried more cars than people. A motorized road; pedestrians now housed in cars. I managed thirty in the nose-to-tail . . . How was I feeling? Good, yeah, good. Free, and swapping between the London road and the action road movie that spooled in my head. This movie had weather, red-eyed sun setting past the tumbleweed plains, a hot breeze carrying the scent of horses. The movie I was playing in – *The London Road* – had no weather. Not today. Just the flatulence of passing lorries, the cloud of drivers' vision, the cyclones of colliding airspace. This was the real movie, it was life drama and it took place every day – you paid only with your time, which was your life anyway. So it just happened and you couldn't stop it.

I coasted the roundabout, the car no more than a subatomic particle orbiting its nucleus until it had enough energy to break free and go elsewhere in its atomic world. Round and round, with the crazy thought crossing my mind that I could do this all day and no one would ever know, such was the transient life cycle of a roundabout. At last I placed the car in the correct lane and with a burst of indicators, right then left, headed down the slip road. In fourth gear, and with the pedal flattened, I waited patiently for something to happen, for the car to enter a power band, for my speed fear to get left behind in the extreme burst of acceleration.

Instead the dial counted the speed increase slower than a second hand in analogue time. It went: 30 . . . 31 . . . 32 . . . Taking a line from the slip road and a long wedge out of the hard shoulder, I eased on to the inside lane: 44 . . . 45 . . . 46 . . . The needle hovered. In my mirrors the angry face of a lorry came looming with headlights blazing and two-tone air horn pumping: 47 . . . 48 . . . 49 . . . Ahead there was a long falling stretch of carriageway: 50, 51, 52. Acceleration increased. A little brown Fiat comeback at the end of the century. At 55 I began pulling away from the lorry, so I rolled the window down, shook a fist at him and gave him a middle-finger gesture – a love-finger fuck off. With declining gradient I zipped across into the outside lane: 68, 69 and 70.

Then my vision failed. Startlingly every object had countless edges and the road was going everywhere: into the sky, underground, to my left, to my right. My eyes were vibrating, so was my body, shaking down the highway like a road drill. Initially thinking that some secret fear had taken a grasp of me and was riddling through my body, I then realized that it was the Fiat. The car was juddering like an overcharged sex aid. Slowing down allowed me to regain vision; gradually the sensations went and everything returned to its rightful place or shape. I remembered it happening in Andy's Mini. But he kept going, throwing in a conceit about how Annis enjoyed it. Something to do with the wheels not being circular or wheel-shaped . . . Back on the inside lane, doing less than sixty, the decline was flattening and the lorry was coming up behind me again. Giving the car some more power, I made an attempt at escape. No use, the Fiat was intransigent, it wasn't designed for speed. Quickly the lorry was right behind me, a couple of feet. So close that the lorry's company name filled my rear-view mirror with some of its letters: HOMO was glaring in the glass, HOMO in my mirror. This is some way to be insulted, in your *own* rear view, in your *own* car. Twisting over my shoulder, I read the full name ZOOMOHOME barely ten feet behind. What a way to resume driving after two years, with the hulk of a lorry trying to hump the back of my little Fiat. What a way to resume with an arsehole in a lorry trying to shaft me. What a start. What an arsehole.

So I tricked him. At the last minute I spun the wheel to the left, rumbled over the chevrons and executed a difficult angle into the last of a slip road. He carried on, the lorry less agile – with none of the car's grace or manoeuvrability – trundled down the carriageway.

The rise in the exit road scrubbed speed from the car, but I kept my foot firmly down, ready for the next confrontation. A few yards before the give-way triangle I planted the brake pedal to the floor; this was my brake test, another of my fear tests. The energy did its conversion thing and heated up the brakes, remembered d'Alembert's principle and slowed me down. Then an icy lurch, the back of the car came out, skidding sideways, all screeches and squeals, as though the car was auditioning for an American movie car chase. What could I do? What was I meant to do? I kept my foot on the brake pedal and we lurched backwards into the roundabout. I allowed my kinaesthetics to settle and then looked around and worked out where I was. Don't be surprised to hear that another lorry was clattering towards me and screaming its two tones.

Panicking slightly, I found a gear and headed back down the same slip road I had just come up. And now there were two cars driving towards me. With a presence of mind that many drivers would do well to take note of, I indicated and pulled on to the grass verge. The cars did their road-swear at me: horns and bursting headlights. I wound the window and gave a reactionary finger, turned the car round and decided it would be a good idea to drive home.

And that wasn't much better. The signals and the lane changes were up against me. And other road users seemed to know I was about and were making life hard. A white-haired woman in a Metro played chicken as she drove towards me in the middle of the road. When she didn't hit me, I noticed she was reading a newspaper. I had a tussle with a red Porsche. Its number plate was C DUST. It was doing twenty when I nipped past . . . There was a time when I used to swoop along at that kind of speed. I apologize if I held you up on your way to that important meeting with that important associate, or was it your wife, your husband, some lover, your dominatrix – where were you going that day? But I was a gentle mover in my Fiesta back then. I was in no rush to get anywhere.

Now I'm a gentle mover in this traffic and rolling along in my little brown Fiat. Gently moving on through the angry traffic with my angry road-face. Look at my graphic: pure assumption. It says, *Move. I'm coming through*. Look at me: too car-scared to know any different. Look at that fucking cunt in his company Ford, what's he mean: circled forefinger and thumb describing an imaginary shaft? Wanker? Hey, Ford, this is my piece of road, I got here first! Look at the angry road with its angry faces.

A great success. Yes, I truly class today's driving as one of my best achievements. By my own admission I may well not be able to perform the cut and thrust traffic slices of the more experienced motorist. I may not be up to much when compared to a driver like you, or your friend if you're not so hot yourself, or don't drive. But if you'd seen me two years ago sitting in my stationary Fiesta with road terror in my eyes and my anaemic knuckles gripping the wheel, you'd see the comparison, the improvement, and be quick to congratulate me. What Spritz would say, I do not know. Probably it's best he doesn't find out. If I see him out here in his low Saab, I'll take the next junction and plan another route.

Turning the last corner, I entered my mean street and almost crashed into . . . into *smoke* – from which a van then appeared. I heard some hooting and swearing, but when the smoke had cleared I looked around and the van was gone. Then I coasted the grey to my flat. The car received its criminal attention from the mean car-snatchers. They eyed the car and considered it as stock, as a commodity. They scored the Fiat and looked away. That was that. Their heads dropped in criminal pity. Poor guy, they imagined, what did he do to deserve *that*?

I slanted in next to a shift of builder's sand that was now weeding over, and ground the door open. As I did so a car slithered to a halt and gave a hoot of protest. I looked at the driver. I looked at the girl with dying eyes sat at the wheel with a mad flowery hat staring straight at me.

Apology, I forgot to mention that she'd been following me all day. Always there, a cover distance behind. Hers was one of the two cars I had driven at when I went the wrong way down the slip road. She was one of the drivers who swore at me. That was when she blew her cover. That was when I knew it was her, the brief stare burning into my retinas. Now she was in my street once again, hands drooped over the wheel, engine idling . . . Her door swung open, she stepped out, a billowing flowery dress (a hat-match) trailing through the door.

'You bastard!' she shouted. She started towards me. I went to the right of the car, aware that a slap was ready in her hand. She went the other way. And then the other way. She came to rest, the aggressive red blur of the car's roof between us.

'You *are* following me. Why?'

'The roads,' she said, 'were safe before you started driving.'

'Why are you following me?'

'You tried killing me out there. I loved you, and now you're trying to kill me!'

'If you weren't following me it wouldn't have happened.'

'I'll never go in a car with you again.'

'You've never been in a car with me *before*.'

'Oh, Doug. How easily you forget. To think it meant so little to you. To think I gave you everything I had . . . To think I gave you my love.'

'Well, now you're giving me a headache. Just fuck off.' For a moment the eyes looked deader. But this time there was something else: there was sadness.

'It's strange. Edmund is adamant that you're scared of driving. He told me it was your biggest fear. He won't be happy to hear you've bought a car. Why do you lie to him? Why do you lie to me?'

'You haven't spoken to him recently?'

'Of course I have!'

'You haven't asked him?'

'Asked him what?'

'About his novel.'

'Doug,' she said sympathetically. 'Edmund is not writing a novel.'

'Ask him,' I said. 'Ask him about Simon Sole.'

'Who?'

'*Simon Sole*.'

'All right. If it will make you happy, on Monday I'll ask him about this Simon Sole. And I'll ask him why you lie to everyone. I'll ask him what's wrong with you.'

'Yeah, you ask him. Now fuck off.'

'Goodbye, Doug.'

She climbed into the red car, the engine still idling, pushed the lever forward and accelerated down the street. The car's drag lifting a layer of dust and litter from the road. Crisp packets caught in the air followed her and fell in empty space. The red car swung into the main road and disappeared.

A late Saturday mood was spreading through London and filling the road network. It came from the shops, it came from the streetlamps as they flickered on and the shoppers started to go home. It came as it did every Saturday to plug the void of early evening: after the shops closed; before people went out. And yes, thanks to the movement of change, it did apply more to the young – the young who filled pubs and clubs . . . It came down on the arching shoulders of Doug even though he had no social plans for the night. The mood was pervasive and eagerly aware of every Saturday, but unaware of Saturday, 1 January, year 2000, when everybody was planning to be too fucked with festivity or fatigue to notice. All rejoicing at the birth of their child Millennium. Born at midnight and weighing in at a massive eleven and a half pounds. Millennium, who had come bounding into the next 1,000 years with the words, 'I'm here. It's started.' And the exhausted mother slowly closing her legs and wondering where the heavy youngster had disappeared to.

At the top of the stairs there was an outdoor smell. A smell of freshly penetrated wood. A large chunk missing from the doorframe and the door gently swaying in the windless day.

The TV – third-hand crime, now fourth-hand – was stolen. Most of the resaleable technology was gone. So was the food from the cupboard: instant fry-up, plastic cups of gourmet eating, the milk, the bread, the margarine . . .

Nothing else: they'd left the bed, the clothes, the furniture and, incredibly, the wine – perhaps the burglar-eye not seeing what the burglar-mind believes should not be there.

No doubt the criminals were now down in casualty complaining of headache and flash-blindness caused by the colours. The colours that were already criminal. The criminal colours that now bore witness to others' crime. All this in the hollow shakes of city rape.

I didn't win the lottery. I didn't even *nearly* win the lottery.

Seven

I called the police last night. I used my telephone; hidden under a pile of clothes, they'd not stolen it. In the shock – the burglar-shock, the shock the burglars had left on hold for me – I assumed they'd taken it and added it to the list, but then I heard a muffled ringing and found it beneath the empty arms and legs of a clothes pile. It was Andy – was I coming to lunch tomorrow? Yeah, I'd drive over in the morning – today. Oh, and I've been burgled again. 'Neighbourhood watch working well then, is it? Your stuff's likely to be in the flat next door.'

Two hours later they arrived. Through the door, without knocking, paced Moustache. Shooter stood in the doorway, scouting the dark corners for a terrorist or a haul of semi-automatics. Moustache, with one hand on his upper lip, the other hooked into his police belt, appraised the door. 'Usual MO,' he told Shooter. 'Five seconds with a jemmy and they're in. No more than thirty and they're out.' Finally they looked at me: the victim. 'Hello,' said Shooter, 'it's Mr Down. Owner of London's finest example of Italian car design.'

'Hold on,' I said, 'you're traffic police, this is a burglary. Don't detectives come round to take photos and imprints?'

'Detectives? At this time on a Saturday?' Moustache

turned to Shooter. 'Mr Down don't know much about the force, does he?'

'Nope. I reckon he's pretty much in the dark.'

'Mr Down, the police is like any other organization. We're short of money, short-staffed and now have shorter officers. Undermanned, so to speak, we have undertaken job-sharing. The police have limited resources. You just think of us as your detectives.'

'He probably believes that if his *real* detectives did the crime scene he'd get his belongings back.'

'He probably does. Very naïve.'

'Very naïve.'

Moustache called me over. 'Look at this. You see these large marks in the dust? That's glove marks, there'll be no prints. All these *in-and-outs* are similar, there'll be no clues. All we can do is make a list of the stolen items. Now, what's missing?'

I told him.

'Did you hear that, Shooter? They made off with Mr Down's food.'

'They did leave a clue,' I said. 'You could take a genetic fingerprint from this.' I handed him a Pot Noodle, some damp food still at the bottom, and a protruding spoon. 'Forensics could get the DNA from the saliva and make a match. Then we'd have our man.'

'Forensics! DNA!' exclaimed Moustache. 'Very naïve.'

'It works in America,' I said.

'It costs. It's money, Mr Down. This is the Met, not the LAPD, we don't have the same budget. No, we'll take notes, make our reports and that's it. It's all we can do.'

So they left, no crime solved. Shooter led the way. By now he was twitching and scanning the stairway, his hand cocked by his side, ready to go for his gun. But Shooter didn't have a gun. He had a truncheon. The criminals had the guns. The criminals had long set aside their truncheons. The criminals were ready with more effective arms.

Down the road I knocked on an old boy's door. The same old boy I'd sold my wood vice to. The old boy who was called Old Boy. He'd mended my door before. He knew why I was there. He said, 'Been done over again, have you, old boy?'

'That's about the size of it, Old Boy.'

'Wait up. Let me get me plane, me bastard and some four-be-two.' He wandered over to his tools. 'Now where's me wimble?'

Obviously I had no idea what he was talking about, so I stood dumb and watched him rooting through his tool bags, a stained roll-up hanging from the corner of his mouth. Fighting with respiration, he would sneeze occasionally as a shower of dust fell from his cap and was caught in his wheezed breathing. 'Ah! Here's me priest. Thought I'd seen the last of it. What's it doing in 'ere? Do you fish, old boy?'

'No,' I told him. 'I haven't got the patience.'

'Bin fishing since I was this high.' He held a flat hand less than a foot above the workshop floor. 'Used to go with me old boy. Here, grab this.' He handed me a plank of wood. 'Course, I don't go these days. Not since the old boy drowned.' I told him I was sorry to hear that. 'Here it is. His old wimble. Fifty years old, still does the job. Not like these modern electrical ones.'

'So you don't like modern technology, Old Boy?'

'Tell you the truth, I can't see the point of it all. Nothing wrong with the old ways. If it ain't broke, don't fix it.'

'You haven't got a computer then?'

'You're having a laugh.'

'Let me carry that.'

'No. You'll be all right with the timber. 'Ere! Mind me cornices!'

The whole street knew I'd been burgled. The police car would have suggested it. And now with Old Boy creaking up the road with his arthritis and rural voice they all knew for sure. He mended everyone's doors and windows. He did the job cheaply. He didn't charge criminal prices. Not like the cowboys who were always brothers of, or in business with, the criminals, who supplied them with power tools from DIY store jobs.

It took him half an hour. During, we exhausted all talk of technology. We exhausted television in four seconds: Have you got a television, Old Boy? No. We talked about – *he* talked about the old times for most of the time. I listened and felt glad to be young. Get this: when he was a teenager he lived in the country – in the fucking countryside. He and his first girlfriend (he said lady friend), whom he ended up marrying, had had to use pebbles as a contraceptive. *Pebbles,* like the Romans. So I asked him whether he thought modern girls should use pebbles. He suggested that it might curb the problem of single mothers. These girls might be less hasty to get so many old boys into bed if they had to use pebbles. These modern girls are so promiscuous, not like the old girls *he* used to know. It's frightening, he said. It's frightening.

Yeah. Absolutely terrifying.

I parked the little brown Fiat in front of Andy's motorbike. The machine's rust was darker today as the Sunday drizzle stained its porosity. The oil slick beneath engine was vaguely iridescent in the low light, like the sheen of damp hair. And the discarded skip now full of broken homes and sinking into the liquid road surface.

The Victorian street-door of the townhouse buzzed back,

clicked and let me in. I did the long haul up to the top floor, over the worn carpet and under the hanging walls of peeling paint that sprung flakes into my hair and clothes. Out of breath, and on hands and knees, I thumped on Andy's door. The door thumped back at me with the jungle bass from Andy's stereo. Slowly I stood up and shook the paint from my hair and over the magnolia snowstorm on the door mat.

Annis swung the door open and stood in the backdrop of smoky light. There was warmth around her and in the room; unlike the damp London day outside. She was wrapped in two heavy pale blue towels, one bowdlerizing her body, one spiralled on her head. Her face and shoulders still bore the wet lustre of shower water that could not permeate her velvet skin. The big eyes addressed me. 'Doug, come in. We were just talking about you. I expect your ears were burning.' She kissed me (ten per cent lip contact) and said, 'Andy, turn the music down.'

'These are volume-vibes!' shouted the dancing man. 'All right, mate?' In the stereo corner he turned the knob and the shooting columns fell a few decibels. 'Bought the album yesterday. It's recorded in quadraphonic: amazing affects – effects. The sound goes all round the room, even with two speakers. Listen to this bit. Sit there.'

'I'll get dressed,' said Annis. 'Fix Doug a drink.' She disappeared into the cleaner, less friendly light of the bedroom and closed the door.

The low lengths of the room were then filled with music. Andy dancing a tribal jig. 'This bit!' A drum roll followed the walls, went to my right, went behind me, went to my left and exploded somewhere in front of my face. Next, a scream came out of the left wall, passed through my ears and travelled through the right wall and out into the drizzle.

'What did you think of that?' asked an excited Andy, the rhythms gradually shaking from his taut body.

'Excellent. Amazing what technology can do.'

'Yeah, man. Fuck knows how it works!'

'They said on *The Future* that it's got something to do with phase lag. Sound waves or something . . .'

'Sounds like surf-talk to me. Now what would you like?' He swept an open palm over the drinks. 'Lager's in the fridge if you prefer.'

'I'll have a Coke.'

'With rum, or vodka?'

'With ice and lemon.'

'OK, Doug. But this non-drinking's gonna have to stop. You're the only friend I've got that doesn't drink.'

I was tempted by a lager. An icy ice lager. But with a sober hangover, I said, 'I'll stick with Coke.'

'Annis was telling her parents about you yesterday. They think you'd be good for her. They disapprove of me. Never liked me – old cunts.'

'Didn't you try selling her dad some acid once?'

'I didn't know it was her dad. I assumed it was some dero she was giving money to. How he ever had a daughter like Annis—'

'You'll never know, will you, Andy?' interrupted Annis. 'Yesterday he was so embarrassing. For a start he was high and my parents didn't know how to communicate with him. All he could say was, "She's hot, ain't she? Done all right, haven't I, Gordon?" '

'You are hot though, babe. Isn't she, Doug?'

'She's very attractive.'

'Mummy didn't know what to say or where to look.'

'Did you hear that, Doug? She calls her old lady *mummy*.'

'It's kind of sweet,' I said.

'Thank you, Doug. Thank you,' said Annis. 'You can see why they prefer him, Andy. That reminds me, Esfyn says, "Hi." '

'Does she—'

'Why does *that* remind you? What've your parents got to do with Esfyn?'

'Andrew, will you get Doug a drink!'

'He's got one.'

I had to raise my glass, like an exhibit, to appease her.

'Good,' she said. And returned to the bedroom.

'What's up with her?'

'You know. It's a girl thing. Or us. Maybe we need some time apart.'

'You'll work it out,' I said encouragingly. 'You always do. Look at young Vanessa. She tried electrocuting you but you still made up.'

'Vanessa was off her head all the time. Annis is more difficult. She's too fucking independent. I can't control her. Now where are my Rizlas?'

He was constantly losing his Rizla papers. It didn't help that he was colour blind and orange was one of his missing colours. Maybe if they were to produce them in that size, but in a colour he could see . . . He tried putting them in an old tobacco tin. But then he was forgetful too and always lost the tin.

This time I picked out the jagged outline hiding in the orange-tinted hair of a model posing on the cover of Annis's latest fashion magazine.

He made a joint, crumbling in the blond resin and sprinkling a shower of cocaine. 'Saves my nose,' he said, and lit the eight-incher. Standing up and coughing, he announced, 'This will put her in a better mood.' He slid a CD into the player. 'She likes Bach.'

Hovering over the stereo, and still coughing, he began wrestling with the remote control. As he pressed its buttons strange things happened in the room. The TV blinked into life and died as quickly, a video cassette popped out of the machine and popped back in again, like a provocative tongue. A long blast from the stereo ground into the thick air. 'Fuck,' said Andy. 'I fucking hate these programmable remotes . . . CD, CD?'

The news on the radio started up: 'Bong. Ten die in freak stock exchange crash. Bong. River Thames floods underground as new superferry takes wrong turn. Bong. Lighthouse collides with big rock. Bong. Women's Institute in Mafia crack war – we talk to the Godmother. Bong. Lost master found in Louvre. Bong—'

'This is my fucking Archibald Prescott tape,' said Andy. 'What's wrong with this remote?'

'Health inspectors find egg in chicken. Bong. Arctic lost in massive snowstorm. Bang! And we talk to the three-legged man after he wins amputation battle.'

'Annis has connected the video to the stereo again!' He threw the remote control across the room and said, 'It fucks everything up when she interferes.' Round the back he swapped some wires; Bach boomed into the room. With the volume of the suite lowered, Andy asked, 'How's the car?'

'Going good. I think we're going to get along very well. I took it out on the dual carriageway and managed to do seventy, but then it started shaking like fuck, so I slowed.'

'Need to get the wheels balanced.'

'I thought they weren't circular.'

'Same thing.'

'You know I got stopped by the police? They want me to take my documents down the station within seven days.'

'Ah. The seven-day wonder.'

'How much is car tax?'

'Fuck knows!' He didn't know. He didn't believe in it. Try the post office, he suggested, they might know.

'The same police then dealt with my burglary. Moustache and his mate Shooter.'

'*Shooter*? Fuck me!' Andy didn't believe in the police either. He felt they treated him unfairly. I mean, after all, he had paid for the drugs with his own money. They were his. What right did the pigs have to come and nick them off him. Especially when it was such good shit. He'd have to go and get some more now. 'Soon they'll have names like *Frame Up* or *Brutality*.'

'They don't reckon I'll get my stuff back.'

'No. You never do. How many times you been done this year?'

'Twice.'

'And three times last year?'

'Four.'

'Move out, go to the suburbs. You're not insured, are you?'

'I can't afford it.'

'Kidder'll have some gear. Get him when he's desperate for cash and he'll do you a bargain. That video only cost twenty quid. They're three hundred new.'

'It was probably Kidder that nicked my stuff.'

'No, he can't remember where you live. Anyway, he only does stores.'

'Seeing as I hardly watch any TV I might not bother with another one. Maybe I'll have to start reading books,' I said with resignation. 'Oh yeah, I had something I was going to show you, a booklet called *Cooperage in the Late Twentieth Century*.'

'Cooperage? That's horses?'

'Barrels.'

'Barrels?'

'Coopers make barrels – they used to make barrels.'

'Why would I want to see a booklet about barrels?'

'It's not about barrels. It's a film script.'

'Fucking stupid name for a film script. What is it? A film about how to make a barrel?'

'No. It's about a pub landlord who wants to chop a punter's cock off.'

'Eh!'

'Well, there's this punter, Chattaway, who goes to the pub every day but never buys any beer. So the landlord decides to chop his cock off.'

'That's a bit drastic, isn't it? You wanna watch out. You haven't bought any beer in a pub for months. They're probably sharpening the knives in the GoodBye as we speak.'

'The landlord suspects that Chattaway is queer.'

'You're all right then.'

'And Chattaway suspects that the landlord is queer. Plus they both fancy the same girl, but only the landlord is actually shagging her. She's a barmaid . . . Does all this make sense?'

'As much as it's likely to.'

'My idea is that you and your old acting mates could borrow a couple of camcorders and make the film. It's only a short script.'

'I don't—'

'I mean, you won't need to really chop someone's cock off. You could use a carrot or a sausage or whatever.'

'Carrots! Sausages! I'd use a *prosthetic*, Doug. Yeah, bring it round, I'll have a look. Rhubarb would be in on it.'

'He could be Chattaway. Chattaway doesn't talk much.'

'I could be the landlord—'

'Andrew!' Annis opened the door and broke into the conversation. 'We are not having sausages again. I told you to put a chicken in the oven.'

'Nobody suggested we were having sausages.'

'*You* did. You told Doug we were having sausages and carrots.'

'No, I didn't. We having the chicken. It's in the oven. Take a look.'

'I thought—'

'Jesus, Annis. Relax. Come and have a drink.'

Annis was dressed now. Dark velveteen covered her dark velvet skin and the pampered hair scattered over her face in shards of highlight. Her large eyes – eyes she retained from childhood – that said so much, yet kept her secret, were the brightest stars in this shadowed day; darkness shuffled and made way when she awoke in the black night. She spoke.

'Have you basted it?'

'I'll do that, Annis. I need another Coke. I'll baste it.'

'Thank you, Doug.'

It hardly need be mentioned that the home comforts – food in the oven, detailed interior, sterile bathroom – which struggled for a place in today's domestic discord, were the result, or the influence, of Annis. This does not presume that if you met her you would expect to see her roasting a lunch, matching curtains with friezes or boiling the toilet. It suggests that if you met Andy you'd spend a couple of minutes with him and quickly realize that he couldn't cook, that he wouldn't even bother with any curtains, that he thought the dark calcium rings in the toilet were there to measure water level. You'd realize that he'd sooner get on with something else, something more immediate, something coarser.

Even now, as I ladled the juice, Annis was wearing the

trousers (dark purple with near-metallic shine) and casting a didactic eye my way . . . After a couple of drinks Andy would say, 'She just needs a firm hand,' and proudly hold up the firm hand. But it tended to be less simple than that: an undeclared battle for control seemed to pervade the relationship. In closely guarded talk, away from the other, each might acknowledge this. But in open speech it was unmentionable. It just happened and ran its course, throwing up casualties of vituperative locution. And then the grand, the *emotional*!, make-ups in the aftermath of nearly non-physical contact. This was how it had gone on for months. And it was soon to change.

(Is it the power, the inaccessibility, the vulnerability, that sucks me into the clean air that surrounds Annis? That vulnerability: a shared weakness?)

'Thank you, darling,' said the actor to his girlfriend. She, his understudy, handed him his drink, smiled intimately and began stroking his knee. You expected Andy to shatter the union by pointing at his crotch and shouting 'On This Now!' But he said nothing. He gave her a sick little grin . . .

This euthymia settled in the Sunday room. For the first time since I'd arrived I now felt as though I had, after all, come to the right place. Now the *invited*, not the *un*invited guest. We had the room with all its history and future finally framed with happy resignation. It took on the melancholic air of the steady drizzle outside. This was correct, this was striven for in all the dust and smoke and low lighting. This was most definitely a wet Sunday afternoon in early spring and the inside had adjusted to match the outside. The drizzle went on. It was the air. And the air was thick in here too: something was burning . . .

'Can you smell something?'

Andy: 'No.'

Me: 'What?'

'What is it?'

'I don't know. I can't smell anything.'

'Doug?'

'Burning?'

'Can't be the chicken,' said Annis. She leant over the cooker. Her nostrils glared at it. 'But it seems to be coming from here.' She opened the door. 'Doug! You left the bloody tea-towel in the oven.'

'I'm sorry. Fuck.'

Having stepped back, Annis stood there, with her semaphoric arms, and began coughing with baffled incomprehension at what the smoke was trying to do to her throat. Briefly disappearing, we heard the window open. Upon reappearance she was mediating her coughing. Tears were in her eyes, she was laughing – it was funny. She didn't mind the burnt tea-towel whose smoke was slicing past her and into the wet outside.

She came over to me, the smoke shifting as the room arranged it into hot and cold layers. She placed a mocking hand on my shoulder. And now, with the force of a hiccup gathering in her voice, said, 'Doug, Doug, Dou-Uurghp. What can we do with you? You need looking after. You need a good, Uurghp! – woman.' The hand moved across my shoulder, rested on my neck and stayed perhaps a fraction longer than some old Buff Moth would suggest is correct.

'No harm done then? The bird's all right, is it?' I asked.

'It's fine.'

'Sorry about the tea-towel.' It was gently hissing and spluttering in the sink. 'I'll buy you another.'

'Don't be silly, Doug. It's only a tea-towel.'

'Chuck it out the window, Annis,' said Andy. 'It stinks.'

'There's already enough rubbish out there.'

'Exactly. A little more won't make any difference.'

'Guess so.' Annis launched it into the fleshy piles of rubbish that lay in the rubbish front garden. From the window, she said, 'Someone's vandalizing that skip again. They're using one of those blowtorch things this time. Why do they bother?'

'They're just trying to prove a point,' said Andy.

'Which is?'

'Ask them. I don't know. *They* probably don't know.'

And there was some sense in this statement, some quiddity. People spend much time trying to prove something. Ask them what they're doing, and why they're doing it, and there'll be no answer. We all toil away and then find we're not quite sure why there's a hammer in our hand and nails between our teeth. Why do such a thing? Is there a point to it? There must be. Well, I'm . . . because . . . *you know*. But you don't. No one does.

Annis closed the window and sat down. Wriggling into an armchair until she felt comfortable, then picking a magazine from the glass table, a glossy fashion-life with its flickable pages and sticky smell. Finding a suitable article, she ran a flattening palm down the spine and began reading. Here she looked at home, as an autochthon of this perfect world of photos and touch-up hints for the spotless goer. Here she was mingling with her own. She could see herself in these pages. And with good reason: she looked like they did, she looked like them. She was at home as a slender finger traced the page.

Andy said, 'You know I'm doing a slot next week?'

I told him I didn't know.

'Yeah. Down at the Miser Club. I thought I'd told you.' A midweek special set aside for first-time stand-ups to ply in front of real punters. Five minutes each, the best – as adjudged by decibel reaction and Miser Jack's caster – getting a quarter-hour on a future Sunday night – where he or she could well be spotted. There were famous graduates, Archibald Prescott – a favourite of Andy's – had followed this route, though not through the Miser. Of course he had now advanced into TV, where the rules of comedy engagement were slightly different. You got a second chance, you could wipe the digital information and do it all over again. Whereas the Miser was raw and live, and the crowd was fair, but drunk enough to kill if they didn't like you – they nurtured stage-death. In short, they could be expected to heckle.

'Are you nervous?'

'Shitting myself.' But he didn't look it. Eyes rolling and bloodshot as he drew on another, larger, spliff. 'Terrified.'

'And the material – you've got a routine?'

'Getting one. It's not perfected yet. Five minutes is a long time in comedy. Especially at the speed it goes these days.'

'Not like Shakespeare any more, is it, Andrew?' interjaculated Annis, suspended for a moment from her magazine article – it had *SEX* in the title.

'Shakespeare's not funny. He's shit.'

'A lot of people would disagree with you.'

'Let them. It's not the comedian's place to follow convention,' said Andy, in what sounded like a well-rehearsed line. 'I acted in his stuff and found it a drag – boring.'

'What are you going to do on the night then?' I asked. 'They can be wankers in the Miser.'

'Heavens!' said Annis, who was reading again. 'Did you know that a man can channel his orgasm?'

'Too right,' answered Andy. 'He can channel it right out the end of his dick. As you know.'

'You're always so crude, Andrew. It says here that they can channel it up their spine and into their head and make it last for thirty minutes.'

'Bullshit, Annis! Thirty minutes? Thirty *seconds* maybe. On a good day.'

'Doug?'

'I'm not saying anything.'

'Yes, you are. You are saying something, you're saying, "I'm not saying anything." '

'OK. I'm not responding then . . . What's in your performance, Andy?'

'As I've said before, I can't really tell you the jokes as such. It's general humour. Birds, sex, drugs, the weird things people do, some stuff on domestic life and infidelity—'

'Amazing!' said Annis, clearly excited by new knowledge. 'Have you ever had a multiple orgasm, Doug? I know Andrew hasn't.'

'I'm not—'

'Jesus, Annis. Those magazines are full of shit. It's all bollocks. By women, for women.'

'*Doug*?'

'Not exactl—'

'Annis! Blokes don't have multiple orgasms. *Chicks* do, we don't.'

'Doug?'

'Well, it depends what—'

'Annis! Leave it! – And a joke or two about a couple who go their separate ways.'

'Take no notice of him, Doug. He's only feeling insecure.'

'Why? Why am I feeling insecure?'

'Because you're nervous.'

'Read your magazine.'

'Anything else?' I asked.

'You'll have to wait until the big night.'

'Did you know—'

'We don't want to know, Annis,' interrupted Andy.

'— that the male orgasm will be redundant within a hundred years?'

'That's it! I'm going to peel the potatoes.'

Annis continued, 'Hilda Slough says that sooner or later baby-making will not require a male and sex will become a sordid thing of the past.'

'What a depressing thought.'

'Yes, Doug, I have to agree. Even if Andrew has got a small willy.' She giggled mischievously. Andy chuckled confidently – perhaps suggesting that this was not actually true. He stood over the sink, the joint in his mouth, the ubiquitous fat-lady apron wrapping him with its tired illusion. He peeled slowly, with herculean dedication, and with plenty of swearing: 'There must be a fucking easier way to do these cunts! Ow! Fucking peeler! I fucking hate potatoes.'

'You like them when someone else does them,' Annis called to him. 'When I first met him he could barely open a tin. You can cook, can't you, Doug?'

'Yeah, tea-towels!' shouted Andy.

'I'm not much better than Andy, I'm afraid.'

'Well, you couldn't be much worse.'

'I read in the papers about someone who definitely can't cook. There was this story about an old man who sued a tinned-food manufacturer. Apparently it read on the label, "Place tin in oven-proof dish and cook at gas mark six for fifty minutes." So that's exactly what he did. He put the tin in a dish and put it in the oven, waited fifty minutes, then came back to it. He was about to open the oven when there was an explosion that blew the door off. The tin had blown up. He sued the company for a new oven and for shock, and won. They were forced to pay and told to change the instructions to say that the tin had to be *opened* first, and then *emptied* into the dish . . . I'm not that bad, thankfully.'

'Sounds like the kind of thing Andrew would do. Wouldn't you, Andrew?'

But he wasn't listening. His upper body and face were painfully contorted as he focused on the vegetable. Head hanging, elbows tucked hard into his ribs and mechanically crouching, Andy processed potatoes. His swearing now muted, comments came, such as, 'Oh, now I understand,' or, 'Ah! That's how it works.'

Annis, the girl most on my mind, swivelled, her face petitioned me, she said, 'Where's my present then, Douglas? Did you bring it?'

Quietly, so only she would hear, I replied, 'Don't call me Douglas. It's in the car and I'll give it to you when I leave. Remember the condition.'

'The condition?'

'It's a gift that can be shared. And I want you to share it with me. You can say no of course. But I hope you don't.'

'It's not baby oil, is it?'

'It's not.'

'Shame.'

'What are you two whispering about? Not me I hope,' said Andy.

Part Two

Eight

Dear Mr Down

Further to your letter inquiring of employment in the Shoe Shop, we would be interested in interviewing you. It is no coincidence that we presently have a vacancy for a salesperson – we are expanding. Please bring with you details of past employment and any information of relevant experience.

As you mentioned in your letter, the Shoe Shop is at the forefront of retail footwear. We feel that the Shoe Shop will be the main contender in shoes in the future. More importantly, the Shoe Shop is . . .

And so it went on: the Shoe Shop doctrine. The Shoe Shop's proximity with feet, with people, with shoes. Appended at the end, almost as an afterthought, were date and time at which the interview would take place. Then there was the signature: Colin Rumble, manager.

The letter came as a surprise. A surprise because it was such an early reply to my letter. A surprise because it arrived in an envelope shaped as the sole of a shoe; address printed where the ball of the foot would stand, stamp stuck obliquely to the heel. It was there on the doormat when I woke up, upside-down – showing only white. With no other post it looked like the police outline of a murdered one-legged stand-up comedian.

Without the perverse connotations, I can safely state that I look forward to a career in leather, rubber, laces and man-mades. I hanker after the foot and its fitting. Its wonderfully horrible shape and frightened skin. Boy, feet sure are strange, hidden like genitals, with whom they share a similar purge from common sight. Feet with their wear and tear and smell and penetration all crumpled together in polished leather compartments. I want to house feet. And I want to do it in a shoe shop called the Shoe Shop. It is something, I feel, I could be good at.

The Shoe Shop is indeed a big mover in shoes. It's out there on the leading edge with a chain of shops eager to satisfy your feet. Revolutionizing the market by supplying a free foot massage with every purchase. They're bill-boarding on the streets, slotting adverts into TV-time and familiarizing newsprint with their claims. Tying all this together is the copywritten strapline, simply 'FOOTWEAR'S FUN!', and advocates on TV business programmes stating, 'The Shoe Shop kicks arse.'

So the surprise, then, that they are interested in me. The experience I have in shoes has always been at the other end, the customer end, and has entailed me taking another pair of fucking shoes, that have fucking fallen to pieces, back to the Smell of Leather and saying, Give me another pair!

And the money: 'blow away Frenetic Phones' money. I'm going to blow Frenetic away anyway, unmindful of induction into the Shoe Shop, or any other job. I just need one last time down there. I'm going to return all the insults I get, I'm going to give as good as I get on the Frenetic phone line. The next time an arsehole threatens to come and stick his Frenetic phone up my arse, I'll calmly swear away into my microphone. I'm looking forward to it. All this to come after months of subservience to these cunts calling me up and shouting away. Hey, arsehole, it's not my fault that Frenetic's phones are no better than a couple of empty margarine containers and a tight length of string. I just happen to work for them.

Something else: I've decided to move out of the colour spectrum of this tired flat. Wait a couple of weeks and I won't be here any more. I'm moving across town to kinder pastures, out of harm's way. Away from the burglaries, the threatening mail, the night visits from insane girls with dying eyes, from the hang-up phone-callers, away from the blinding colours. I intend to leave the mean street, and the mean streets that surround it, to the mean people who don't want me here anyway. They deserve it. They made it this way and they're all far meaner than I can hope to be. I mean it. I'm outta here soon.

Maybe I'll miss the tramps who huddle together on the dog-stained corner – their young and their old, their women and their men in desperate conference on the dark concrete. Maybe I'll miss the old man drunk who – with shoulders drooped by the weight of his world – repeats the same word over and over. 'Palilalia palilalia palilalia . . .' he says quickly. I don't know what it means. I've looked it up in my old school dictionary, it's not listed; there's pale ale, paleface, palette, palette knife, palfrey, palindrome, paling, palisade . . . no palilalia. Maybe I'll miss their begging, which they now affect with a personal lilt. 'Hello, Mr Down. Do you have any money for my tea today, Mr Down?' And now that they're all criminals, now that it's an offence for the poor to beg, they have made it their business to know the names of all potential benefactors. Then they can say, 'No, officer, I'm not begging. I'm only asking my friend Mr Down for some money. I'm not *begging*.' Ah, the way the criminal mind works. And have you seen how many beggars there are around these days? How their criminal numbers have increased? Now that they're no longer allowed to beg, they're worse off and need the money even more. How did all this happen to them? How did they suddenly all become criminals? How did this criminal thing happen? . . . Maybe I'll miss these mean streets after all. Maybe they'll miss me. But I don't think they'll know I'm gone. Not until they come round to burgle me and there's nothing left. Maybe then they'll realize I've left the mean streets.

Meanwhile I'm still here.

Huge news: he's going free. In five months he'll walk out of the courtroom an innocent man. Innocent after nearly five hundred jail days. There'll be massive divides, black and white ones, there'll be political division. But the clerk will read the verdict, stuttering slightly as she does so. She too sees it as black and white: written down, it reads, 'Not guilty,' twice. No reasonable doubt will be cast, and that's important. There must be reasonable doubt. Someone had to make the decision, *someone* had to be bold and say that there was reasonable doubt. Never mind what we will think – we didn't have to decide . . . But what will the nations do with their news? There'll be so much more time as we rocket into the lights and tinsel of another Christmas.

No more suicides in the last few days. The dead rock star's dead influence is wearing, losing momentum. Around the country, mothers clasp their children less tightly as the weeks pass and the deadly longing retreats from the stare.

And students are poor again, almost criminals. The government insists on giving them money, and now there's a tide of old copper coins spilling into holey pockets and campus nooks. But they can't spend it; they can only look after it until the government asks for it back.

Technology's doing its thing too. It seems that it has begun to teach itself. It has exhausted our knowledge and is now going it alone. We're shunned, our days might be numbered . . . Me, I'm looking for a clever friend. One who understands the language, the electrical lingo. I'm looking for a modem into the modern.

Through the mean streets and past the bounty of beggars (one of *his* collective nouns) came Spritz, a hand held to his head, the head that contained the twisted telemetry of his writer's mind. There he was: fat man, arms adrift in the odd colours of his odd suit, his tie backed out over one of his shoulders and pointing back at the way he'd come, like the severed rope on a man escaping a hanging. The grey hair awash in the grey light, and the bullied look on his face that exertion had forced on him. He looked up at my window, my silhouette black against the Egyptian jasper – he looked bad. Dr Spritzer was moving towards my flat and moving fast and effortfully through the movement of change. A movement that was covering the ground faster than his shagged body could manage. It was about to slipstream him and rush past with a valedictory zap and boom in the quaking air as it flew into the future.

I lost sight of him as he swooped under the crumbling wall that lined sentinel pigeons and headed for the concrete steps that would lead him to the closed door of my flat. Then heavy footsteps hit the tensile concrete, sending strophic echoes through cold passageways. Without knowing these belonged to Spritz, I'd have feared that they belonged to attackers, or bailiffs, or police coming for someone – coming for one of the building's fearless.

He didn't knock on the door; he slapped it. Three times he brought the open palm against the wood, punctuated by internal speech: You will, *slap*, enjoy, *slap*, this, *slap*.

'I want to come inside, Doug. Let me in, it's Edmund. Doug?'

I let him in. He tumbled into the room, headed for the armchair and fell helplessly into the upholstery. From his odd jacket – the room's colours destroying any appeal it might once have had – he pulled his tobacco pouch and started rolling one of his terrible roll-ups. Gradually his breathing started to settle and he lost the appearance of a rabid dog hiding from quarantine in a port. I asked him a question. Anxiety scurried across his face before he answered.

'Yes please, Doug.'

'Milk? Two Sugars?' Doing my best, like the WPC in the rape crisis centre, I made him a cup of tea. Not Valium, whisky, opium. Just tea. 'What's up with you? You look terrible.'

'I'm not feeling too well, Doug. Something bad has happened. I've come to warn you.' Such premonitory advice came as no surprise from Spritz's fragile mind that asked of itself so many terrible questions. It came with the regularity of a chain smoker's next cigarette.

'What's happened?'

'She's gone mad.'

'Who's gone mad?'

'*She* has.'

'The girl?'

'Her.'

'Lucia de Londres?'

'Yes, her.'

'No need to worry, Spritz. I already knew that.'

'No, listen to me. She's coming after you. You must not talk to her. Don't listen to anything she says. She's gone over. I can't help her any more.'

With the roles reversed I asked the psychotherapist to tell me all about it.

'I arrived at the office this morning. The door was open – Oh dear, have you got a light? – and Lucia was there and reclining in my chair. "Tell Mr Down that I'm going to kill him," she said. "Why?" I asked her. "Because of the awful things he does to people. People like me." She's procured a knife. I saw it. Watch out for her, she's going to use it.'

'Don't worry. She's all talk and slaps. She won't hurt me.'

'She will!'

'Spritz, why do you look so worried. She's not a problem. More of a nuisance than anything.'

'I'm worried for *you*. Go and stay with family or friends. Get away from her, don't let her anywhere near you. If she does get you, don't listen to anything she says. Remember she's ill.'

'I'll keep an eye out for her.'

'I've told the police. They're going to pick her up and question her. I'm sorry, Doug.'

'It's not your fault. Here's your tea.'

'Promise me that you will run if you see her.'

'Yeah, sure.'

'Promise me!'

I promised.

Edmund Spritzer looked happier, calmer now. Some professional equanimity found its way back into his doctor's face.

'I might give up practice. She's my first failure and it's hard to deal with. I'm extremely saddened by this turn of events. It hurts when people let you down, don't you think?'

'I guess it does—'

'Makes me angry as well. I don't deserve it. I've done *nothing* to deserve it.'

He talked on for a few minutes. Then arranged his body and stood up to leave, saying, 'Thank you for the tea. Be careful, Doug.'

'See you on Thursday.'

'No,' he replied from the door. 'I have to postpone. I'll call you with another day.'

He left. Looking more relaxed than on his flustered arrival. But he wasn't right. Something wasn't tuned in, some frequency was wrong. But there you have it: Spritz and his terrible ways.

So I've got a mad girl on my trail. What's new? What's new about having a mad girl on my trail? What can she do to make the world any more crazy or dangerous than it already is? Can she really tip London over the edge and into organized chaos? What would chaos make of her anyway? What fractal image would the super-computer come up with for London in disarray?

The girl is mad though. I wouldn't disagree with Spritz about that. I'd have her swimming in the molten lake deep down in the crazies' crater and making salads from forbidden fruits. Fuck, I wouldn't be surprised to hear that she drinks the blood from road-kill, or – what's the expression?

– 'eats of herself'. And right now she's probably slamming the knife into the table between the spread Vs of her fanatical fingers, or carving the word *hate* into park benches.

So yes, I am worried, but it's not going to spoil my plans. In no way will the threats change my attitudes. No way . . . Well, a little maybe. But I'm already tempered by the lunatic on my heels. And I do look behind me, cast a rearward eye and quicken my step. Only then to turn a corner and run slap into the tortured face. If she wants to find me, then somehow I believe she will, whatever I do to avoid it. But, Jesus, Spritz is such a *sensationalist*.

Onward, to happier times. One just knocked on my door. Tap, tap. And I let her in. 'This is a surprise,' I told her. 'What are you doing here?'

'I've come to see you,' she said, Annis said . . .

Yesterday at five o'clock we finally sat down to lunch. The three of us gathered around the circular table and raised our cutlery. The three of us gave the table symmetry, triangular symmetry. But there was a form of asymmetry, asymmetric moods, asymmetric sexes, two men, one woman, Annis – the floater. We were missing a fourth person. Someone who would shift the whole thing into the balance it was looking for.

In the low light I forked some food and aimed it at my hunger-struck mouth. As I did so an old bluebottle came humming into vision like some shot-up bomber limping home on one engine, lopsided and gravity-defying. This sure was a ponderous old fly, corroded, even dusty, with its bushed drone . . . As its flight path homed in on Annis, she pulled an arm back. With a javelin thrower's groan she struck it. A hard hit, the fly went somersaulting through the smoky air, hit Andy on his forehead and bounced on to his plate, landing upside-down (and probably dead) in his gravy.

'You stupid fucking bitch!' shouted Andy. 'What did you do that for?'

Now Annis was caught. As the fly had bounced she had begun to laugh. A split second later Andy was swearing at her. What could she do: carry on laughing or retaliate?

She chose neither. Instead, she burst into tears. Tearfully she said, 'I couldn't help it. I didn't mean it.'

'I can't eat this shit now,' said Andy, sliding the plate to the table's centre.

Then I came in: 'Come on, Andy. She didn't do it on purpose.'

'It's not the first time. Believe me.'

I tried to envisage a constant stream of flies bouncing off his forehead and landing in his food.

'Oh, Andrew Cipolin, you're such a wanker!'

'Don't fucking flick flies at me.'

'Fuck off, Andrew,' she said. Big tears from the big eyes now dropping into her gravy. The insults continued, a whole volley of them: backhand, forehand, dropshots, one hundred and thirty mile-an-hour serves – the aces. Continued until I said, 'Children!' This made them both stare and glare at me, and made me wish I hadn't said it. Bashfully I apologized, 'Sorry.' Annis said, 'Have mine then,' and slid her meal on to the heat-pattern that Andy's plate had left on the table. Then she fled. Ran into the bedroom and slammed the door. Bang! It sounded injurious.

Bang! This came from downstairs. Somebody knocking on their ceiling: the floor of the townhouse top floor. 'Fucking cunt!' screeched Andy. He stood up, left the flat, clattered the stairs, started shouting at the tenant below . . . Three meals on the table, one person: me. I thought about eating, there was nothing else to do. Bang! This was something else.

As I seriously considered my food the noise below escalated. And the silence in the silent bedroom remained silent and totally clueless. This was to be my first meal for over seven hours. For the last three of those hours it had always been nearly ready. 'Yes, it's nearly ready,' one of them would say, 'almost ready.' And the reasons, the delays: macedoine muddles, temperature fall-offs, gravy restarts, plate problems (availability and breakage) . . . I scraped some carbon-deposit from the quasi-barbecued chicken and decided to give it a go, to get some food in me. Then the timbre of the silence changed: I heard quiet movement. I put the fork back on the plate and looked behind me. Annis's head popped round the bedroom door, like a puppet. Her eyes red, darker, from the art that crying had left with them.

'He's downstairs?'

'Yes,' I replied.

'Good. I'm absolutely starving.' She sat down with her pathos and her ruptured pride and with those eyes.

Probably slightly high, delirious even, from hunger, I told her she was beautiful.

She said, '*Doug*.'

I said, 'You are. Now eat your food.'

She said, 'Thank you, Doug.' And picked her fork up.

Bang! A door slammed downstairs. Annis put her fork down. The comedian's heels kicked over the worn stair carpet. Annis picked her fork up, prodded the food and started to eat.

'Fucking arsehole!' said Andy from the door. 'There's a million flies down there. He must be fucking breeding them.'

'Come and sit down.'

'Sorry, Annis. It wasn't your fault. But I still ain't eating this.'

'Out the window?' I asked.

'Best place.'

'Share mine,' offered Annis.

'Thanks,' he said. 'I can't believe how fucking hungry I am!'

As soon as the food hit the rubbish front garden three dogs attacked it. Then they attacked one another. While the larger two were busy trying to bite each other's teeth, the little dog nipped in, grabbed a drumstick and ran off. Switching on to this, the other two chased after it, their feet scrabbling like plastic on the damp pavement. The little dog slipped on a coil of dog shit and was then attacked. Then the larger two started attacking each other again, so the little dog returned to the rubbish front garden and started eating. Until it was attacked and had to run away once more.

There was now a large chunk missing from the discarded skip, and burn marks had atomized in the paint that surrounded the hole like the brown over-spray on my Fiat's windows. The missing part now being used to repair a damaged skip, or tethered to the front of a ram-raider's car. The discarded skip was being recycled. Once rubbish, its decay was now reversing, it was becoming ante-rubbish.

Back with the domestics, Andy and Annis were sharing her lunch, playfully duelling with knives and forks over the cooling meal. So they were friends again. Or at least they thought they were. It's hard to tell with their roller-coaster love ride. I don't know. And I don't think they do either. There goes a potato . . .

The fact that we had pudding was more of a reflection of the

Sunday drizzle than of any normal meal that might be served in the townhouse top floor. It was an English pudding.

I just couldn't eat it, it wasn't my kind of food. It was, I think, an attempt at something else: some insult or hint. I just couldn't eat it. And the cook didn't seem to mind.

'I don't mind,' she said. 'Not everybody likes spotted dick.'

'I'm sorry,' I apologized, 'but it looks . . . it looks regurgitated.'

'It's from a packet.'

'No wonder then.'

'I'd go as far to say,' said Andy, 'that it looks like a mixture of fartleberries and used toilet paper that has been pissed on and then cooked.'

'Ugh . . . What are fartleberries?'

'Apparently they're little beads of shit that accumulate in arsehair if you're a filthy bastard.'

'Andrew, how do you know such disgusting trivia?'

'I just pick it up in my endless search for comedy. It's amazing what I find on my comical travels. Like, I went to Tower Bridge to do some background on a sketch and ended up being told all about this disease called Peyronie's Disease, which is where a bloke can't get a proper erection. And then the other day I was having a drink with Bobby Kock, who's already on the circuit, and he gave me all this shit about bananas. Did you know that they were herbs? No, me neither. And that they're getting straighter? "So much potential," he said, "in bananas." His is a more basic humour than mine though. As you might expect.'

'I don't think I want my dick now,' revealed Annis.

'Whoa, steady on, darling,' said Andy. 'No one's offering!'

'My *spotted* dick. Sorry about him, Doug.'

Turning to me, Andy asked, 'What do you think of this

weather, mate? Depressing, no?'

'It can't go on. Can it?'

'I've never been so pale,' said Annis, who certainly wasn't pale. 'I must look positively ill.' And she didn't look ill either.

'No, you look healthy. Unlike Andy, who looks like a bag of shit. Don't you, Andy?'

'It's my image. No point looking like I've just come off a health farm if I'm going to stand up on stage and tell jokes about shitting and shafting.'

'But you do look worse than usual,' said Annis. 'Maybe you should cut your drug intake a little.'

'No need. I feel fine.'

'Well, you can't—'

'Annis, don't bother finishing that sentence. Doug doesn't want to know.'

'Don't I?'

'He can't—'

'NO. Shut it!'

'Family jewels,' whispered Annis, as Andy frisked his pocket for drugs, 'at the jewel repairer's.'

After hours of waiting for the meal and then watching half of it go out of the window, Annis decided that there was only one thing she could do. She said, 'I'm going to wash my hair.'

'Again?'

'It's greasy.'

'If you say so.'

Andy, who had been smoking and drinking throughout the day, and was now beginning to look as though this valiant attempt was about to fail, said, 'Make yourself comfortable, Doug. I'm going to do the washing-up.' With a spliff modelled on a traffic cone, he walked slowly to the kitchen and peered vacantly at the stainless-steel sink. He picked up a scrubbing brush. He was clearly confused by it.

After ten minutes he had half-cleaned half a plate and spilt half a bottle of washing-up liquid over half of the kitchen floor. After picking himself up and abjectly staring at the sticky green substance that had floored him, he wearily said, 'Fuck this,' and lay down on the long sofa. His snoring made the same sound as his motorcycle when he tried to kick-start it, and sounded just as tiring.

Once again I was alone. So I opened Annis's magazine and quickly found the article about the male orgasm and its bleak future. What I read gave me the opposite of an erection. It gave me an inversion: my genitals tried burying themselves like females'.

Right, so when Annis reappeared – her hair looking exactly the same as before – I said, 'That's better, your hair looks full of life.' And she said, 'I didn't wash it in the end, I did my nails instead. Look.' She held her hands down to me, flattening them like she might if she was doing press-ups or crouched in preparation for the starter's gun and an Olympic sprint. 'Do you like them?'

'Exquisite. It's amazing what you girls can do with your hands.' Of course what I was really thinking was how they would look wrapped round my cock. 'You're lucky to have so much potential in your hands.'

'Do you think so?' Now, Annis knew that she had more low-down on hands, especially her hands, than I did. But she still asked me, so that I could say *yes*. So I said, 'Yes.'

She assessed Andy, asserted that he was asleep and said, 'Doug, will you do something for me? I *can* trust you, can't I?'

I said she could. This was one of my more truthful statements of the week.

'Come with me then.'

I followed her hand into the bedroom. 'I've got something I'd like you to take a look at. No one else has ever seen it.' She bent into the wardrobe and came back with a folder. 'This is my portfolio. Take a look inside. You're the first.' I pulled out its contents: photos. Glamour photos of nearly naked girls. No: not *girls*. Photos of the photogenic Annis. 'What do you think? Have I got a future?'

'Yeah,' I said, turning a photo on its side. 'Definitely.'

'Good.'

'You've certainly got the . . . er . . . the body for it. And this one, it hardly even looks like you. Amazing!'

'I don't look silly?'

'No way. They're very artistic.'

'Thank you. Now may I have them back?' After hiding them under the false floor of the wardrobe she told me that they were our secret and waited for me to swear that I'd tell no one. I swore. She said, 'I feel better now that someone has seen them,' then she kissed me.

'Thank you for showing them to me. I enjoyed it.'

She considered this and said, 'So did I.'

Thinking about the photo of the naked girl on a barrel, I asked, 'Have you ever done any before? More amateurish ones?'

'No, they're the first. If you'd told me a month ago that I'd do them, I would have violently disagreed with you. But then I saw this documentary on telly about glamour models and they said they did it because they could. I thought "I can do that." I mean, I know I'm not ugly. So I went ahead and did it. On impulse really.'

'Impulse?'

'What's wrong with that?'

'Nothing. Impulse is good. I wish I was more impulsive. No. Well done.'

She led me out of the bedroom – the bedroom that had its secrets, like all bedrooms. Andy was still asleep and stretched over the sofa and dangling on to the floor. He looked like he had fallen off the ceiling, or out of an aeroplane, and this was where he had happened to land. He was still energetically snoring and busy preparing his body for its next intake. He was busy; even though he lay asleep, looking like a piece of rubbish.

'OK. Your turn,' I said to Annis. 'Come with me.'

'Where are we going?'

'To the Little Brown Fiat.' The way I said it made it sound like a pub or a New Age health shop.

'*Where*?' she asked.

'My car.'

'Oh, yes. You've got something for me, haven't you?'

'I have.'

She followed me down the dark and discordant stairs into the neighbourhood watch street where the neighbourhood was running about with one another's TVs and videos.

'Is this it? It's *very* brown, isn't it?'

'It has the beauty,' I told her, 'of being unstealable. No one would want it.'

'I think that's what Andrew said . . . It really is quite disgusting.'

'That's what I like about it, the fact that it's so revolting.'

'Well, as long as it gets you from A to B, it doesn't really matter what it looks like.'

'Doesn't it?'

'I wouldn't have thought so. But, maybe this –' she indicated the car, but was unable to look at it – 'is the exception.'

I opened the unlocked door and leant into the back and pulled her present off the seat.

'Your present,' I revealed, 'is in the bag.'

Her hand, with its fixed fingernails, reached in and pulled out the wine. 'A Margaux! How wonderful! I expect this will be delicious.'

'I hope so.'

'How did you think of such a gift? You are clever. Come here.' I expect I was blushing. I expect that was the idea. She kissed me. No. She didn't kiss me, she virtually got off with me. Now if I'd opened my mouth a little more . . .

'Remember the condition? Let's share it. Let's drink it together.'

'With pleasure. Does this mean you're going to start drinking again?'

'Hopefully. Definitely. Yes. *Definitely*.'

'I've lost my job. Can I come in?'

I invited my second unexpected guest of the day to be seated in the big armchair. She lowered herself into the two deep buttock-dents that Spritz had left in the cloth and straightened the stained antimacassar.

I asked the question.

'Yes please, Doug,' answered Annis.

'One sugar?'

'Yes.'

Annis looked good in the chair. Its inflated proportions enhanced her girlishness as some other prop might, a bicycle or diamond engagement ring perhaps.

'Tell me what happened.'

'They sacked me.'

'Why?'

'Partly it's your fault – though I don't blame you, of course. Remember when you phoned up for your car insurance and I charged you fifty-one pounds when it should have been two hundred and fifty and I told you that I could get away with murder because the company is so inefficient?'

'Yeah, but I didn't realize it should have been that much.'

'They were listening to my phone that day, they recorded everything I said, like charging you ninety-nine pee if I felt like it, and all the rest. It's on tape. They called me into the office and played it to me. The senior supervisor was really happy about it – he never liked me. He said, "I'm sorry, Annis, but the company is going to terminate your employment." Then he started laughing and told me he thought he'd better phone the police, unless I – Oh, he's such a letch! I told him to fuck off. I told him my lawyers would be in contact.'

'Have you got a lawyer?'

'You know they escorted me off the premises? I didn't even get a chance to say goodbye to my friends. No, I haven't got a lawyer.'

'You never liked it there, did you?'

'Couldn't bear it.'

'Look on the bright side then. You're out of it now.'

'But what a humiliating way to go. They had no right to sack me like that. I'm not the only one who gives their friends special prices. Everyone does.'

'Milk?'

'Hum. Andrew wasn't bloody at home. I don't know where he goes during the day.'

'Comedy research?'

'I doubt it. He's not funny.'

'No, he's not.'

'Doug? Are you busy? Are you doing anything today?'

'I've got a couple of supermodels who want to consult me for dietary advice.'

'Sounds interesting.'

'Yeah, they're flying in from the States. My driver's picking me up at noon.'

'Really. If you could fit me into your schedule I have a proposition.' From her bag – which, with its lumped and overweight demeanour, had gained overnight status – she pulled out some fresh bread, some cheese and a bottle of wine – the claret. 'If you're ready to break your vow of abstinence, I thought we could share this.'

'Absolutely. An excellent suggestion.'

'The tea will spoil our palates, but since the wine should be opened and left for an hour before drinking—'

'Why?'

'To be honest I don't know. Wine snobbery, I think. But seeing as it *should*, I'll open it and we'll have it later. Now. Have you got a corkscrew?'

'I think *everyone's* got a corkscrew.'

She tore the lead foil from top and asked what made me choose this particular wine. I told her: impulse.

'So you can be impulsive then? Ever thought of becoming a calendar model?'

'Never. Here's the corkscrew.'

She twisted the cork out, gave the wine a long and interested sniff and said, 'This is a good choice. We're going to enjoy it . . . You do *like* wine, don't you, Doug? Only, I've never seen you drink it.'

'I like everything about it,' I said, trying desperately to sound as though I meant it.

'Later then. Now where's my tea?'

An hour later I said, 'Here goes. Cheers,' and began pouring the wine down my throat.

'NO. Not like that!'

With a mouthful of wine I gargled a bubbly, 'Huh?'

'First, tip the glass to its side and check the colour of the wine's rim.' She scrutinized her wine and appeared satisfied.

'Annis, I want to drink it. Not look at it!'

'Then, swirl the wine, smell it, sip a little, breathe through it. Here, like this.' She showed me. All twists and choking sounds; I expected her to drown.

'I never realized you were such a connoisseur.'

'I'm not. I simply adore a good claret. It turns me on.'

'Really?'

'Yes, Doug. You're not safe now.'

'Here, have some more.'

Half an hour later I was feeling the best I'd felt for months. My first drink for all that time was going straight to my head and doing its alcohol-thing up there. Now that I wasn't sober . . .

Now that I wasn't sober I looked at Annis. Drunkenly I executed my line, 'Annis, I want to f— sleep with you.'

So immediately I regretted it. So immediately I snapped back into sobriety. 'Sorry. Ignore me. I'm just drunk.'

She gave me her big-eyed look. The colours in the room began attacking me with added ferocity. The big eyes kept on looking. I felt sweat on my back.

She said, 'OK. Let's do it.'

I didn't need to imagine that I was anyone else.

I didn't need to imagine that *she* was anyone else. In the past I had closed my eyes and imagined that many girls were Annis – but they never actually were, until now. Now I just kept my eyes open, stared at what was there and let my imagination do an erotic recce.

Immediately after – in post-coital glee – I gave up trying to give up smoking and started smoking again.

'I'll phone Andrew and tell him I'm staying at Esfyn's. He never comes here, does he? . . . Good. Can I borrow the phone?'

Picture me. Revitalized and kicking towards the century's end with mad heart beating, finally after all this time, at a regular rhythm with no jump-starts or shock-stops.

And now the night was crystal, black crystal – jet, black tourmaline. The night moving onward too. Onward and out of the frost-bitten hand of winter. The summer, while a long way off, was now visible and in sight when you cocked a leg over the crow's nest and looked hard into time.

Annis by my side. We were ready to go again. Fuck. I can't believe my luck. What a bit of fucking luck.

Nine

Early in the morning I was actively awake. I knew last night had not been a dream, I only had to consider the quiet body next to me for confirmation, confirmation that the night's events were real.

But was it a mistake? On her part? Not on mine, certainly. But would she be washed over with powerful defiance? Would she say, 'I'm sorry, Doug. It should never have happened. That's all'? I made a tentative move, or rather, part of me made a tentacular move. In her lower back she felt the disturbance, she moved closer. No. No mistake. Watch that hand, Annis, carefully now . . . I discovered past midnight why she was called *Annis*. 'Since I was seventeen,' she told me, 'the name just stuck. Yes, most girls like it, though they prefer not to admit it. What about you, where did you get your name *Down* from? Or is it just family?'

Freeways of sun were stretching into the room. Earlier, ahead of schedule, today's light marked the end of winter. Not the start of summer, but the end of winter, and this was something. The colours in the flat were subdued. The light did this, so did my hangover, so did the new scenery: Annis. There was now something more eye-friendly to look at, something animate with its own surging presence, something that the colours could only be a background to.

Naked, and with light slipping over her, Annis walked to the cooker and told me she was going to cook me breakfast. Now, when was the last time this happened? I thought the cooker had broken, I thought it had died, I thought it was trying to get me out of the flat. Then, with the frying pan spitting and clinking, she delivered me a lit cigarette. I gave it to my mouth, and smoked, the cigarette rising and falling between my lips, like a conductor's baton, conducting. I have started smoking again and this time I'm not stopping. I'm very happy about all this. Things are definitely looking up.

She was saying she had to feed me well. I was going to need the strength. Sensibly, incredibly boringly, this should all be too much. I am meant to be ill. There I was a couple of years ago believing that I was dying of some medieval illness where the mind simply fades away and then hollows out the entire body. But never mind sensible. Fuck sensible.

Sensible stops me smoking and stops me drinking. And what good does that do me? It gets me relying on the guidance of Spritz and believing that I've fucked someone up nastily. Sensible is out.

'I want to thank you, Doug.'

'Thank me?' What could she thank me for? Fulfilling my fantasies? Doing me more good than two years of therapy?

'I want to thank you for helping me make the decision that I had been putting off for months: the decision to leave Andrew.'

'Oh,' I said. I felt guilty, but not guilty enough to stop me saying, 'Come here.'

The contents of Annis's bag were scattered into the folds and ripples of the duvet. They were the contents of a bag belonging to somebody who didn't plan going home first thing in the morning after fucking her boyfriend's best mate. They belonged to someone who had longer-term plans, someone who was making a change in their life, someone who was breaking out and moving into something new. There was money, banking paraphernalia, hair dryer, cosmetic kits, clothes, towels, nightie (unworn), jewellery, pregnancy tester (unused), CV . . . Her life. She found what she needed and went to the bathroom. Then the phone rang.

I answered it with a distracted 'hello'. There was silence, 'Andy?' I asked.

'No,' said the voice. 'I've just called to say I *don't* love you.'

Framed by the bathroom doorway, Annis's lips framed the word, Andy?

I shook my head. To the voice I said, 'That's great news. I'm so glad to hear it.'

'Good luck,' said Lucia de Londres, and put the phone down. Well, at least she's not going to come round and eviscerate me, I thought. I checked the phone for the incoming number. Nothing, sorry, no number.

'Good news?' asked Annis.

'Yeah. I've been offered an interview tomorrow. At the Shoe Shop.'

'You deserve it. I hope you get the job.' Back in the bathroom she resumed her teeth-hygiene, the brushing sounded like someone removing lime scale from a kettle element, it sounded vigorously efficient. It was the pertinacious preening that most of us lack the stamina to bother with. And we've got those side-effects to prove it: from the nicotine and caffeine, from the glucose and sucrose.

Over breakfast she asked with casual cadence, 'So you

don't mind if I stay here for a few days?'

'Stay as long as you like. But remember, Andy will find out eventually.'

'I'll move in with Esfyn. Andrew doesn't know where she lives.'

'Don't rush it. Stick around for a while, you make excellent breakfast.'

'I was right, wasn't I? All you needed was some female attention to bring you out of your depression. You were depressed, weren't you?'

'I was.'

If you got Andy drunk enough you could ask him anything. If you got Andy drunk enough you could ask him a question and be sure that he would have forgotten it the next morning. If you got Andy drunk enough you had to make sure that there were no drugs lying around that might enhance his memory that should be fading into the night.

Andy got himself drunk enough a few months ago and, unusually, there were no drugs. So I asked, 'Say one of your mates slept with Annis. What would you do? How would you feel? What if it was me?' The sheer questioning – not the question's content – was more than his bloated body and unhurried mind could cope with. He was too drunk to understand. I tried a more direct approach, 'If I fucked Annis, yes?' He stirred and showed drunken concern. 'If I fucked Annis, would you mind?' He formulated the answer, slowly but not intently. And with no inflection – so I didn't know what it meant – he said, 'Fuck her.' My last attempt was a lie: 'I *have* fucked her.' Again he thought through his own aeons and came up with, 'Me too.' Then he slid off his chair and fell asleep, a tangled body on the townhouse floor. I said, 'Goodnight,' and slowly left.

'What did she say?' I asked. Annis had ended her long and difficult call with Esfyn. She stepped back, and at arm's length replaced the receiver.

'He found her number, God knows where, and he's been calling her non-stop. He couldn't understand why Esfyn would not let him talk to me. She kept telling him I was asleep – for fourteen hours! She's pretty angry with me, but at least Andrew doesn't know where she lives. He'd have been there by now – don't you think?'

'Probably—'

'Maybe I ought to call him again . . . No, I'm not going to. I bet he's already in bed with someone else. He was incredibly unfaithful to me.'

'Was he?' I asked. The *was he?* as a reaction, not to his unfaithfulness, which I already knew about, but to her tenses, she was already talking in terms of 'was' unfaithful. Either because he used to be and had now stopped, or because he still was but would now not get another chance. 'Do you think you'll ever go back to him?'

'I doubt it. It's unlikely.'

'But possible?'

'Isn't everything?'

'Apparently.'

She decided to stay until the end of the week. 'I really enjoy being here,' she said. 'You and me, maybe there's something there.' She surprised me with her next statement – with female embarrassment she said, 'You were very good in bed, Doug. I wasn't expecting you to do all those things. Quite a stud, aren't you?' I don't know, maybe I was trying harder. Maybe I had more to gain. Maybe she was contact-erotic and simply demanded that her partner did his (or her?) best in the sack. Whatever the reason, I felt that I must have been quite good, I was now drained from the vigorous thrusts and body U-bends. I felt like a yogi who hadn't exercised for ten years and was now unfolding himself from the tight ball he had foolishly attempted. The aches and pains would go, all they needed was my new-found freedom: alcohol – or—

'Annis? My shoulders are somewhat sore, would you—'

'Where? Here?'

'Yes.'

'Take this off. I've got some balms in my bag. Lie down on the bed, I'll get them.' She took control – as she always would – and soothed emollients into my skin. I think I lay there cooing and *ah*ing. I think I told her all sorts of schmaltzy things. I think I did all that before her soporific hands took effect and I fell asleep. I think . . .

My house guest shook me awake. I came round spurting Fuck offs and What?s. 'What's happening?' I asked, confused by the lingering dream. After staring at her (she later said that I looked stupid), I worked out where I was, who she was, I worked out that I was in fact a human being. I asked again, still mistrustful of my words, 'What is it?'

'Answer the phone!' The phone? The *phone*. I'm going to throw that fucking phone out of the window – all it ever does is wake me up. 'Answer it!'

'Can't you?'

'It might be Andrew.'

'Andrew? Andy.'

It stopped ringing when I touched the receiver, as if some-one in the tower block opposite had kitted themselves out with phone, directory and telescope and this was how they spent their jobless time. I dialled 1471. At the other end the computer arranged a woman's voice and interposed the numbers. She read the telephone number to me; her voice was up and down, suggesting she'd had a sore throat on the day they recorded numbers zero to four and had her usual nasal coherence on the day they did five to nine. She gave me Andy's number and advised me to press the digit 3 if I wanted to return the call. I obeyed her. When he answered I moved the piece three inches away from my ear.

'You'll never guess what she's gone and done! Stupid bitch!'

'What now?' I hoped to sound detached, weighted by my own problems.

'She's only gone and left me!'

'I'm sure she hasn't. Annis, I presume.'

'Who else?'

'How do you know she's left?'

'She phoned to say she never wanted to see me again.'

'She didn't,' I said, which was true: she never said 'never'. 'She didn't?'

'She fucking did. Listen, Doug, help me out. I need an address, Esfyn's address.'

'Esfyn's got a boyfriend.'

'What? I know. I don't want to shag her. Annis is there and I've got to go and pick her up. You get on with Esfyn, call her and get the address.'

'I haven't got her number.'

'I have.'

'Can't you call her.'

'I have. Come on. For me.'

'I'll do it.'

Five minutes later I twisted my cigarette into my Anglo ashtray and called him back. 'She wouldn't tell me. She knew why I was phoning. Not stupid is Esfyn.'

'Fuck.'

'Sorry.'

'Never mind.'

'No?'

'Forget it. I'll see you tomorrow night at the comedy?'

'You're still doing it?'

'Of course.'

'You're not too depressed?'

'You know me better than that, Doug. I'm cool. She had to go in the end. She was bound to go in the end. I'm making all this fuss cos she'd expect it. It's a game, Doug. Annis loves games. See you tomorrow.'

Annis asked exactly what he'd said. So I lied to her. I lie to everyone these days and they all believe me. I'd lie to you if I met you. 'Yeah,' I'd say, 'I'm an honest bloke. Tell me about your problem, it will go no further. I won't use it, honest.' I don't like lying, but what can I do? What can I do now that the truth is all lost in fiction? Now that fiction is the truth.

Annis had a proposition. She would like to buy me lunch. And no, she didn't mean going down the supermarket, buying a bag of frozen chips, some reconstitutables and a cauliflower, or a cabbage. Instead, she wanted to take me out to lunch. 'Where?' I asked her. 'Where did you have in mind?'

She told me. I couldn't believe it. She wanted us to drive out into the *countryside* and find a village pub.

'A village?'

'Acorn.'

'What? Where?'

'Less than an hour. I used to go there with Christopher.'

'Who?'

'He was before Andrew.'

'From London?'

'No. He was a public school boy. Talk about chalk and cheese.'

'Bit of a wanker, I expect.'

'Not at all. But he did turn out to be gay. He went off with his old housemaster.'

'His who?'

'Housemaster. It's a lovely village. Lots of trees, lush grass, streams, wildlife, farmers mucking the fields. It smells different too, like another world . . .' She could have gone on about this for ever but she faded it and said, 'You have *been* to the countryside, haven't you, Doug?'

'I've flown over it a couple of times. In a plane.'

'It'll do you the world of good. I guarantee it.'

Hurriedly I thought of some excuses. 'The car might not make it. We might break down.'

'I don't mind sleeping in the car, it would be fun.'

'I haven't got any money.'

'I told you, *I'm* paying.'

'It's dangerous. There are lots of wild animals.'

'There are not. It's the countryside. Not the jungle.'

'I've got to go to work.'

'You haven't.'

'No – Yes, I have! Shit, I'd forgotten. I'm on this afternoon.'

'Cancel.'

'Yeah. Fuck 'em. Let's go to the *countryside*.'

'You're not a very safe driver, Doug. Can I drive?'

'You're not insured.'

'I am. I made sure I was. Mind the lorry!'

'What lorry?'

'That one!'

'Shit!'

'Pull over.'

The lorry bounced loudly past us, its huge wheels jumping off the road surface. A brick shot off its bed, missed the Fiat and exploded on the tarmac. We were on bumpy roads, worse even than London's hummocks and craters; country roads. Annis pointed a bird out to me, 'Look!'

'That's a big parrot.'

'No, Doug. It's a pheasant.'

'A pheasant? Are they edible?'

'Of course. They're game birds.'

'Are they? Why are they called *game* birds?'

'Because they're hunted and shot as a sport. That's a game, I suppose.'

'I bet the pheasant doesn't see it as a game.'

'No, probably not. Now move over, let me drive.' Annis took the driving seat, as was her prerogative, as was her aim in life. Andy had perfunctorily mentioned this habit, in case I ever met a girl like Annis. He didn't expect it to *be* Annis. Neither did I. 'Gracious,' she said, 'the steering wheel is massive. It's as big as my first hula-hoop.' It was oversized and overworked, the rim was burnished with the twirling of its many owners' hands. No one kept this car long, I was owner no. 48 in the logbook. No. 47 was a Chinese name, he'd kept it less than a month before passing it on to No Name Motors. So the rejected little brown Fiat had its big brown steering wheel, which Annis was now addressing as we headed up the road towards a bend.

If I was not a safe driver then Annis was not a slow one.

'This is fun,' she said. 'I haven't driven for ages. Andy won't let me.' With the engine revving she managed to squeeze more speed from the car than I had achieved in all my fear-confrontation tests. Maintaining a ridiculous velocity she turned into the corner. I swore loudly, then held my breath. The tyres were squealing. The car went into a broad slide, gathering up the rural rubbish on the road's edge, Annis's hands flicked the big wheel and the car balanced itself. Coming out of the corner, the car was pointing straight up the highway, but we were still going sideways accompanied by the howling rubber. Incredibly, during all this, Annis had started singing. 'Get your motor running,' as the car lurched, 'Head out on the highway!' as we neared the rambling hedge, 'Looking for adventure,' as the ditch beckoned the car, 'And whatever comes our way!'

Once travelling towards the next vanishing point, and realizing that I was still alive and not dead in some parallel world, I said, 'Fuck, Annis, I thought we were going to die. Don't do that again!'

'Sorry, Doug. I couldn't resist it. It was such a lovely corner. Double apex actually.'

'No wonder Andy doesn't let you drive. You're crazy!' With an unsteady voice I opined that she had learned all this from somewhere.

'Christopher taught me on his parents' farm. We used to race over the tracks in their old cars. One time we were both going for a corner and I accidentally pushed his car, an old Jag I think, into the ditch. He wasn't hurt, just pissed off that he'd have to drive the tractor nearly three miles to pull it out. You should have seen him, he was covered in mud by the time he got back on the track. Then we . . .'

'Where did you meet him? You never actually *lived* out here, did you?'

'No, I met him in Florence on a school art trip. We were the only two who agreed on the dimensions of a statue's penis.' She slowed the car, pulled on to a muddy verge and slithered us to a stop. 'We both agreed it was too small.'

'Now what?' I asked. 'A pit stop?'

'No.' She pointed across the road at an entrance. 'There's a beautiful house up there. Look at the drive, it's a lime avenue. Doug, even if I have to be buggered by a seventy-year-old owner I'm going to live in a house like that one day. I don't like London any more. I have aspirations.'

As the big eyes drooled I could see that she was moving away. She had imagined her life, set it out like a flow chart that belonged to an early-nineteenth-century novelist. Her plot did not include Andy and it did not include me. It went much further and delved into Romanticism. It went back in time. It went forward in time. Yet somehow it skirted history and the future. And it completely ignored the millennium.

'What do people do in the countryside? They can't race cars through fields, shoot pheasants and live at the end of long drives all day long. Do they go to the pub? *Are* there any pubs? Are there any *clubs*?'

'It differs from town life in that everything is more stretched out. People do the same things, only differently, and they take longer. Really life is more sedate.'

It sounded as though green and rustic patches on England maps were offered up on a different time-basis. It sounded as though time was elongated and ticking away within different parameters. It sounded slower.

'There's something you can do out here that can't easily be done in towns. I'll show you later. You'll enjoy it.'

Driving into the pub's car park – which would have been full of non-patrons' cars while they did their banking, shopping and sightseeing if it had been in London – I told her that the country folk dressed like yuppies. However, it appeared I had got it wrong, the wrong way round. For some reason the *yuppies* had dressed like country folk.

The pub itself seemed unaffected by its location. It still looked like a pub and not like the mud hut that I had feared. I think it was called the Plough or the Tractor or the Combine Harvester or something.

Obviously not from around these parts – but this not mattering because she was tall, blonde and beautiful – Annis caused her usual stir among the pub-drinkers. Of course they ignored me, or pretended I wasn't there. In an alcove she ushered me into an opsit-bank and asked, 'Wine or beer?'

'I presume they have bitter,' I said, 'I'll try a pint.'

As I sat in the seat designed for courting couples I realized what was different about the countryside. It was the point I had missed all along. Even with the idling jukebox and the folky chat about horse manure and field-drilling, everything was much *quieter*. When there was a sound it meant something, or had some definite origin, whether it was a bark, birdsong, tractor furrowing or a lone car travelling the lane, it was labelled, it was assigned. This was unlike the city, where there was always noise and it was never quiet. The background hum had to be blocked out and this was the nearest you got to silence. The city itself could never be silent, only acclimating your imagination could manage that.

Annis placed my froth-topped pint on a coaster that had a picture of a cow on it. The beer was the colour of damp tree bark and it tasted different. It tasted silent – there was none of the usual popping and jostling on my tongue.

'You're quiet,' said Annis quietly.

'I know,' I whispered.

'Why are you whispering?'

'I don't know.'

'Sorry, I can't hear you . . . Speak up!' Mid-sentence a jet dive-bombed the pub. In the boom the building felt as if it had been lifted from the ground and dropped like a Monopoly house.

'Bloody RAF!' shouted a farmer. 'Who do they think they are, spoiling our countryside? They wouldn't do it over a town. Can't they practise over the sea, for pity's sake. My cows won't calve if this goes on! Where's that petition?'

Briefly there was silence. Then two more jets cat-and-moused through the air above the quiet country pub. The building did its bomb-shake again.

'It's bad for business,' revealed the landlord. 'The folk don't like it and every time planes come that close they throw the yeast up in the real ale. It takes two days to settle. Give us the petition. I'm going to sign it again.'

Five pints and a meal later Annis was back behind the wheel and steering us through the impossibly narrow lanes. We were heading for the place she had predicted I would enjoy. When we stopped we were in the middle of nowhere. So I said, 'We're in the middle of nowhere. What are we doing here?'

'Down there –' she gestured towards some bushes and trees – 'is where we're going.'

'To see the wildlife?'

'Sort of. Follow me.' I followed her across the lumpy field with its aculeated crop and over the remains of old carrier bags that had *fertilizer* or *poison* written on their sides. Five minutes later I was grazed and bleeding from the thorns, but we were where she wanted us: a bed-sized clearing in a spinney.

'Get undressed,' she commanded. 'You will enjoy this. Open-air sex is so free.'

'People might see us or hear us.'

'Don't be silly, Doug. We're in the middle of nowhere. You said so yourself.'

'Come here.'

But she was wrong. People could hear us. After, as we made our way out through the vicious thorns and furious brambles I heard a gunshot. Then another. Coming through the hedge were men with big sticks. I grabbed her hand and ran her to the car. Other guns had started firing now, and there were more people with sticks, even women and children. 'Fuck Fuck Fuck. Get us out of here quick, Annis! They probably think we're aliens. I've heard about these country people, they don't even know what a town is. Drive!' She made no move. 'Come on. We're in danger. What's so funny? This isn't funny. They going to shoot us – or *beat* us to death.'

'Doug! The people with the sticks are beaters.'

'I know! Please drive the car.'

'They're shooting at pheasants. Not us.'

'Peasants?'

'*Pheasants.*'

'Pheasants, poor bastards. Now can we go?'

'OK,' said the pussy-whipper and pointed the Fiat into the muddy lane. Behind us the beaters continued hitting everything, they continued with their game. A game, Annis later admitted, whose season should have finished earlier in the year – this was an illegal shoot.

'They're a funny bunch out here,' I commented.

'Merely different,' said Annis. 'You'd get used to it.'

'I wouldn't.'

She drove us through the demanding roads with their unbelievable angles. There was a whole alphabet to describe them, Z and S bends, C curves, N turns, T junctions, A-shaped give-ways, D-profile lay-bys, acute X crossroads and V-layout genua. We took a left off a K junction and entered the I of a straight road and eventually slipped on to the dual carriageway, which was a road that had been plough-planed though the valleys and the hills and then covered with a length of graphite tape that the surveyor had rolled at London.

On the inside lane, the car fatigued from Annis's expressive driving, we were rocked from side to side in the parallel tracks that the heavy lorries had set down. Darkness, which the road reacts to before anyone else does, was coming at us. Cars had side-lights switched on and their drivers were leaning further forward in their seats, hoping perhaps to see their reflections in the Catseyes that glinted like the fillings in the teeth of an old sweat-eater. Annis had her foot flat to the floor, we were doing forty-seven miles per hour and steam had just begun to filter through the air vents and into the car where it assumed an ephemeral form, then disappeared into the car-air as the ghost of a cat might. 'Don't worry,' said the driver, 'I know what's wrong.'

We pulled into a service station.

In *Cooperage in the Late Twentieth Century* the action is starting to hot up. The landlord is constantly scuttling over to Chattaway with free pints. Soon he intends to administer the poison. Then he's going to call his cabby mate, Cabbage, help Chattaway off the premises, bundle him in the taxi and drive to the deserted house where he intends to do the cutting, the cock-cutting.

Chattaway – blissfully, and soberly, unaware of what is being planned – is extremely weary of all the beer that the landlord keeps buzzing over with. He is convinced that the idea is to get him drunk so that the landlord can have his gay sugar-daddy way with him. But cunning Chattaway has a means of secretly staying sober. Whenever no one is looking, he pours the beer into an empty three-litre lemonade bottle that is hidden in a supermarket bag. Then he leaves his dark pub-corner and goes off to the dirty pub-toilet. In here he locks the cubicle door and sprinkles the beer away. He is careful to maintain a normal speed of micturition. Of course no one ever takes the time he takes, sometimes more than three minutes, and he hasn't heard the pub-rumour concerning his gargantuan bladder. Chattaway has his schemes whirring as well: he wants to get rid of the landlord so that he can make his move on poor barmaid Bella. His plan also involves poison (and I think this is where the film takes its creative licence). After poisoning the landlord he will call a taxi and aid him on his way to hospital. During the journey he will plant the drugs and forged cash (he bought these at the beginning of the film) on the landlord and then poke holes into the veins of the landlord's arms with a hypodermic needle. He describes this in his narration as 'a nice detail'.

A couple of pages later the landlord is in the toilet and admiring the graffiti that he has scrawled on the tiles. 'The landlords fucking Bella.' Not very imaginative, but he's proud of it. While he's in there he notices that the cubicle door is locked. In later dialogue he explains that this is when he decided to vandalize his own toilet and rip the cubicle door off, 'since if a bloke ain't got a cock he can still piss sitting down in there, chick-style like'.

Next there is an awkward confrontation as Chattaway (finally!) stops urinating and joins the landlord in the once-white reflet of the graffiti-tiled toilet. Difficult glances are exchanged as Chattaway slips past him and returns to his dark corner. The landlord feels uneasy about the whole thing, so he decides to pull a couple of pints and join Chattaway with some smoothing conversation.

Chattaway doesn't know that his pint has twenty sleeping-pills dissolved in it. The landlord doesn't know that when he left Chattaway for a moment to greet his mate Cabbage, Chattaway seized his opportunity and tipped a phial of bromide into his pint.

'What's that you're reading?' asked Annis, who had woken from the restorative sleep that alcohol had persuaded her to take. 'I didn't know you liked books.'

'It's nothing,' I replied, and threw it back into a pile of clothes. 'Just some junk that I found lying around.'

'I'm sorry about your car. Are you still angry with me?'

'Not a problem. At least it still works.'

'Only just.'

In the service station the car had pulled itself to a steaming stop and started snorting boiling water from under the hood. Then there was a bang and we were engulfed by an ejaculation of steam and hot mist. 'It's overheated,' Annis told me.

'Yeah. I'd guessed that.'

'I'm sorry.'

'What do we do now? Scrap it?'

'We wait.'

So we waited. And while we waited Annis explained why she had to leave Andy. Why she *had* left him: she was too independent. 'I've got my own thoughts, Doug, and a lot of men don't like that. They want to fuck me, tell their mates, then go home and masturbate over their magazines. They want to treat me like pornography. They want me to be a photograph.'

'Aren't those glamour shots pandering to that, surely you're *becoming* pornography?'

'Certainly not. Men don't fuck *with* pornography. They're all too frightened. If the spread-legged beauty in their centre-fold came to life and climbed out on to their bed they'd run a mile.'

'*I* wouldn't.'

'Yes. Yes, you would. Let's put it this way. If I was a porn star and used to group sex with men who had twelve-inch willies, wouldn't you feel a little insecure taking me on all by yourself? Wouldn't you feel inadequate?'

I didn't want to answer that one, but I did ask, 'Have I got a small one then?'

'Well, it's not twelve inches, but it does the job.'

I said, 'Thank you,' and placed the road atlas over my crotch.

She came back from the station shop with a container of oil and a bucket full of water.

'This is the radiator cap,' she said, holding a twisted disc of metal, 'and it wasn't on properly.' She poured the oil and water into various gurgling orifices. The literature on the oil container claimed that this oil could add five-thousand miles to the life of the engine. What a bargain, I thought, and went to buy some more.

The little brown Fiat was then running again, kind of. As we drove it did its impressions of a dustcart eating rubbish. And it complained of mechanical abuse at top speed: twenty-five miles per hour. It complained at *twenty-five*; even *bicycles* don't mind that sort of speed. An hour later we arrived at the coloured flat. My driver's eyes were searching in her mascara sockets, so she lay down and sought sleep.

How, I had asked her, did she know so much about cars and radiators and where to put the oil. Partly Andrew, she explained, but mainly Christopher. And, ostensibly, she was still sad that she had lost him to men. Sad, because he was the only man who had the credentials and references needed to fit into her life-plan. Sad, because he was now gay and had his own pornography. Pornography that Annis couldn't enter: women were not welcome.

So she had fallen asleep and dreamt of the royal family. A childhood dream which she kept on believing in. A dream that would come true. It was all a matter of time, just time.

She was rubbing the snow that had come at her eyes while she slept, and saying, 'I dreamt I was a princess. And you were a prince. At least I think it was you. The prince had blue eyes. What colour are yours?'

'Blue. But a little faded around the edges.'

'Maybe it wasn't you. His were bright blue.' She opened her eyes fully now, and said, 'Honestly, Doug, all this upheaval is having an awful effect on me. Right now I feel like a drink. Not like me at all. Shall we get some wine? How about a trip to the Wine House?'

Down in the Wine House there was still plenty of wine. In fact there was still so much of the stuff that it was impossible to tell whether any had been sold since I was last there.

Annis was not alarmed when I told her that we had to buy a minimum of six bottles. 'Don't worry,' she said, 'I'll buy you a *cellar*.'

Wendy pulled me over, indicated Annis and questioned

me: 'It worked then?' I nodded. 'It always does. Wine always does,' she promised.

'Would it work on you?' I asked.

'Yes, it would,' she said. 'I'm married to the owner.'

Over with the ranks and rows of wine (arranged with military precision), Annis informed me that it was not necessary to spend twenty pounds to get a good bottle. 'I'll buy you a selection and we can have a tasting. I'll drink you through the basic grape varieties. You'll be amazed how quickly you pick them up and how much fun it is trying.'

'Chardonnay?' I asked, holding up one of the many wine glasses that we had purchased from the Wine House in order to accomplish this educational drinking session. 'It is, isn't it?'

'No. It's Riesling.'

'This one's Chardonnay?'

'No. That's red, it's Pinot Noir.'

'This is the Chardonnay.'

'It is.'

'I agree that this is all very interesting. But I'm getting too drunk to learn anything. Can't we just drink them instead?'

'Certainly. Why don't you put some music on?'

'I haven't got a stereo. It was stolen.'

'What about that radio alarm clock thing?'

'It sounds like a Coke can with pebbles in it . . . I'll put it on.' I tuned in to a station that sounded the least like sandpaper and set the alarm for eight o'clock in the morning – I had my interview with the Shoe Shop at nine a.m.

The table with its full, half and empty glasses, and its six bottles, looked like a large drinks tray belonging to a drinks party where all but two guests had rushed outside to witness the main event. And we were those two lone guests. By midnight we had killed off four of the wines and they had all begun to taste the same – they could have been the same for all I knew. The last leg proved to be the most strenuous. Annis said, 'You drink the red. No, the white. I'll tackle the white, the red, or do you want the white? Or the red?'

'We should mix them.'

'No! No.'

'No?'

'Here's the white. Cheers.' Holding a nearly full bottle Annis stood up, straightened the short length of her skirt, unruffled the drifts in her blouse and considered herself in the tall mirror. 'Mirrors,' she began, 'are a very useful invention.'

'They are,' I agreed and jumped up in time to catch her. 'They're very honest, aren't they?' I lay the droops and loops of her body on the bed and sat down to challenge the rest of the wine. It beat me in the closing stages and with defeat sounding in my ears, with its warm hiss and whistle, I fell asleep next to the shape of Annis, who had drunkenly assumed the recovery position.

Excellent result! When I was woken by the exaggerated claims of advertisers on the local radio station I had no hangover whatsoever. Not a glimpse. Happily I was still drunk. It crossed my mind to forget the interview and attempt to drain the wine that had baffled me in the endgame last night. I decided against this and did my morning wash. Boyishly I brushed my teeth, I spat the vinic fur from my tongue and astonished my face with water. Then I directed three slabs of Haligum at my mouth and masticated dynamically. I left a note for Annis – who remained suckered to the bed in the previous night's pose – telling her not to do anything, not to bother clearing up. I drove to the Shoe Shop at maximum speed, at twenty-five, and parked next to the publicity car, which (you guessed it) is shoe-shaped.

Mr Rumble came rumbling into the room and said in a loud rumbling voice, 'Mr Down! How the hell are you?'

'In fine fettle,' I assured him, immediately relieved that I was still drunk.

'Take a seat, Douglas! May I call you Douglas?'

'Doug,' I said energetically, 'it's Doug.'

'And so it should be, Doug! So it jolly well should be!' Rumble flung himself into his revolving chair and revolved. After ten revolutions he anchored his feet and in a bellowing voice said, 'Tell me, Doug! Why do you want to be in SHOES?'

'Well, Mr Rumble—'

'Colin! *Please*!'

'Well, Colin, I've always been interested in shoes. After all, where would we be without shoes?'

'An excellent point! Indeed, where *would* we be without the little devils? Tell me, Doug! What are you packing on those feet of yours?'

'Shoes— boots, Colin. I find I am very hard on my feet.'

'They don't look like the Shoe Shop to me!'

'Regrettably they're not. These came from the Smell of Leather.'

'THE SMELL OF LEATHER! WHY WHY WHY?' So I told the man with the huge voice how I had unwittingly bought a pair of shoes from the Smell of Leather which had kept fucking falling to pieces. And finally, I told him, the manager had settled with these boots.

'You understand the problem, Doug! The problem of quality, the QUALITY concept! Here at the Shoe Shop we are not cheap! And there is a reason for that. Is there not? QUALITY QUALITY QUALITY!'

'Quality,' I repeated.

'QUALITY,' he repeated.

'The quality, certainly. I can see that the Shoe Shop is quality.'

'It is, Doug! I think that you'll be a great asset to us! Bravo! Welcome on board! When can you start?'

'Two weeks. I have some loose ends to tie up.'

'Two weeks! Bravo again! We'll see you then!'

He wished me well and tortured my hand by shaking it. Then, with my ears ringing and my shaken hand shaking, I made my way back home through the dry and bright of the greyly shod streets. I drove back to Annis. I drove back to the wine. I drove back to the colours. I drove back at a new maximum speed: twenty-four miles per hour. Or thirty-eight *kilometres* per hour, which sounds faster to the English.

And there she was, up and awake, and not so steady on her feet as alcohol knocked her about with its morning knee-trembler. She was doing exactly what I asked her not to do: tidying up. Her greeting was wordless, it was unrehearsed. Her crescent eyelids rose and fell, the semi-mooned forehead pressed heavily on the frown, the lips were arched and out of place – she looked like the Sydney Opera House in failing light. 'The note,' I asked, 'did you read it?'

'No. Yes,' she replied through the architecture of her paralexic hangover. 'I think I've got a hangover.'

'Yes, I think you probably have.'

'And you?'

'Not yet. Later.' And it's true. Sometimes my hangovers have a nasty joke waiting for me, a joke that isn't funny. They come at me when I've stopped expecting them: maybe a day, maybe a week, maybe never. Sometimes they lay dormant for long periods, they hibernate, then pool resources and come rearing at me with everything they've got . . . 'Luckily for me I'm still drunk.'

'I wish *I* was. I wish I was drunk. Or sober.'

'Have some wine.'

'No thanks. I don't feel like drinking.'

'Do you feel like eating?'

'No.'

'Paracetamol?'

'Yes please.' There was a tub – a tub I hadn't touched, or needed, for the past few non-drinking-months – filled with white pills, part of my self-help medical kit. 'Did you get the job?' she asked. 'Or do you have to wait to find out? I hate the way they keep you hanging on before they tell you.'

'I got it.'

'Well done, Doug! What was it like, the interview?'

'Quick, very quick. And loud. The interviewer, Colin Rumble, was a very loud man.'

'Not one of those motivational types?'

'He might be. I don't know.'

'He didn't talk to you about hierarchies of human needs? Or hygiene factors and motivators? I hate it when they do that. They all do these days. It's so boring!'

'No, he just talked about shoes and quality – loudly.' I gave her the pills. She swallowed them dry, with great difficulty, with plenty of throat action, like a snake swallowing an animal or a safari trekker's suitcase that was four times its diameter. 'Go to bed,' I advised, 'get some sleep. I'm going to finish the wine and then I'll join you.'

'You don't mind me being here, Doug?'

'Absolutely not. I enjoy having you around.'

'Give me a hug then. I'll feel better if you do. I feel so fragile, I need someone to squash me back together.'

'Sure. Come here.'

Annis sleeps quietly. Even with a hangover she makes little noise, no more than a purr really. There's none of the keel-hauling sound of a ferry grounding in Calais, none of these windpipes and nasal cavities blocked with contraflows and diversions, none of the steady wood-sawing that keeps so many of us awake through the night. No, she sleeps quietly, as babies are supposed to, she sleeps like the new-born: silent and unknowing.

When she wakes she'll be happy to hear that she fell asleep quickly. 'So my head hit the pillow,' she'll ask, 'and I was asleep?' 'Yes,' I'll answer. 'I don't know how you do it.' To which her response will be, 'Neither do I. I guess I just have a talent.' And if that's her talent, then what can you do except congratulate her on having discovered it when she did? And explain to her that she was lucky not having to wait a whole lifetime for it, by which time it would have been too late and a talent wasted.

I have a refound or rediscovered talent. My talent is once again in the area of smoking and drinking. Two pastimes in which I really am quite a high scorer when I put my mind to them. As I say, these are *re*discovered and the *re* prefix features as a major player in the Down household. My father has a talent for brushing his hair in such a way as to hide his receding hairline. He has a talent for receiving stolen property and renamed credit cards. My father is a talented and receding recidivist. Last year he was reimprisoned for the sixth time, he has no talent for staying re-released. My mother works in the social services and does her best to reclaim such people from repetitive crime, she tries to reintegrate them, to rehouse and re-educate them. She tries with all her female knowing and wife's technique to reform them. Currently she is contemplating remarrying. My sister's talent is for retakes. She loves to resit the exams she has resat many times before. Regardless of all the revision that she rereads and relearns she repeatedly fails. She and her fiancé have just reapplied for a council house. They have just been rejected. They have rejoined the despairing masses.

I drew heavily on one of Annis's heavy cigarettes and drank faithfully from the last bottle of wine. I learned all this at school. How to smoke the tar-laden cigarettes which gave the girls husky come-on voices and made the boys cough and spit. How to make yourself sick when you'd drunk too much so that you could carry on and drink some more. I learned how to cheat the cigarette-vending machine and how to con the condom dispenser. I learned how to read and write and how to apply it to what the school felt would be necessary and useful to me in later life. I learned about reference books from a back-to-basics English teacher who made us look up the word *dictionary* in a dictionary, the word *thesaurus* in a thesaurus and the word *encyclopedia* in an encyclopedia, and because he also taught woodwork he showed us how to carve the word *wood* into a piece of wood. I learned a lot at school; but not from the teachers.

The wine I was drinking was red, it wasn't French, it came from Australia and it was two years old. Any more than that I can't tell you. I don't know what grapes made it, how it would be described in those playful wine terms, whether the heavy cigarette was its worthy accompaniment, whether the glass was of the correct dimensions and shape. I do know, however, that my long-running dispute with grapes was finally coming to an end. Thanks to Annis, it was now possible to enjoy the white wine that she chilled and the red that she had begrudgingly poured into a pint glass for me. What I like about wine is that it's three times stronger than beer and a lot easier to down than spirits. It is – and you may not appreciate me saying this – a ready-made cocktail. Oh, and the other thing it does – something beer and spirits can't manage – is marry off girls like Wendy and get me into the sack with Annis.

And there's some good news on the wine front, the front concerning all alcohol. It appears that in moderation (a couple of glasses now and again) alcohol is going to reduce your chances of heart disease by a half. That's half the chances of people who drink too much, and it's also half the chances of people who don't drink at all. It seems the teetotallers of this world are more prone to death than they had expected. It seems that they were wrong after all. It seems that their attempt to dupe death has all been in vain – they would have been better off drinking all that time. There's a J-shaped curve produced by medical experts to prove it. It's in a glossy about death that people can consult to see why they're dying. It's probably the ultimate reference book – chances are that if you consult it you think there's something wrong, you might think you're dying, or you might be pessimistic or hypochondriacal. I consulted it when I didn't rate my chances quite as highly. I looked at it because I was meant to be ill. But I wasn't dying. I am aware of that now.

Grappling with the remaining wine (there was less than half a glass left), I remembered a conversation I once had with an economist. The economist (a teacher, I think) was getting high on one of his microconcepts. He was conceptualizing *marginal utility*. He told me that the more a consumer consumes of a consumerable the less utility he will gain from said product, its marginal utility will decrease with consumption. Now this statement was in awkward contradiction with my current predicament. As my wine neared its end I was savouring every last mouthful and was hoping that this alcohol might be just what my body needed to drift into confused bliss. Its marginal utility would in fact be increasing, its marginal utility as the final alcohol units hit home might be what was required to make the equation whole. Then my wine would have cumulative utility. And there would be nothing marginal about it. Nothing at all.

Keenly dispelling this myth I sent the wine at my bloodstream and slid over to join Annis. She lay there modelled by Greek mathematics: the hyperbola of her waist, the parabolic evolutes of her elbows and knees, the helices that formed her ears and the ellipses that were her eyes. She made no sound as I kissed the nape of her neck and as I pulled her hair between the lazy Vs of my fingers. I leant and kissed the slightly proffered lips; she gave a warm sigh but was still asleep and dreaming her own special dreams. She dreamt once again of her prince. This time the prince had kissed her. This time the prince had saved her.

Hours later, some time after she had disclosed that she was in love with a prince (not an English one, surely – too old, too young, too unpredictable), hours after her dream she was groping mid-sentence: '. . . I used to love him . . . Still have a love *for* him . . . At least I can support him . . . I don't hate him.'

'Come then. It would be a good idea. The two of you can talk.'

'What about you?'

'Don't worry about me. Esfyn's coming too, she can be our cover.'

'Right, Doug! I'm going to do it. I'll come.'

'Good. Call Esfyn. You can borrow some of her clothes. No, you're taller. Oh, I'm sure the two of you will think of something.'

'You know what, Doug,' she said confidentially, almost with embarrassment, 'you're right. I'm still the same person I always was. What've I got to fear?'

'Nothing, except the usual things.' And the usual things were: death, prolonged life, murder, rape, traffic – the insanity of cars, the insane cars that people wanted to ban. Yes, apart from the usual things she had nothing to fear, and nothing from Andy, who after all, when all was said and done, at the end of the day, was – what was he? He was a comedian. Surely no need to fear a comedian, even an untried one, who probably, when he did try, would not be very funny. But this was *his* night and Annis needed to discover whether he could be funny when he went live with his act and there were *all* those people looking on and hoping (jealously) that he would be bad – that he would be unfunny. And the unfunnier he was, the bigger, the better, the *funnier* the stories would be the next day between work mates as they discussed the previous evening over pint and pie. But give him his chance, he hadn't tried yet, and he did have that bravery, a special courage that persuaded him to stand up and do stand-up. Could he be funny? He truly hoped he could be.

Pulling clothes from one pile and throwing them on to another, I was searching for money that a vague memory suggested would be working its way down towards the orange carpet. It turned up wedged into the butterflyed spine of *Cooperage in the Late Twentieth Century*. Which reminded me: I had promised to show it to Andy. Be he warm or cold, from the weather front of his reception, I would show him tonight. It would provide stabilization either way, from his comedy-high or his comedy-low. The money was on the page where I'd left the action: the poisoning in progress. I'd have thought that it was drugging, not poisoning – I mean, they're not trying to *kill* each other. But this is intended as a film script, it can get away with it – films do. Chattaway and the landlord about to go down, the action at the peak of its cinematic mons. One, or both, about to tumble its speckled gradient. Personally I'm with Chattaway, he might soon be penis-less and I wouldn't wish that on any man, not even . . . If it goes ahead there'll be a purple ridge circumscribing the base. This will go dark red, red, light red and fade as the years pass. This will be where the surgeons do their microsurgery and stick the missing member back on – that's if they ever find it; a dog might eat it or something. All this if it ever comes off, we don't know yet, the film's not over, there's still chipped polystyrene covering the base of the cardboard tub: the remaining popcorn to dry the mouth out and get stuck between teeth and gums . . . *Cooperage in the Late Twentieth Century* fitted perfectly into the pocket of my wool jacket. It was a transition fit, where external matches internal, a sexual fit. Or, as my mother would have said, *Cooperage in the Late Twentieth Century* was made for my pocket.

When it came to clothes, Annis was catwalking the main contenders. She asked if she could borrow a shirt she'd seen hanging around, but she had some questions. Had Andy ever seen me wearing it? Would he know it was mine? No, he wouldn't, it was for work; Andy had never seen me around work. Yes, she could borrow it. In that case, did I have an iron? Look at it! *Do you?* I pointed at the unused iron in the corner, the stolen iron in its stolen box. Unstolen too by my many burglaries. Unnoticed perhaps. After all, who wants an iron? Needs one, sure. But do people really *want* such a boring object. And its name: *iron*. Nothing given away there, is there? Give it a consumer name like *Diamond* or *Cruiser* and people might get interested. People might start stealing them from me.

'I would imagine that an ironing board is asking too much,' said Annis.

'Stolen. Use the table. I'll wipe it for you.'

She started ironing, a towel placed on the table. I watched: the precision sweeping action, the run-offs past the creases, the pancake reversal; so unlike men. Men, who attack the clothes – the iron is after all a weapon, many opponents have fallen under its massed yield. 'That should do it,' she said. 'It looks like new.' She referred to the iron. 'Has it ever gone wrong?'

'No, it's very reliable.'

'Mine keeps burning Andrew's clothes.'

With the shirt checked, mirror-judged, removed and rehung, she said, 'All that leaves is my hair. Can I borrow your Body Blow In? I'm all out.'

'It's dry dry.'

'No problem. I'm dry.' She amassed what she needed and went to do her diurnal hair-thing. There was a call for another towel in the closing stages, mine weren't as absorbent as the fleecy ones she was used to. After the hair was done (warmed and dried, the intimate smell of treated-hair lingering in the room like salon-scent) she was almost ready. Just a touch of make-up, not too much. She didn't need much, but then neither did the models in the magazines who were paid so highly to advertise it. She then said, 'What else do I need to do?'

I told her I couldn't think of anything.

'Right then, I'll get dressed.' And so this part of the process began.

'Don't you usually do stuff like make-up after getting dressed?'

'Depends what I'm wearing. The order is dictated by the clothes.' So that was her schedule then. First she decided what to wear, then arranged everything around it. This, she informed me, meant that she knew where she stood for time. She knew she'd be late, but she knew *how* late. Then there'd be no last-minute panic or mind-changing.

During all this time (and there was a lot of it) I had to find something to save me from boredom. The answer was easy: I tripped down to Gary's corner shop and bought lager and cigarettes. With my hands full of beer and smouldering ash, I waited for the make-over girl (who didn't need a make-over) to complete her make-over. I waited as I would over the coming months for the same hold-ups. But then I would be waiting for a different girl, a less complicated one, a girl who didn't have the same scheduling. Still, she would make me happy. The relationship was going to be less fraught – the control-emphasis would be more in my favour.

When you looked at Annis from her left, the abbreviated skirt formed part of a callipygian comma, and her legs, frighteningly exposed, were exclamation marks. This was her punctuation. She was punctuated and this was what made men stop, pause and exclaim, 'Boy, look at that!' and then question their own symbols who weren't by their sides.

As I stopped, stared and swore under my breath, she

walked round the car to the driver's door and asked with some concern, 'You're not planning on asking Esfyn to marry you again tonight, are you?'

'Not tonight.'

She turned the key and waited with her patience for the engine to fire up. Eventually it wheezed, spluttered, gave us a pulmonary hawk and then went into the pulls and pushes of its Otto cycle. 'Sounds awful,' said Annis, matching my own thoughts. She found a gear, a lottery now since the gearbox was no more than a box that happened to have gears in it, all broken and twisted and probably back-to-front. Pulling the big wheel with both arms, she hoisted the car into the road and said hopefully, 'Here we go.'

Driving down the street our ears were fed with whirring, wearing and metal-tearing. A red traffic light (only recently repaired: it had been a victim of road-rage) halted us at the end of the mean street with its orb indicating danger. On amber we were out-dragged by a night-stalking runner who, with all his thin fluorescent strips moving on his body, looked like a swarm of fire-flies accelerating down the pavement. Twenty-two and we passed him. Twenty-three and we hit maximum.

'This is so embarrassing,' said Annis. 'Why didn't you buy a proper car?'

'You broke it.'

'What was that?'

'Something falling off, I expect.'

There was a definite change in the streets tonight. Sure it was dark and of course it was still light, we, after all, were adding to astronomical pollution – light pollution, the most up-to-date variety of pollution. But the air was drier, it was less massive, and it was devoid of its normal presentiment.

London's inhabitants walked straighter, taller, with shoulders not as tired or hunched, expecting nothing quite as bad as the early year had brought.

'Take a look at them,' said Annis. We passed two men. Two men whose upper bodies wore T-shirts, thin white T-shirts. 'I can't wait for summer.'

'Neither can I. Neither can London.'

'That's Esfyn's house. You'd like to live there, wouldn't you?'

'Yeah, probably.' This was more like it. There was less decay, less rubbish, less wood – less of the splintered wood that boarded up windows and waited for graffiti. Better cars, better houses. Better people? There seemed to be less meanness and I saw no dead cats. The street was kinder. Yeah, I'll move in around a place like this soon, I could get used to it. I won't move in with Esfyn though, she's got a boyfriend and I wouldn't – well, I have with Annis; forgive me, another lie.

'Careful what you touch. Esfyn is very house-proud.'

The panelled door opened, petite Esfyn asked us in. She checked our feet as she checked us in. Wipe them please. We wiped.

'Go through. Powell's in the living room.'

'*Powell*?'

'My boyfr—*fiancé*.'

'Congratulations,' said Annis. 'At last.'

'Thank you. We're very happy. Sorry, Doug.'

'I hope it works out. When's the big day?'

'In two or three years.'

'Jesus!'

'Doug!' Annis scolded me.

'I'll make you both a coffee. Go on, the door's open.'

Turning to Annis, I asked if Powell was coming tonight.

No, he wasn't. 'He doesn't go out,' she whispered.

'Jesus!' I said again.

'Shshh, Doug!' I followed her through Esfyn's fantastically tidy house and into the fantastically tidy living room. I contemplated *living* and looked the room over. It was catalogue-control, mail-order content, TV-advert shimmer and shine. Unliveable really, you wouldn't want to sit with booze and fags and cheer the football on, you wouldn't expect to fuck in front of the fire.

Annis said, 'Doug, Powell. Powell, Doug.'

'Good move, Powell,' I said. 'No more lonely nights for you, eh?'

'I don't . . . We don't . . .'

'What are you watching?'

'*CrimeTime.*'

'My mate was on that, he was in a train and—' I stopped because the mate was Andy and Annis didn't know about his TV appearance.

'I recognized the hat,' she said. 'Kidder's girlfriend, Trish. I know all about it.'

'What's that, Annis? What did your friend do, Doug?'

'Nothing serious. Only infidelity.'

'Do you smoke, Powell?'

'I certainly don't.' He pointed at the large No Smoking sign on the wall, a sign that really did make the place look like a brand-new room layout in a department store. I gave him one of the looks I gave non-smokers. One of the looks a lot of people had given me recently, and he said, 'We don't allow it. If you must smoke you can use the garden.'

'You can wait, can't you, Doug?' This was Annis, heavy smoker of heavy cigarettes.

Not so long ago I'd gone for well over a week without

smoking. What problems would a few minutes present? I can survive without one now – surely. 'Where's the garden?'

He gave me directions. I went for a smoke. Annis joined me, no surprise.

On a patch of dry black grass we smoked and talked. A clear night was above us, posing like a huge Hallowe'en hat with its moons and stars. And the full moon was a chromium bull's-eye in the sky – and no one was up there tonight.

'They're an odd pair,' I said. 'Especially Powell. What's wrong with the guy? What's she see in him?'

'She felt sorry for him. Then she fell in love with him.'

'Shame. It's a waste of a good-looking girl.'

'I can see why you and Andy are friends. You don't really understand women, do you?'

'Of course not. I'm a man.'

'Well, I can't deny that.'

'Exactly. Come here.' I wasn't expecting her to, but she did. She refused to take up my offer of giving me a blow job, though she did kiss me. 'It's not always necessary for us to understand you,' I said. 'Sometimes we men can still empathize with you.'

'Don't you mean sympathize?'

'I don't think so.'

'I hope you feel better now,' said Powell. 'I'm sure your families do, too. It's not just you that gets hurt when you die; there are other people to consider as well.'

'Here, have some chewing gum.' I handed him a slab of Haligum.

'It's not nicotine gum, is it?'

'No, it's for people with bad breath.'

'But I haven't got bad breath. Have I, Esfyn?'

'No, you haven't. Here's your coffee.'

Silence. Silence as we drank our coffee (decaffeinated – these two are health freaks!). What was there to say? Sex and drugs were obviously out. I watched Powell as he had his trouble of chewing gum and drinking coffee all at once. Now here was a guy, I guessed, who had plenty to say, a whole list of strange ideas making nonsense in his head. Given the chance – the chance of a soft, or dead, audience – he would probably air them in his difficult voice. Luckily he didn't get this chance, no one asked him: we were all still alive. Anyway, here was a *man* I couldn't understand. What chance did I have with women?

At last, Annis said, 'Shouldn't we be going?' And to Powell, Esfyn said, 'Are you sure you won't come, darling?'

'No, I'm sure. It's the special tonight, ram-raiding. I've been looking forward to it.' She made him promise to record it. 'I always do, you know that.' He gestured a cupboard, hermetically sealed with polish. Presumably it contained a whole library of *CrimeTime* tapes – a cupboard of crime.

'Of course, I've always liked comedy,' announced Esfyn in the car. 'It's the new rock and roll, you know. That's what the pundits say.'

'That's certainly what Andrew believes. He wants on the bandwagon.'

'Maybe you're being cynical, Annis. He seems very serious about it all.'

'Doug, if *poetry* was the new rock and roll, Andrew would be busy with his rhyme book constructing verse.'

'I don't think poetry has got what it takes to be the new rock and roll.'

'Neither do I. But at least it would encourage the poets.'

Five silent minutes later Esfyn had a question: 'What I want to know is, what has happened to the *old* rock and roll?'

'Rock and roll doesn't exist any more,' said Annis, and turned the car into the busy street.

The Miser was a tumbledown place, a lot of cheap thought intended it this way. Someone would flatten it soon, and then recycle it, into house and office, into pub and leisure centre. Built only a couple of blocks from the GoodBye Bar – which trounced it in the desirability stakes – it was a loose stockpile of tarred wood, sooted brick and lagging canvas that had once been an oast house. Now it had scaffolding holding up a corner where the builders refused to rebuild. This was the condemned corner, no one was meant to go near it. Ragged tape that said KEEP OUT and DANGER covered the owners' backs, but ensured that children would explore its prohibited recesses and that junkies and prostitutes would use it for injecting and unsafe sex – unsafe because the building would collapse and take a john and a whore with it sooner or later.

'Is it safe?' asked Annis, as the Miser gave us a faint groan. 'It all looks very precarious.'

'It's been here for over one hundred years. I see no reason why it should choose tonight to fall down.' Christ! I've got to stop lying.

'I guess you're right,' she said, and stepped inside. 'Bloody hell! The floor's sticky. I can hardly walk!'

'Yeah, so are the walls. Keep away from them.'

We paid our comedy money and received our comedy tickets. The big ticket man directed us up some steps to the main floor. Swirling letters painted everywhere gave us its name: the Hop Floor. Really no more than a large room with fool-the-eye partitions and a brightly lit stage at the far end.

Brightly lit with pure white so it looked like the interior of a village hall disco, or an operating theatre, or a crime scene.

'No wonder Andrew never brought me here, it's a disgusting place.'

The girls made their minds up. Changed them a couple of times. And eventually told me what they would like to drink. I then ambled away and hid myself in a dark corner. I was looking for Andy. If I saw him I was going to simply explain that I had bumped into Annis and Esfyn. He'd believe me. There was no reason for him to suspect that I was fucking his girlfriend . . . Before tonight he had maintained that his stage presence and confidence would be enhanced if he turned up to these events at the last minute. He'd then give the organizers some shit, stagger on stage and do his slot. At the end he'd leave with whichever girl made him the best offer. I think he had mentally rehearsed this more than the actual comedy, and had said, 'I don't care which girl sucks my comedy cock. Just so long as she's good at it.' As I scanned around I had no idea when he would be on. The show started at eight but the Miser did not believe in a play list and we'd have to wait on the MC, Miser Jack, to talk us through the young, and the old, hopefuls.

Music in the room was subdued. It was background, as it had to be, as it would be at a rock concert so as not to detract from the main event. So as not to overshadow it – and there was always a danger of music surpassing comedy of this type. The Miser didn't want the crowd to start calling for music while there was some lonely comedian stood on stage under the terrifying light – like a griot orating to a bored tribe.

Back with the girls – and with alcohol all round – Esfyn said, 'It's very courageous of Andy to do this.'

'I'm sure he's got plenty of drugs to help him out,' said Annis.

'Well, I wouldn't do it. No, that's not true – I *couldn't* do it. Excuse me,' I said, and wandered off again.

In the Miser's toilets, which were so sticky that they might have been the source of the entire building's stickiness, I found myself standing next to a worried comedian. With a fixed face of concentration he seemed to be having trouble urinating.

'Hello, Andy. How are you feeling?'

'Good as can be expected. Is she here?'

'With Esfyn. I found them in the middle somewhere.'

'It's over,' he said. 'This is my future now.' The blockage cleared, he began with a thankful sigh. As if pissing was now his big future.

'Watch my shoes. You sure about that, are you? This is your future?'

'It is. Do you want some coke? Fuck! Have you been drinking?'

'A little—'

'At fucking last!' He slapped my back. I flew at the wall. Thrust my hands at it and was then helped by Andy to pull myself away from its adhesive surface.

'I'm on in half an hour. I'll meet you after and we can go on somewhere. To the GoodBye.'

I wished him luck as he went off to get nervous or high in a corner somewhere.

What could Miser Jack possibly say to the crowd? What could he possibly say in this rundown and crippled building? What could he possibly say except, 'Please give a warm welcome to our first hopeful. Place your hands together for

Billy Williams.' Billy Williams walked uneasily across the stage and into the unfriendly stare of the interrogative lights, and said, 'Good evening. I'm Billy Williams.' Apart from a shrill and encouraging cry of 'Go, Billy!' from some woman, there was no response. Straight into his act, he gave us his first line. 'I'm from the future.' Pause. 'My watch is five minutes fast!' Pause. 'So you've all got five minutes before you need to laugh.' He stared into the audience. A man at the front started coughing. 'No, sir! You're too early.' The man stopped coughing, told Billy Williams to fuck off – which got a laugh – and started coughing again. A girl shouted, 'Show us your willy, Billy!' She got a laugh. Then Billy Williams said something that he would soon regret in his short comedy career. Referring to the man with the cough, he said, 'My old man had a cough like yours, sir. He used to swear when he coughed too. He would go, "Fuck-ough, fuck-ough! Coungh cough cunt." ' Billy said this from the back of his throat. It did pass as coughing. Trouble was, he hadn't reckoned on the audience, who immediately started mimicking him. So with mock coughing they all swore at him, 'Fuck-ough, cunt, cun-ough, fuck-fuck-fuck-ough!' Poor Billy Williams, the first hopeful, opened his mouth ready for his next line, decided against it and took his only option: he left the stage and went to the bar. The place was still coughing, but now it was real coughing, everyone had fucked their throats by pretending to cough. Even Billy Williams held a cupped hand to his mouth and had a quick hack as he waited for his drink and tried (unsuccessfully) to push back the tears.

In favour of the followers, but of no help to the thwarted Billy, the audience seemed to have settled down. They still heckled, told comedians to fuck off, asked little Mark if his mother knew where he was and demanded to see Charlotte's flaps. But they did laugh occasionally and had agreed to clap at end of slots and sometimes while the comedian was still on – if they could be bothered.

Andy came on dressed like a flasher. He went to the microphone and lazily looked into the crowd. 'He's looking for me,' said Annis, and half raised an open palm. For a long time he continued looking. The crowd started muttering, coughing, talking and finally, and inevitably, began shouting fuck off. He just stood there, taking no notice until he appeared to find what he was looking for. He concentrated on this. Some of the crowd sound fell away. He tapped the microphone. Steadily and loudly he said, 'SEX-UAL IN-TER-COURSE.' This gave him his silence. He went on, maintaining volume, 'IS GOING ON OVER THERE!' He pointed with both hands at a couple. She was sat on his lap. He had his arms crossed over her breasts. 'I'VE BEEN WATCHING THEM ALL NIGHT. EVERY TIME SOMEONE'S UP HERE, HE STARTS *PUMPING* HER.' The couple now looked embarrassed, the whole room was staring at them. Andy continued in an incredulous tone, 'HAVE YOU JUST COME, SIR? HERE, YOU MIGHT NEED THIS.' He threw a toilet roll at them. The female attempted to get up. 'NO. DON'T MOVE, LADY. WE DON'T WANT EVERYBODY SEEING HOW SMALL YOUR BOYFRIEND'S DICK IS, DO WE?' Now she didn't move. 'HEY, MAN? ARE YOU PROTECTED? . . . NO? . . . NO PROBLEM. YOU CAN USE MINE.' He reached under his flasher's coat and into his groin, struggled and pulled out an unrolled condom. He chucked it at the couple. It didn't get that far, it landed in a space that people had made for it on the floor, a space people made by getting out of its way as if it was radioactive, as if it was shit, as if it was *radioactive* shit.

Leaving the couple, but sticking to his favourite material,

he went on: 'OK. WHO IN HERE IS A WANKER? WHO WANKS?' No one answered. No one heckled him either. 'What about you, mate? You do. *DON'T YOU*? OF COURSE YOU DO. EVERYBODY DOES. In fact, YOU'RE ALL A BUNCH OF WANKERS. So why don't you admit it? I will. I'M A WANKER. I'M A REAL WANKER. What else does every fucker do yet not admit? But if you did, if you admitted it, conversations might be better. You get to work one morning, you're late, "SORRY I'M LATE, BOSS, MY WANKING OVERRAN." Or when your girlfriend's mother phones and asks to speak to her, tell her the truth: "NO, SHE CAN'T COME TO THE PHONE. SHE'S IN THE MIDDLE OF A WANK." And what about those teenage years? You're alone in the room, doing the business as it were, and there comes a knock on the fucking door, a little voice goes, "Can I come in?" So you make up some shit excuse, you're reading or asleep or something. WHY DON'T YOU SAY, "NO YOU CAN'T COME IN, MUM. I'M HAVING A WANK"?' Andy took a breath and pointed at a feathery-haired old man. 'YOU'RE BLUSHING. WHERE ARE YOUR HANDS? ARE YOU HAVING A WANK?

'AND WHAT ABOUT SHITTING? NOW THAT'S ANOTHER THING . . .'

The material became less crude after that, though he did end on a high note by going into buggery with plenty of frustration. OK, so the audience wasn't in hysterics, but they didn't heckle him and that was important. He had mastered crowd control. Being funny, he later admitted, was less important than that control. Playing the crowd was the key. The world-renowned Archibald Prescott could tell you that.

Annis had not spoken for quite some time. She hadn't laughed either, though she had donated some fluttering and unenthusiastic applause earlier. And now Andy was heading from the far end of the room. To me she turned, she said, 'Andrew and I have no future. He's not me.'

Andy took in the whole table with the unmasted sails of his flasher's mac and shook my outstretched hand. 'Well done,' I said. 'Very, er – very sexual.'

'Crude. You mean *crude*.'

'Yeah, crude.'

'Hello, Annis. You're looking hot. How are you?'

'Well, Andrew. Yourself?'

'Kickin'. Man, am I flowing.' He guided the off-cuts of the huge coat and sat down, and helped himself to some of my drink – relishing it, as if he had a new-found interest in alcohol, as if he was the one who had spent the last few months drinking Coke and water. Annis tapped my knee, moved over quickly and whispered, 'I'm going home with Esfyn tonight – *now*.' Then she stood up and said, 'Esfyn. We're off. Let's go and get the taxi.' Esfyn, who had seemed to drift in and out of reverie all evening, said, 'Yes, we must. Powell will be waiting.' It all gave an impression of being planned – it probably was. Andy asked me who *Powell* was.

'Esfyn's boyfriend. No, her fiancé. They're engaged now.'

Andy peered up as Esfyn and said, 'So when's it due?'

'What?'

'The *baby*.'

'What baby?'

'Your baby.'

'I'm not having a baby.'

'But you're engaged.'

'Come on, Esfyn,' said Annis, 'we're going. Andrew thinks people only get engaged or married when they're having a baby.'

'*Babe,*' called Andy, 'come back.'

But she didn't.

With no girls hankering after his comedy cock, Andy said, 'I feel lucky tonight. Let's go and celebrate. My comedy. Your drinking.'

'Sure. Give us a cigarette.'

He flicked me one from his soft American packet, said, 'Good to have you back, man,' and lit it with his tarnished brass lighter. 'Time to get drunk.'

On the way out I asked, 'What about Miser Jack, has he spoken to you?'

'He said he'd call me. He sounds real interested. Fuck! This floor is sticky. What's it made of? *Glue?*'

In the GoodBye, the waitress with great teeth greeted us at the bar with the words: 'Shit! It's Mineral Water Man with one of his weird friends.' She prepared my water and pushed it at me.

'NO!' said Andy. 'TWO LARGE WHISKIES! Sorry, two large whiskies, please. And two lagers, Doug? A pint as well?'

'Good idea,' I answered, deciding that a lot of alcohol would stop any guilt that might bounce at me later on – when I would think about Annis.

As we had walked in, the landlord was reading the answers to the midweek pub quiz. 'Number twenty, nothing rhymes with the word orange. Orange. Number twenty-one, Necessary is spelt EN, E, SEE, E, DOUBLE-ESSE, EH, ARE, WHY.' Andy handed the money over, it received its checks: eye check, light check, metal check, ultraviolet check. It checked OK. Change was handed over . . . 'And finally, number twenty-five, Manchester United.' . . .Then there was shouting: 'No fucking way! . . . It weren't fucking Man U! . . . *Hey! I'm telling you . . .*'

'So what made you start drinking again? Does this mean you're no longer ill?'

'It seemed like the best thing to do. And no, I'm not ill. I don't think I ever was.'

'Me neither. Here, have another smoke. And drink up, it's your round next.'

'About tonight, are you always going to make comedy out of that subject – sex and bodily functions. I know that comedy is meant to be free, but you were quite avant-garde. Especially in the delivery. You were very loud. Some people were scared.'

'All an experiment, Doug. I enjoyed myself out there tonight. I got a lot of shit off my chest. You should try it. It's a real buzz.'

'Not me, I think I'm too serious a person. I don't know how to be funny. It's not one of my talents.'

There had been an adumbrate calm surrounding the landlord. And now it looked like some fight was about to break out. The ardent sources of hard football knowledge were shadowing him with cocked bodies that were ready to unleash their kicks and their punches. The bouncers, who were actually rather effective (maybe because years of stray bottles and knife attacks had left them with nothing to lose: they were all out of vanity) came in and approached the quizzers, saying stuff like, 'Calm down, soldiers', 'Put that down, soldier', 'Listen to the landlord, soldier, the landlord's the man with answers. Right then, you. Yes, *you*, soldier, you're out of here.' Slap! . . .

'They're all wrong,' said Andy. 'It was Nottingham Forest.'

'Are you going to tell them?'

'Fuck off!' he said, and swallowed the rest of his pint. Then belched. Then laughed. Then looked at me.

'Same again?'

He nodded.

And I went to the bar to spend some of the money I had saved by not drinking.

Cooperage in the Late Twentieth Century was open on the table. It lay among tall and short glasses, empty matchboxes, crumpled fag packs and the ashtray, with its dump of tarred butts and crumbling cylinders of grey. It lay in this cityscape, and bridged the amber river of beer that ran through it. I was talking Andy through the action and referencing a passage here or a line there. We got up to speed, where I'd left it, the drugs administered, Landlord and Chattaway about to go down. Audience on the edge of its hard seats.

'You be the landlord. I'll be Chattaway. Start here.'

'Long time since I read a script in a pub,' said Andy. 'I'm the landlord?'

'That's right.'

'OK.'

Landlord: Running a bar's got its problems.

Chattaway: My dad had a dray.

Landlord: There's the punters, some lower the tone.

Chattaway: It was wooden. Are you drunk?

Landlord: Am I drunk? Are you a poof?

Chattaway: You are drunk.

Landlord: Fuck off, cunt. What was wooden?

Chattaway: *I'm* not drunk.

Landlord: Bella, two pints over here, darling.

Chattaway: No.

Landlord: Yes. What's a dray?

Chattaway: You *are* drunk. You're dribbling.

Landlord: I ain't, I . . .

Chattaway: Beer's strong.

Landlord: Tis too. Fuck it. I'm . . .

Chattaway: I'm going to lie down.

Landlord: Bella? Cabbage here?

'I'll do Bella. You do Cabbage.'

Bella: He's just arrived.

Cabbage: Toss the—

At this point there was a throat-clearing interruption from a nearby table. A voice said, 'Toss the cunt in the cab and let's get this over with. I'm not happy about it as it is. I'm parked on doubles. Shit! What's up with you, Landlord? Are you drunk?'

We turned in search of the voice, the voice that had the Cabbage lines verbatim. We saw a girl twisting her face to us.

She came over. Purposefully, confidently, she introduced herself. 'Hello, Doug. Hello, Andy. I'm the author.'

'What's your name?' I asked the second attractive girl of the week who had come my way. She was shorter than Annis. Darker hair: black. Sharper, less innocent eyes – life's eyes.

'My real name? Or my pseudonym?'

'Your real name—' I began, and then, realizing who she was, said, 'I know your pseudonym, it's Lucia de Londres.'

'That's right. Well done, Doug, you've sprung me.'

'Where are your eyes?'

'Her *eyes*?' interrupted Andy. 'Who is she?'

'Contact lenses, coloured ones. Edmund's idea, he said they would scare you. Sorry, Doug.'

'And your real name?'

'Lucy, Lucy Smith. Not very exciting, I'm afraid.' She put an arm round Andy, pulled their faces together and said, 'Andy, could you leave me and Doug alone for a while. We need to talk. Join your friends, they've just walked in, over there. When I'm finished I'll call you back and you can take me to the townhouse flat. We can both help each other. Right, off you go.'

He picked up his pint, his whisky, his flasher's mac and walked to the table. Rhubarb, John, Jon and a roughed-up Kidder were there.

'We're alone.'

'You're not going to slap me, are you?'

'No. And I don't love you either. Let me apologize straight away for all that.'

'I'm confused. You and Spritz are lovers, aren't you?'

'No. Definitely not.' She took a prognostic pause. Then continued, 'I became a patient of Edmund's sometime before you did. It was the usual kind of problem, I'd split up with my boyfriend, lost my job, didn't get on with my parents, you know, all the normal angst. But it really got to me, so I went to Edmund. My ex-boyfriend recommended him.

'He said he could help me. But I would have to be prepared to wait. He said he could "get to the root of my problem".'

'Sounds familiar.'

'After a few months he told me what I was suffering from. He told me I put it from my mind, blanked it out.'

'Yeah, that sounds familiar too.'

'And then, when I broke into his office, I found his novel. The story is about a psychotherapist and two of his patients. For the past few months he has simply been manipulating us and writing down what happens. Edmund's novel is not fiction. It's real life. Our lives.

Andy came over – laughing, presumably at one of his jokes he had just laid on the boys – and said, 'Are you ready to go yet, babe?'

'No. Go back to your friends, Andy. I'll be with you soon,' said Lucy Smith. To me she said, 'I can't believe I fell for what Edmund told me; he said I'd been raped. The bastard. He said it was you.'

'Well, you're a great-looking girl and everything, but I don't think I'd rape you. I didn't, did I?'

'No, no, you didn't – although for some time he convinced me that you did. That's why I wrote *Cooperage in the Late Twentieth Century*: as a warning to you. I planned to cut your penis off.'

'You mad bitch.'

'Sorry, Doug. I did get a little carried away. Never mind, now it's payback time, and your friend Andy is going to help me.

'*Andy*,' she called, 'I'm ready.'

Andy came back.

'Andy, you were very funny tonight. Now I want to thank you.' She led him off by his penis. And Andy didn't seem to mind – this was what he did stand-up comedy for anyway.

I joined the others and got drunk as I wondered what to do next. They couldn't believe Andy. 'How does he do it?' they asked. 'He's not that good-looking.'

'No,' I said, 'he's a comedian, that's all.'

At least I knew I was right about one thing: I wasn't ill. I'm not mad. Thank fuck.

Ten

'Where is he then?'

'I've told you, Mr Down, I *don't* know.'

'You must know. Who are you anyway?'

'I'm his cleaner.'

'So he let you in. Then where did he go?'

'I let myself in. I'm putting the phone down.'

'When did you last— Hello? Oi! Pick the phone up. Hello! Bitch . . .' I put a line through the second number on my list. The first one was a dead end:

'Please could I speak to Dr Spritzer.'

'I'm sorry he's taking no calls.'

'It's an emergency. Put me through.'

'Sorry I have no number for him.'

'So he's not there then?'

'I can't tell you that.'

'Where is he?'

'Sorry. I'm sorry.'

'Stop fucking me about—'

'Sorry. Goodbye, whoever you are.'

The third number that might reach him came from my paranoid list of telephone numbers. The list I had made while I was paranoid. When I was paranoid that I was paranoid.

Looking back, I think that I was acting perfectly normally and was convinced otherwise by the wayward novelist Dr Edmund Spritzer. Enough.

I'll speak to him. I'll tell him that his story is coming to a close, time for him to draft his final chapters and wrap up the action. Now, because I'm not a very vindictive person, and because his plan for me and Lucia de – *Lucy*, ultimately failed, and because he's weighted by all his terrible questions, I'm going to hint that Andy and Lucy are out for him. I'll tell him I have my own plans. He'll react badly to the whole deal, he'll worry and the questions will mob him. All this: an unexpected twist in his plot.

The paranoid number was answered. A male voice, modelled on gay American, said with twangy speech, 'Terry's and Jerry's. Hello?'

'Is that Terry?'

'Jerry.'

'Can I speak to Terry?'

'TERRY,' called Jerry. And then to me, 'He won't be a moment. Are you the one?'

'The one?'

'From last night? He said you'd call. You sound wonderful, I can't wait to meet you.'

'No. I'm Doug.'

'So am I, so am I. Ooh, here he is. Terry, it's Doug.'

'Hello, Doug?'

'I'm a friend of Edmund. Edmund Spritzer. You know him. Help me out, tell me where he is.'

'I'm sorry, you've just missed him, my love.'

'Where's he gone?'

'Straight to bed I shouldn't wonder. With his new

friends.' Aside, to Jerry, he said, 'Boy! Is Edmund a sucker for punishment.'

'And where is that? Bed?'

'I don't know. Listen, why don't you come round, we would love to meet you, Doug.'

'I'm looking for Edmund.'

'You can dig me if you like, Doug.'

'No thanks.'

'Goodbye, Doug.'

So Spritz has disappeared. A good move on his part, immersing himself in his other world, his terrible sexual world. Take your mind off your problems with sex. Yeah, sounds like good advice. Not the kind of advice he would hand out though. But still the kind of advice he follows through the confusion of his terrible insecurity.

I'd like to immerse myself in sex. Sounds like something worthwhile to be immersed in. Unfortunately Annis is across town in Esfyn's spare room. So it wasn't going to last – no one really expected it to. Me and her? Then again . . . Maybe she needs some time out. It was pretty intense back there for a few days. I lost count of the number of times, and that's got to be good. The break will do me good. If it is a break.

And the missed chance: Lucy. Shame, waste. She did offer, didn't she? If I'd known what lay behind that bag-lady disguise I could have agreed to her love, pushed her under the shower for half an hour, hidden her clothes and waited for the change. I would have needed to take those contacts out, those frightening contacts, and flush them away. So, a missed opportunity? Perhaps it was her plan. You know, get me naked in bed, hover over me with hardening talk, pull the razor from its hiding and with madly flowing arm chop away until I became non-sexual. Do a Chattaway on me. No cock. What a life.

At least I'm safe from her now. Though I never felt that unsafe before – she seemed too crazy to be scary. But maybe if I'd known then what I know now, I would have been terrified, a jabbering semi-erect figure of a man fearing for, well, fearing for his very manhood. And if she'd gone ahead with it I would have blamed Spritz. He'd come back with his excuse: research, research for his novel. Research? Get your material elsewhere. Leave me out of it. I'm happy the way I am. No need to write me into your 'real life' novel, your little piece of *cinéma vérité*.

In *Cooperage in the Late Twentieth Century*, which I found in my jacket pocket, I have finally got to the end of it. If you can call it that, call it an *ending*.

We're in the dirty deserted house, our author – the recently revealed Lucia de Londres – has found new and deeper depths: her ideas are right down there in the earth, under the crust and in the mantle where the hot rock sluices around. This house is setting to the final act, the 'cock-cutting act' (and even she calls it that, there it is at the top of the page in small caps: FINAL ACT: COCK-CUTTING). The house is full to its smashed windows with piss and shit. She intends to have excrement positively oozing in the finished film. But it won't get made. Nobody makes this sort of stuff. It just doesn't have its place: too depraved for commercial cinema; too much story and not *enough* depravity for porn or nasty-nasty or cock snuff.

So, with filth making a big impact, in this, its final cameo, Cabbage kicks Chattaway and Landlord out of the cab and into the house – then takes Bella down the park, where, she has been informed, he will 'give her one'.

In the house, Chattaway and Landlord – barely able to walk due to the effects of the drugs they have laced each other's drinks with – are busy getting on with a slow-motion fight. The landlord is grabbing at Chattaway's jeans and trying to undo them so that he can get his penis out and cut it off. Chattaway, not realizing this, and naturally thinking that the landlord wants to shag him, is slurring back all the euphemisms for homosexual he can think of. Lucia obviously had some fun here, and came up with a few new ones, I think. With his plan to get Landlord arrested still firmly in his head, Chattaway is also stabbing at him with the hypodermic needle and trying to stuff a few hundred quid's worth of drugs into his waistcoat pockets.

And then we get our ending. Her words: FREEZE FRAME. THEN RETREATING SHOT OF LANDLORD WITH HYPODERMIC STICKING INTO HIS EYE AND CHATTAWAY, TROUSERS REMOVED, WITH CHEESE WIRE TWISTED ABOUT HIS PENIS. Next line: THE END.

The end. This, the film script written by a girl who thought I had assaulted her. And now she wants to get even with Spritz. Oh dear.

What, I wonder, does she have in mind for the doctor. Will her reimposed sanity hold a worse fate for the hapless Spritz? When crazy she came up with a drastic remedy for me, a violent piece of retribution from a semi-fucked-up mind. What violence could her fully functioning head come up with now? . . . Or will sanity curb her anger and allow her to settle with a side-glancing blow from the front corner of her red car? A bruised leg, worse perhaps?

I have one last call to make. I'll make it later. I'm being watched by a supervisor. A Frenetic supervisor – my manager. Personal calls are strictly forbidden, Doug. Don't even think about it. Well, I didn't until today – my last day. They don't know it yet, but I'm handing in my resignation after I've had my fun, after I've sworn at a few more customers.

It was a nine o'clock start this morning. Nine o'clock. I wasn't here on time. I was late by half an hour. *Only* half an hour. An outlandish feat after all I drank last night. Drank and drank. The boys insisted, who was I to argue? They all bought me a drink. Constant toasts to the return of the old Doug, Doug the drinker, the Doug they'd all missed. Down the hatch, Doug. Good to have you back, mate. Here, Rhubarb, go and fetch Doug another whisky. Whisky, Doug? Whisky, Rhubarb.

If I'd known how many people I could bring happiness to by renewing my drinking I would have renewed it a long time ago. Don't ever do that to us again, Doug, they were saying. Tears, big rolling tears, welled from their eyes. 'It was like losing a bird,' said Jon, 'to another fucking bird.' And Jon knew how sad this was, and how it made you feel, it had happened to him twice. Probability had ganged up on him; twice was a lot. 'You can't not drink,' said the other John, 'it ain't right.' Rhubarb said, 'Rhubarb,' and went to the bar.

So when I arrived at Frenetic I was half an hour late. It was nine-thirty, I knew the time because the little brown Fiat had a little brown clock in it. And for some reason the little brown clock still worked.

Swooping in through the double doors, burping whisky, and farting, I think – I can't be sure – I knocked into the frail frame of my supervisor, a kid the same age as me. He asked me a question, one of his favourites.

'What time do you call this, Down?'

'I don't know,' I lied.

'I *said*, what time do you call this?' He was angry. I never liked him.

'I told you. I don't know. Ask someone else, I don't wear a watch.'

'What time *should* it be?'

'You've got me there.'

'It should be nine o'clock. But it's not, is it?'

'No?'

'*No*, it's nine-thirty.'

'There you go. Problem solved. Now if you don't mind, I'd better go and do some work. I'm a little late.' I began walking.

'Why are you late?'

'I was having a wank,' I muttered.

'*What*?'

'BANK. Now please excuse me. I must get on.'

The first call that came fizzing into my earpiece was disastrous. The caller, who had a legitimate complaint about his phone, was just too goddamn polite. Please be rude, I was thinking, then I can swear at you. But no: 'I feel awful to be bothering you. You seem like such a helpful young man. I'm just a silly old fool who doesn't understand technology.' Politely we settled on a remedy. He went away happy.

But I didn't have to wait long. The phone beeped, a voice said, 'Cunt!'

'Shithead,' I replied.

'What did you fucking call me?'

'Cunt.'

'You called me a shithead.'

'Sorry, cunt.'

'I wanna speak to your fucking manager.'

'I expect you do. He's a cunt too. I'll put you through.' Then I cut him off.

A minute later a girl stood up, her face was troubled, she called for the manager. 'A gentleman would like to talk to you. He's completely horrible.' The manager put himself on. 'Hello, sir? . . . Don't call me that, sir . . . I don't care what he said. I'm not one of those . . . I *am* the manager . . . If you feel you have no choice . . . We'll be sorry to lose your custom . . . Goodbye, sir.' The manager put the phone down and said, 'He called me a cunt! I don't believe it.' 'They all do,' said the girl. The manager stared angrily at her. 'Not you,' she said. '*Us.*'

I made my call to the townhouse flat. The comedian answered the phone, I asked the question.

'Lucy's told you all about the trouble she's been causing me?'

'She has.'

'Anything else?' I wondered whether she'd mentioned Annis. My little affair with his ex.

'No. Should she have?'

'I don't think so. Is she there?'

'Certainly is. On my todger as we speak . . . Hey, come down here, darling, Doug wants a word.'

'Hello, Doug.'

'What are you going to do to Spritz, Lucy?'

'I haven't decided yet. He seems to have disappeared. Any idea where he might be?'

'None. Are you going to hurt him, physically?'

'I think I'll have to, won't I, Doug?'

'Whatever. Tell me, did you send me a photo of yourself on a barrel?'

'Yes, Edmund took it.'

'And a black balloon with a pin inside?'

'That was my heart.'

'And how did you know I'd pick up *Cooperage in the Late Twentieth Century?*'

'I didn't. Not that time. I can't believe how unobservant you are. I must have thrown it in your path more than ten times but you just walked over it. You notice money though. All that time you were picking up coins. And remember the time you found that five-pound note? You looked like you'd won the lottery.'

'I was pleased. OK, call me if you find Spritz. You've got my number.'

'Yes. Yes I have. Sorry about it all, I'm sorry I frightened you.'

'You weren't as scary as you might think. But then I had no idea that you were planning to chop my cock off. Fuck.'

Now that the *non* preceding smoker had become forcefully *pro* I found myself welcomed once again into the car park's circle of pro-smokers. As I smoked with them for the last time – scrolls of smoke unrolling in the light air – they asked me why I was leaving. I asked them why not. They stood there coughing and searching for a reason not to leave, a reason why they too could not leave. They asked again. I'm moving into shoes, I told them, I'm going to the Shoe Shop.

Back in the office I was giving my manager the good news. He gave an unexpected reply: 'You can't leave.'

'I am leaving.'

'You can't leave since you've not handed in your notice. We need a week's notice.'

'I am leaving.'

'We've got a week's work out of you first, young man.'

'Sorry, no.' I stood up, left his office and burst through the double doors for the last time.

Outside I found myself in the sights of the supervisor who had asked me the time. He looked ready to censure me, he composed his expression as I approached. He said, 'Now where do you—'

'Thank you for all the shit you've given me. You do your job so well.'

'Insubordination, Down, is a sackable offence.'

'Oh, fuck off. Go and worry someone else instead.'

'I'm warning you—'

'Let's hope our paths don't cross. See ya kid, I'm fucking off.'

Strolling over to the car I removed the thick jacket, yanked the tie from my neck, rolled my sleeves past my elbows, to reveal skin that still had winter in it, and felt in my pocket for the numb car keys.

Now there was no mistaking the burning star up there, close enough to touch, yet so far away its distance remained incomprehensible. This was it then, the sun in the blue sky. And the sky was blue, blue from Raleigh scattering: the scattering of blue light by galactic dust and aerosol into the atmosphere, glowing blue in the ozone. The sun wasn't yellow, and it wasn't white, it wasn't coloured, it was something more: something you couldn't look at. Today it was shining at Perspex and glass and bouncing off with such intensity that it left a broken pattern, its light seemed to shatter transparency. This, the weather, on the day I finally leave Frenetic and travel in the knowledge that no one is out to get me.

I pulled into the busy road, shook the gear lever until I found another gear, then accelerated down the street. At maximum speed, twenty-one mile per hour, I generously waved motorists past. They swerved by, staring in, expecting to see the tired face of someone old, surprised and confused to see the sunlit graphic of one so much younger. Everyone overtook me: the best and the worst cars with their unhappy drivers, the HGVs with their industrial groaning and crunching, the fragile electric carriages, the cyclists with their painted-on outfits – and there was a whole smear of them: legs kicking at the pedals, their bright and vivid colours rushing through the air like a long-exposure photograph.

I parked outside a branch of the Shoe Shop and walked from outer to inner light. A girl pounced me: 'Can I help you, sir?'

'I need some shoes to replace these.' I pointed at the boots. 'They give me blisters and I think that my feet will deform if I wear them any longer.'

'You might like to choose from this selection.' I was led to the Soft Sole section. 'Leather, suede or canvas?'

I indicated a pair, she horned them on. I did a circuit of the shop. I walked on the soles of my feet, not the sides. My feet breathed relief. 'It's very important to have comfortable shoes,' she said. 'It can make the day so much more bearable.'

I agreed with her and said I'd take them. She asked me for some money, then sent me through for my free foot massage, my complimentary foot-job.

Jesus. By the time I left I felt as if my feet were no longer part of my body, they felt high. Walking was like hovering, no effort required, like flying in a dream.

Behind the wheel of the little brown Fiat I drove through London to another shoe shop. Maximum speed down to twenty . . . The sun was at work and it was concentrating on flesh. On building sites I saw the swollen torsos of builders exposed in the air. Those not working were anchored to the site by a spade and eager for glimpses of girls, whom they expected to see in the heat. And it was their day, the whistling began its seasonal amplification as the females went shyly past. The black sunglasses, the body-hugging and body-loving shirts and shorts showing skin to a possible summer.

In the Smell of Leather, the manager – an angry man, with shoes always on his mind, night and day – shrugged with deep resignation, and through a painful expression on his face said, 'I thought you weren't coming back. What's wrong with them now?'

'Nothing's wrong with them. I just don't want them any more.' I pushed them at him.

'You won't be coming back?'

'Not this time.'

Two hundred yards up the road I pulled in and slid over to a barefoot tramp. 'They're giving shoes away at the Smell of Leather. Tell them Mr Down sent you. Size nine? You'll love them.'

He offered me a cigarette. He only had two left so I declined and zoomed off to the GoodBye for a drink.

'Why not?' I asked the waitress with great teeth.

'Because I don't want to.'

'These opportunities don't come along every day,' I assured her.

'More than you'd expect.'

'So who else asked you to marry them today?'

'There was one . . .'

'Join me for a drink.'

'If you stop proposing.'

'I will. I promise.'

'And you can stop that too. I told you, I don't need anyone making me any promises.'

She's all right once you get to know her. Admittedly she said the same of me. She said, 'You're all right now that I've got to know you. Everyone thought you were really sad before. We even had a joke that you had escaped from somewhere, some asylum or something. You don't seem as weird now.'

'Thank you. We had a story about you too.'

'I can't wait to hear this!'

'We thought you were in love with yourself because of your teeth. Yes, it does sound rather stupid. But you do tend to show them off a lot. I mean, they're so *white*. How do you do that?'

'My teeth,' she sighed. 'More trouble than they're worth.' She took them out, and mumbled, 'Now what do you think of me?'

'With your mouth closed I'd never know. So you've got false teeth. People go around getting false breasts and false penises. No one's real any more.'

'What about you? What have you got that's false?'

'My tongue. I lie too much.'

'Do you want another drink?'

'Yes.'

'Yes? Was that a lie?'

'Certainly not.'

The waitress with great teeth – great false teeth – was called Sam. Together in the GoodBye that afternoon and evening we successfully helped each other to get drunk.

At about six o'clock I asked her for her telephone number. At first she refused. But I persuaded her.

An hour later I tried kissing her. She didn't let me.

Half an hour later I tried again. This time she did let me. I almost swallowed her teeth.

An hour after that she slapped me when I reached under the table.

An hour later I realized I was losing my memory. So I had another drink and tried to focus. That failed. I tried again.

After that, I forgot that I was trying it on with Sam and went home with the feeling that I'd forgotten something.

Eleven

Bed-clinging sweat awoke me with its damp embrace. Not the sweat from delirium tremors or from an early onset of Korsakoff's syndrome. No, the sweat that awoke me came from the heat, the sun's heat. It came through the window in a shield of light, a bright paly in the dust and fly ash.

Still dressed, and lying on top of my bed, the memory of the evening came back at me in the warm room. That's right, when I'd returned last night I'd placed the key in the door and turned it. I remember now, the door just opened, there was no lock. I'd been burgled again.

Mean burglars, who have no contact with their brethren burglars, kicked the door in and did the place, subjected it to more criminal attention. Now if they'd had their ear to the streets they would have heard the mean-street talk. They'd have heard: No point doing no. 17, The Manors, it's already been done. Shit stuff, poor quality, almost worthless. Fucks your eyes up too, the colours are disgusting. What a place – don't touch it.

But my house-breakers clearly had their ear elsewhere, off the street with its talk and its plans. Elsewhere: drugs, gambling, in the bank? No. They had their ears and their eyes, and stolen lap-top, tuned into the television. They were watching and taking notes from *CrimeTime*, learning and studying technique. No longer was there a need for prison. No point, you could learn it all from the TV these days. Except that Doug Down had been done last week and there was nothing left – *CrimeTime* hadn't told them that.

So what did they take this time? The phone, the radio-alarm clock, my electric shaver, my suit, my shirts, my cornflakes, a chair and *one* curtain. Oh yes, and they stole my stolen iron. The iron would find a new home and remain illegitimate.

There it is then, the wooden door, splintered again. Grating on its jamb as people push air through the building with their movement. And in front of the disgraced door: another envelope. This one from the council. The council officers have hired a firm of money collectors to come and collect my arrears. They will take whatever they feel necessary to recover my debt and their costs. Next week, I won't know when . . . Let them come, they can have what they like. They'll auction it. And what an auction it will be: Lot 12, a comb; Lot 13, half-full toothpaste tube with accompanying toothbrush; Lot 14, a corkscrew; Lot 15, *one* curtain; Lot 16, a booklet entitled *Cooperage in the Late Twentieth Century*. Who'll start the bidding? Ladies and gentlemen! This is a very desirable collection. Now, who'll start? *Please* . . .

At the end of the road I rapped on Old Boy's door. His wife opened it.

'Is Old Boy in?'

'One moment. I'll fetch him.'

Old Boy struggled to the door. 'Sorry to bother you,' I said. 'I've had another burglary. My door . . . Why are you crying?'

'All gone.'

'What's all gone?'

'We've been burgled,' said his wife, putting an arm around him. 'They've taken all his tools.'

'I think I'd better go.'

'Thank you. We would like to be alone.'

I walked to the other end of the street. Here there was less friction, less contact-friction from the confined proximity of houses. There was more airspace between the buildings, the buildings that were once something else and were now home to people. Inside, people went about the business of family life, the import and export of human deals – the generative osmosis. At this end of the street there was the jagged outline of a concrete discoidal area. It contained a bench, a litter box and a troubled willow tree – a tree mistakenly planted where it had no chance of survival; the dogs, the children and the abrasive vortexes that sprayed across the road saw to that. The homeless, the beggars, the hard-up often spent their days here.

Opposite was the steel-girdered outline of the corner shop. Above the faded awning a little yellow box was ringing and flashing a tiny yellow light. No one took any notice of Gary's headstrong burglar alarm, everyone wandered on by and never wondered why the yellow box was making all the fuss. And because alarms had now become background noise it was easier to block them out and pretend they weren't there.

'I can't switch it off,' said Gary, 'it's got a mind of its own. Goes off when it feels like it. Except when I get burgled, then it takes no fucking notice.'

'Try and ignore it,' I said. 'Have you got a phone, a pay-phone?'

'Over there. Next to the Suicider.'

'Suicider! Where did you get that?'

'Cash and carry.'

'I thought you could only get it via the manufacturers, from back-door contacts.'

'Yeah, that used to be the case, but it's going mainstream now, reckon it's due to the launch of that new lager. Have you heard about it? Called Kamikaze, they'll all be drinking it soon. It's fucking disgusting.'

Leaning against a stack of Kamikaze, I called the police. When the phone was answered, I said, 'I'd like to report a burglary.'

'Sorry, the lines are busy. Can you hold? Or would you prefer to phone back?'

'Fuck. I'll hold.' The hold-music wasn't music at all. It was looped *CrimeTime* updates and crime-prevention tips. The industry based on crime was now subsidizing the police. I was clicked through. I volunteered my details.

'Ah yes, sir, we have your file on the computer. A regular victim of crime, aren't you? Have you thought about moving?'

I told him I had.

'You'll be in for the rest of the day? Good. We'll send someone round.' He went on: Had I thought of contacting *CrimeTime*? They could use a victim like me. Statistically I was a great victim, my stats were league-topping material. Would you like to be on television, Mr Down? Would I get paid? No. *CrimeTime* is not permitted to pay the general public. Why? They were only allowed to pay the criminals, they were allowed to pay for criminal know-how and how-to. I know it seems wrong, Mr Down, but I'm afraid that's the way it is. Give me your phone number and I'll arrange for a representative to call.

'I haven't got a phone. It was stolen.'

'Too bad. If you just go home I'm sure a patrol will be there soon. Today I expect.'

'You've been a great help,' I said, and put the phone down.

Next to the crate of Kamikaze was a crate of Suicider – its apple-competitor. Pulling a Kamikaze, I asked Gary if it was really that bad.

'Tastes like shit,' he said.

'Yeah?' I read the can. 'Fourteen per cent alcohol, that must cover up some of the taste.'

'Try it. See what you think. If you like shit then it's the drink for you.'

'All this assumes that I know what shit actually tastes like. I've never tasted it. What is it like?'

'OK, point taken. It *smells* like shit. And it tastes like it smells.'

Curiosity persuaded me to buy a can. It had to have something going for it with a name like Kamikaze. I bought a tabloid to hide it in – or to be sick in.

The down-and-outs, who were busy watching for the law and getting acquainted with future benefactors, pulled me up and asked for their tea money. Instead of giving them cash I pulled the tab from the Kamikaze and held it out.

'Fuck me!' said one. 'What's that smell? You shit yourself again, Boner?'

'Me? No,' said Boner.

'Here, mate, what you got there?'

'Lager,' I answered, 'strong lager. Try some.' He took the can.

'Smells like shit, but's alcohol. No harm in trying – FUCK! No way. I ain't drinking *that*!'

They all crowded round now, noses pinched, all of us. Except the one who kept saying Palilalia palilalia palilalia, all the time.

'Here, Bob. Come here.'

'Palilalia palilalia palilalia palilalia . . .'

'Bob can't smell. He's got anosmia.' He was given the can.

'Palilalia palilalia . . .' He put the can to his lips. 'Palil! SHIT!' Bob stamped his foot hard on the pavement. 'Pal – Shit! Shit! Shit! Shit! Shit! . . .'

'You've fucking cured him! Bob, talk to me.'

But Bob didn't talk to him, or anyone else. From that day on he just said Shit! Over and over and over.

And then, as I walked home with my newspaper and recovering nose, I was harassed for the first time in nearly a week. As I was skipping along in my new shoes (which show absolutely no signs of failure) I heard the sound of modern agriculture: a diesel engine. Briefly I could make out an old gas van with orange lights flashing on its roof, before its own black smoke surrounded it.

Then I heard my name being called. So I held my breath and went in. An old hippie, reclined at the wheel, said, 'All right, Down, you cunt? Wanna buy an iron? New one. Never used. Still in its box. Yours for a tenner. Or, how about a curtain?'

I tried hitting him. But he threw my curtain at me and revved his motor. When nothing happened, when the van didn't move, I heard him shout, 'Fucking automatics!' And then, as I was grabbing at the door, the van lurched away. I managed what sounded like a kick of denting-strength (which scuffed my new shoes). Then I backed out of the smoke and started to breathe again.

Smelling as though I'd been dunked in a pool of diesel and carrying a curtain that had been overexposed to patchouli oil, I reached my flat with the thought: Christ! Fuck! I don't believe this place. Even the fucking hippies are mean!

Then I rehung my curtain.

★ ★ ★

Newspaper news: some guys working underground in France have produced antimatter – in the form of antihelium. It was transilient, it wasn't around for long before it turned into something else. But that's not a problem, because this was the big step, and now everyone is saying, Think of the possibilities: all that energy that might one day be available. And you get a lot of energy from antimatter, for when matter meets its antimatter *doppelgänger*, each is annihilated – releasing 100 per cent energy, from Einstein's $E=mc^2$. This is enormous when compared to everyday nuclear fission, which gives 0.1 per cent, or the hard-to-master fusion with its 0.5 per cent, and certainly not like the old coal fire, which disgraces itself by converting an unbelievably hopeless one billionth of mass into energy. No, these guys in France are really pleased with their antiprotons and their positrons.

More front page: crime is on the increase. Really? Second page: some government ministers might, just might, be sexual deviants. Might be – that's not libellous. The United European States had been called off. There's a new name and a new arrangement. It's going to be called the United States of *American* Europe. Purely to reflect ownership and control. Not everybody is so happy about this.

And the millennium has found its way into the What's Happening section. A full centre spread, the information splayed across the pages like a naked woman. And this woman is called Destiny – that's her name now. She's a big girl and is readying herself for the big night. She's powdering and pampering, combing and rearranging. Yes, Destiny is a happy girl and absolutely can't wait for her night. It's going to be the night of her life. Trouble is, she has lost her watch and keeps annoying passers-by by asking them for the time. Boy, is she excited.

Packed loosely, what's left of my belongings would fit into maybe two or three cardboard boxes. Packed loosely, thrown from a distance or swept from shelves, I haven't got much left of my twenty-five years. When I move, as I hope to in a week or so, it will be an easy one. I'll line the boxes on the rear seat of the Fiat like children and slowly motor out of these streets and make the sweltering journey to more amicable environs of London. I'm looking forward to it. It's time for a change. I'm ready to move.

I'll leave no forwarding address. My landlord won't know I'm gone, not until he sends one of his many and varied sons over to collect the rent. I'll stop signing on and work full-time at the Shoe Shop under the vigorous and watchful eye of Colin Rumble. As far as he's concerned, I was unemployed before he offered me the job, so Frenetic can be wiped from my history, no one need ever know I used to work there. And I'm not going to vote, so the council tax people won't be able to catch up with me. As far as their arrears department need be concerned, I will have simply disappeared, and I'm happy with that.

The newspaper weather forecaster is optimistic. He writes of warm fronts and favourable pressure conditions. He senses a hot spell. He's glad to bring the good news to the readers. It's his pleasure to do so.

Five or six column-inches away I absent-mindedly tackled an abridged article on the future of bridge; it was all stuttered and out of breath. Then I heard the door swing open. It moved with whine and cry, it was the noise trees made when they were felled.

A voice said, 'It was open. I've come to see you . . . for the last time.'

I turned and eyeballed the tall Annis. Her face was cast, she wore the expression of a girl who had made a decision and was sticking to it. She looked older. She had made the decision that had aged her. She said, 'I'm leaving London. In a month from now I'll be in France. My mother's side of the family live in Grenoble. They have the kind of money I need. There's been an open offer for years. Really I should have accepted it earlier.'

'Can you speak French?'

'I don't think I'll need to.'

'No. I don't suppose you will.' Language was not what drove Annis; dreams were. And dreams are universal, they have no language. Or if they do, it is unintelligible and makes no sense as day rushes through the heavy mind – only images remain, and they can be acted out.

'I couldn't have done it without you, Doug. You were my catalyst. You made me decide to leave.'

'I wish I hadn't.'

'I'm glad you did. Someone had to.'

'Perhaps. But why me?'

'Because, Doug, when you're somewhere you're not all there. Part of you is somewhere else. Me, I'm all in one place at once. To go somewhere else, to *escape,* I need to pack my bags and take everything with me.'

'I'm moving too,' I said with mock competitiveness. 'I'm leaving the colours of this crime scene and moving on.'

'Where to?'

'A few miles.'

'That's all you need, a couple of miles. I need a new country.'

'I'll come and visit you in Grenoble.'

'No, Doug. You want to now. You think you mean it. But you won't come. People never do. It's too far, only love can cover those sorts of distances. And we don't love each other.'

'I guess we don't. Shame really.'

'And because we don't love each other I'm going to show you my thanks with my final gift. Something I can give you because love is not involved. This is because of lust. Come here.'

She led me to the bed, her face set; this was still part of her decision. 'You'll enjoy this. You'll enjoy it because when it's all over I'll leave you and you'll never see me again. Fulfil your dreams, Doug, you may never get another chance.' She turned, her back towards me, she arched her shoulders and said, 'Undo me, Doug.'

Steadily, with none of the fervour of before, with none of the exploratory hand-probing and finger-testing, with none of the foreplay that went ahead of the action and did its warming up to ensure that what was going to happen would happen, steadily, slowly, because there was no doubt here that what was going to happen was definitely going to happen, it was unequivocal, steadily I undid her.

Now this was some going-away present, I thought, as I unclipped her bra and slid a cupped hand over her photographed breasts. She kicked her shoes off and pulled the tight skirt from her waist, she was wearing nothing beneath, it fell to the floor and she stepped from it. I went in search of the musty warmth that was on unconditional offer. I moved backwards, tripped and fell on the bed. Annis giggled, crawled over and helped me undress. She crouched on top of me. 'This is for France,' I said. 'No, Doug, it's for us. Something to tell your children.' She came down on me. For a moment I lay back and watched, then she said, 'Remember my name, Doug, remember what it means. Do all the things now that you might not do again.' She got off me, and got on her knees and elbows. I knelt behind, found a good position and spat into my hand. I transferred the slippery wet to my cock (the cock I was lucky to still have) and said, 'This is for you, Annis.'

The sigh she gave sounded helpless, it sounded painfully grateful. The sigh I gave sounded angry, sounded furious, the sigh I gave as the door opened sounded my disappointment.

'Jesus!' I said through the powerful and taut expression on my face. 'Jesus! What the fuck do you want?'

Annis and I sank together, gradually parting. 'Who the fuck is this?' she asked, pulling the duvet over us.

'Edmund Spritzer, my psychotherapist, my *ex*-psychotherapist.' He closed the door, it found its place in the airflow. 'Can you come back in half an hour? I'm in the middle of something,' I said.

'I can't leave, Doug. I just can't.'

'*Why not?*'

'I just can't.'

'You *can* leave if you want, Mr Spritzer,' said Annis.

'I can't leave. I can't.'

'You can. Doug isn't ill any more.'

'No. No I'm not ill,' I said. 'I never was, was I, Spritz? Why did you do it?'

'Do what?' he asked.

'*It*. Everything, the novel. Why?'

'Lucy told you?'

'She did. Sounds like I'm lucky to still have a cock.' He was shuffling round the room, knees bent. He moved carefully, as though protecting an injury. 'What's fucking wrong with you? You look terrible. Was it Lucy?'

'No,' he said. 'Boys will be boys.'

'Yeah, especially your kind of boys. How many?'

'Five.'

'OK, you can stay for a couple of minutes. You better sit down.'

'I don't think I can,' he said.

I heard the door open again.

'ANNIS!' said Andy.

'EDMUND!' said Lucy.

'Oh fuck!' said Annis.

'Jesus!' said I.

'*How long has this been going on*?' Andy asked us.

'*Andy*,' said Lucy. 'This is him. This is Dr Spritzer. Where's the knife? CUT HIM!'

'Sorry,' Annis said.

'Sorry,' I said.

'Sorry,' Spritz said.

'Who's she?' Annis asked, pointing at Lucy.

'No one,' Andy answered.

'No one?' said Lucy.

'That's Lucy,' I said.

'I'm going to cut Edmund's cock off,' said Lucy. 'Andy, hold him down.'

'I can't believe you, Annis. Fucking Doug, he's my best mate.'

'It doesn't matter,' I said, 'she's going to France.'

Lucy had pushed the frail Spritz into a chair and was pulling at his crotch.

Andy came over to the bed, shouted, 'France!' then pulled one of Annis's feet. 'Why did you do it, Doug?' Annis slid off the bed. 'If you're going to France then so am I, Annis.'

'Annis? Are you OK?' I asked as she bounced on the floor and the duvet finally ripped in two.

'He won't hurt me.'

'You bastard!' screamed Lucy. She slapped Spritz hard. 'You deserve this.' She aimed the knife at his opened zipper.

This time I didn't hear the door open; I saw it open. The two policemen walked in. Shooter and Moustache stood on the mat. Moustache said, 'We had a report that you'd been burgled again, Mr Down. But it appears that you're having an orgy. Maybe we should come back.'

'Shit!' said Shooter. 'The girl's got a knife.' He pulled out a gun.

Twelve

HIGH SUMMER

There is a coat of arms hanging in the Shoe Shop. The lion wears shoes in the lower half, and in the top half laces are bowed impossibly. There's a Latin inscription under the shield. It says, *Qualitas Qualitas Qualitas*.

'Tea?' asked Jenny, the plump sales girl. She doesn't ask how I like it. She doesn't need to. She knows. Every morning she brings me my horoscope mug of tea, Sagittarius: I'm described as feisty, ambitious, unlucky in love. She places the mug on the bedside table, then tells me she loves me and goes to make my breakfast. After I tell her what she wants to hear, she drives me to work in her big golden Fiat.

Some weeks ago, on my first day, I told her that I used to have a Fiat. She asked what kind. I told her I'd prefer not to talk about it. When pressed I lied to her: I told her it had been stolen. Then I told her another lie: I told her I liked big women. I told her she was perfect for me. She said I had a way with words. She admired the way I just came out with what I thought. Honesty was very attractive in a man. She hated liars, she hated men who told her that she was thin, she knew it was a lie, why did they bother? Yeah, me too, I said, eye to eye, I hate liars, they make me sick. Hey, Jenny, I know I've just met you but I feel as though I've known you for years, it's an amazing feeling. I'm so lucky. You and me, we should get together. How about a drink? With you, Doug, it's like looking in a mirror, I already know the reflection, but every day, if I look hard enough, I find something new. I'd love to go out for a drink.

'Tea?' asked Jenny again. I pulled the shoehorn from Mrs Matalawn's prospective shoe, her foot-flab dripped over the sides of the leather. 'I think they're you, Mrs Matalawn. Try walking . . . Yes please, Jenny.'

Mrs Matalawn had been my first customer, my first shoe-challenge. Clearly well known by the lively Colin Rumble, he had greeted her with: 'Mrs Matalawn! How good of you to visit the Shoe Shop! This is Doug! He's new! It's his first day! God bless him! He'll talk to you about quality. Remember the Quality Concept, Doug?'

'Quality,' I said.

'Quality Quality Quality!' enthused Rumble. 'Do your stuff, Doug!'

Mrs Matalawn had taken me under her proverbial wing after that: the great pillow of flesh hanging under her armpit. The flesh colour was now seasonally unbalanced, it was confused. Mrs Matalawn had shown her body to the sun and hoped it would go brown. The sun had decided against this and opted for a mottled red instead. So red it was, and sweating on her nearly symmetrical body that first morning. 'I know all about quality, Mr Rumble,' she had said. 'I tell all my friends about the *quality*. I tell them that when it comes to quality, "The Shoe Shop really kicks ass!" '

'*Arse*,' said Rumble. 'The Shoe Shop really kicks *arse*! This is England, Mrs Matalawn, we're not Americans quite yet!'

'Oh, Mr Rumble,' she said with her deep alto voice. 'You're such a funny man.'

'ARSE,' replied Rumble as he returned to his office.

Turning to me, she said, 'I expect you would like to be like Mr Rumble one day.'

'Yes, I would,' I lied awfully. 'Now what did you have in mind? What can we get for those fabulous feet of yours?'

'Ooh, you're learning already.' I thanked her and listened to her dreadful choice.

Today Mrs Matalawn had entered the Shoe Shop to the customary applause that our regulars receive and announced her intention: the purchase of high heels that must be of exceptional quality and astronomical price. She hinted that she was to be a guest at an exclusive function. She regretted that she could not tell us any more than that – though, of course, she did, and advised us to keep an eye on the television, where we would be sure to catch a glimpse of her in the next few days . . . Top-heavy Mrs Matalawn had bowed legs, they looked like cabriole legs belonging to a huge chest of drawers. She tottered around the shop and came back to rest. 'I think blue would be more me. Did someone mention tea?'

'Jenny, Mrs Matalawn would like a cup of tea. How do you take your tea, Mrs Matalawn?'

My first date with Jenny had been a great success. We both agreed about its success. We agreed that we should do it again. Over coffee in her house, after I had finished all her brandy, she said, 'This evening was a great success, we should do it again.'

'It's not over yet, is it?' I drunkenly asked.

'Speak your mind, Doug. You're an honest person. How should we proceed from here?'

I didn't lie, I told her of my emblazoned lust. I told her what I had in mind. 'Now let me be honest with you, Doug. Here's what *I* want to do.' The myth was true: fat girls and beautiful girls, the best in bed. 'Jenny,' I said. 'Where did you get your name from?'

'From my parents.'

'Have you heard of a Spinning Jenny?'

'No, I don't think I have.'

'I'll show you.'

'*How many* spoons, Mrs Matalawn?'

Mrs Matalawn repeated the large denomination.

'I don't think we've got enough sugar.'

'There's another bag in the cupboard,' I told Jenny.

The morning after our date Jenny asked me if I would like to move in. I could pay her a half, she said, no, a third of the rent, I needed the money. 'Doug, I know it seems a little forward but it would make me happy. Come and live with me. Would you like to? Tell me the truth.'

I told her yes, and I told her no.

'What do you mean, "Yes and no"?'

'Yes, I would like to move in. No, because you might not feel the same way about me. You might think you know me really well. But I'm more besides.'

'Doug,' she said, 'I can read you like a book. You're scared. Move in and I'll look after you.'

'OK. Tonight we can go home via my flat and pick up my box. I'll move in. You can look after me.'

'Do you take milk, Mrs Matalawn?'

'I prefer cream.'

'Top of the milk, do you?'

'If it's all you've got.'

Jenny and I left the shop together that night. Colin Rumble asked Jenny why she appeared so happy. She explained her new-found love with some concern. Rumble said, 'It's a free world, by heavens! You two get shacked up together! I'm a liberal!' In the big golden Fiat we travelled into the blinding eye of the low golden sun. In my flat, Jenny said, 'You've been burgled! The door's open and there's nothing here.' 'This is how I live,' I told her. 'Oh you poor thing, you *poor, poor* thing. How could this have happened to you? What did you do to deserve it?' I thought about telling her the truth: crime and government had got together and planned the whole thing. Instead I lied. I told her that the girl I had been living with had taken everything. One day I'd come back to this. I'd come back to nothing. 'Doug, I promise that won't happen with us. I'm going to be there for you when you need me.' I thanked her for her support. 'By the way,' she said, 'who painted this flat? The colours are extremely bright. You, or *her*?'

'Her,' I said. 'She was an art student.'

'And *this* is all she left you with!' She carried the box away. 'An art student!'

The bailiffs came round a week after the threatening letter – before I'd had a chance to move out. The door was open, unlocked, smashed – Old Boy still out of action and hustled into the arms of real old age. 'We've come to collect on you, Mr Down. Either you give us the cash now or we take your belongings.' 'Take what you like, there's nothing of value.'

'That could cause you a problem, Mr Down.' 'No it won't. It's your problem.' So they went ahead. Filled two boxes and then found some paperwork which belonged to the little brown Fiat (maximum speed now in single figures). 'Oi, Cunt,' said one to Cunt. 'Mr Down's got a car. I think we'll have that.' 'Good result,' said Cunt. 'Now let's get a move on. Load the shit in the van. I wanna get out of here. Mr Down's idea of interior decorating ain't my cup of tea. I'm having trouble focusing.' 'Yeah, this place is fucking foul. Cunts wouldn't live here.'

'Now that *is* better,' agreed Mrs Matalawn. 'These blue ones are definitely me. I'm sure that the cameraman will want to film them. Isn't that a thought! These shoes will be seen on *television,* by *millions* of people!' We squeezed her into the shoes, the fat folded over again, she scuffed around the shop. Jenny brought her tea over, 'Here's your tea, Mrs Matalawn. It might need another stir. Call me if it does.'

Jenny gave me a large drawer in her wardrobe. Moving in, unpacking my life, took less than a minute. My belongings barely covered the newspaper that lined the drawer's base. There was a big soft bed in the room. It was very big and very soft. Moving across it through her collection of cuddly toys was like trying to run through deep water. The bed was also pink – very pink. And the walls: every single wall and ceiling in the entire house was magnolia. The painters who specialized in magnolia had sealed the house, poured magnolia paint down the chimney, allowed it to soak in and then drained it all out through the low letter box. I suggested a change, but she told me that magnolia was safe – with magnolia she knew where she was. Even peach, she insisted, was dangerous. Peach had some form, peach could clash. Magnolia was staying. Magnolia was neutral.

The next morning Jenny rolled over to me and said, 'Who's *Annus*? You were talking about her in your dreams.' 'Ann*is*,' I said. 'A French girl.' . . . Annis had dropped a note into my flat. It said we could finish what we'd started. *Meet me at the GoodBye*. At the arranged time I walked into the bar. The tall girl with big eyes wasn't there. But Sam came over, flashed her great false teeth at me, and said, 'Your girlfriend says "Sorry." ' She gave me a note. It said: *Sorry, Doug. Gone to France. Early flight. Give Andrew my love if you see him. Yours ever, love Annis*. I asked Sam if there was any chance of, of you know, Me and You. She said sorry too: 'Sorry, Doug, you had your chance but you blew it. Oh, and by the way, you're barred.' 'Why?' Apparently I had got into some toilet-confusion, apparently I urinated behind the bar. Apparently I pissed into a pint glass and then tried selling it as lager. Apparently the bouncers had called me Soldier and hoisted me on to the street. 'You were harmless,' she said, 'but you still blew it.' . . . To Jenny I said: 'Annis is a French girl I met down at the social security offices – take no notice of what I say in my dreams – I'd never do *that* to a girl, besides Annis is probably a virgin. She wouldn't let me.' 'I would,' said Jenny. 'If you're gentle. What's the time? Have we got time?'

'*More* sugar, Mrs Matalawn?'

'Two or three should do it.'

'There's no doubt about it, Mrs Matalawn, these shoes are you. I think it's the heel that does it. It really says something. Something about *you*, Mrs Matalawn. Something sophisticated.'

With a cup of tea now boosted to near-saturation point – indeed, any *more* sugar and the tea was in danger of starting to crystallize – Mrs Matalawn was ready to talk. She drank the tea in one sickly gulp, then began. The first five minutes (one sentence, without breath or rhetorical pause) was the quickest. Another fifteen and the pace had slowed, but still no pause, or, apparently, inhalation. After half an hour she was beginning to show signs of oxygen starvation. And then, having turned blue and closing in on the forty-five minutes, without a full stop, or even a comma, she halted and started to breathe in again.

Jenny nudged me and I said, 'That will be one hundred and fifty-nine pounds please, Mrs Matalawn. How would you like to pay?'

'Customer credit please.'

I dabbed the details into the computer, it rolled off a chitty from its endless toilet roll. 'Sign here please.'

'Will you do my foot massage today, Doug?'

'You know I'm not qualified. Paul's the one with the magic hands.' These are the kind of phrases I have to use: fabulous feet, magic hands, superb structure, brilliant bones . . . Mrs Matalawn took Paul's arm and was led away.

Jenny told me that I was very patient.

This was when I realized three important points: I realized that I was, yes, very patient. I realized that I was *working in a shoe shop*. And more importantly, I realized that I desperately needed to go out and get very drunk.

Thirteen

Despite today being my day off, Jenny still woke me up and introduced me to another hangover. I'm getting used to them again now, but I still find myself wondering how my own body can really make me feel so incredibly, so *unbelievably,* bad. It keeps on surprising me, no matter how many times it happens.

'How are we feeling today?' she asked.

'Uh, you know.'

'Well, that's the trouble: I *don't* know.' It's true – she really *doesn't* know. I cannot see this relationship surviving if she carries on like this. I'm always trying to persuade her to get drunk – and she nearly always refuses. Unfortunately even when she agrees and goes right ahead and knocks back a few large liqueurs, she still gets away without a hangover – she just seems immune to them. I mean, can't she find it in herself to conjure up a small one? Even a *sympathetic* hangover would cheer me up. 'I've been watching the news, Dougie.'

'Doug!'

'Sorry – Doug. That girl, Lucy Smith, is being sent to prison. You know the one? She tried cutting her doctor's penis off. Look. There's a photo of her here. Pretty, isn't she? I wonder what made her do it.'

'Who knows. Maybe her doctor tried abusing her.'

'I doubt that very much. The doctor looks so sweet. I've heard that he's written a book about it. A novel, I think. I'll buy it for you this Christmas. You really ought to read more, Doug. You can learn a lot from books. Maybe you'd stop drinking so much if you read a book now and again. In fact, why *don't* you stop drinking? You'd feel so much better.'

'I've tried not drinking,' I said truthfully. 'It doesn't help. It causes me all kinds of problems.'

'If you say so. Meet me for lunch.'

She forced me to agree to this, and then allowed me to go back to sleep.

At noon I made another unsuccessful attempt to get into the GoodBye. I ventured into summer. The high sudorific sun was burning everything it could lay its hands on. Trees and shrubs were bursting into flames with intense regularity. The grass that had been black never went green; in a curious twist it had gone from black to brown and now burnt quickly. There were charcoal patches all over London where fire had been. In the heat, crisp packets melted on the hob-heat of the road, children had less than a minute to finish their ice lollies before the sun did, and no one bought chocolate any more.

There was a whole colour chart to describe the endless flesh that walked the streets. Some people, impossibly white, hurriedly passed through any shade they could find, from one dark shop to another and into the white of the subways. Others, men and women, strolled around almost naked. Some men were wearing string that followed their arse-cleft and held a material prow in front, exposing their buttocks as dark leather rugby balls. And the women – what if this never happens again? – bronzed profiles sectioned by thin strips here and there, the sun succeeded in bringing eroticism to every curve and crevice. It was like living in a mechanic's wall calender. Every creed, culture, race, nationality was tanning. Sean, an old friend of mine, bumped into me on the hot streets when he almost cycled over me with his lightweight machine. 'Soz, Duck,' he said in his Midland accent. 'Oi, it's Doug!' He showed me his tan: pulling a sleeve up on his cycling shorts, he revealed where the sun had not been – this hidden skin was almost white. And Sean was black. Tanning had become a national hobby. It was now something that men and women took equally seriously as they applied their factor-cream.

That day the GoodBye had white plastic tables and chairs outside and, in common with air above the square, they shimmered in the heat. Andy was there with a girl I didn't know, I hadn't seen him for months. I waved and tried going inside for a drink, but one of the bouncers – with a fresh knife-wound angrily lining his face – put his body in the doorway and refused me entry into the dark and recycled inner air. Andy called me over. The girl looked away, flung her head back, the sun began its cosmetics. He asked if I'd heard from Annis. No. And neither had he.

'How's the comedy?' I inquired.

'More refined, still crude, funnier. People seem to enjoy it . . . I hear you're working in a branch of the Shoe Shop?'

'Yeah, I'm happy to be in shoes. I'm living with one of the sales girls – Jenny. Good luck with the comedy, I'll see you around.'

'Come down the Grin Club next Friday, 'bout nine. And bring this Jenny girl.'

'I can't bring her,' I said, 'she doesn't know about any of

this. But I'll try and make it though. Goodbye—' I gestured at the girl in the sun.

'Sandy.'

'Goodbye, Sandy.' Sandy's a nice-looking girl. I think I will go to the Grin Club – a replacement comedy venue after the Miser had finally fallen down.

Like lovers we had made a lover's pact. Some time apart we agreed, then we'll go back to being friends. But Andy and I weren't lovers, so it didn't work out. Outside the GoodBye was the first time I'd seen him since the week in which he had fled past Shooter and Moustache and left the flat. A drug-rush made him rush out. He rushed out because he had a large stash in his pocket and didn't want the police nicking it off him again. But they were more interested in the cold blade sticking into the crotch of Dr Spritzer. Lucy was holding the knife and, quite stylishly I thought, said, 'This is an evil man. He does not deserve a penis.'

'Shoot her!' said Moustache. 'Shoot her, Shooter!' But Shooter raised his gun and shot at the ceiling. Dusty red plaster showered over us and I think I heard a muffled groan upstairs. Lucy released the knife and relaxed. Moustache wrenched her arms up her behind back and frogmarched her away.

Stunned, the pale Spritz sat very still in the chair, the hilt of the knife jutting from his flies. 'Oh, Jesus fuck. Oh, *help help help*,' he cried. Shooter pulled the knife out and proudly holstered his gun (apparently he had it on trial). Impatiently, and still shaking with excitement (he kept staring at the hole in the ceiling), he noted the details of the old hippie's van – my mean burglar. He told me that a conviction was unlikely. He told me that I should try to get the registration next time. Then he got his gun out again and went off to assist Moustache with a now screaming Lucy.

There was no blood on the knife and, realizing this, Spritz started sobbing. Then he stood up and vigorously rubbed his genitals to make absolutely sure that they were all there.

'What a vile and disgusting man!' said Annis as she dressed. 'Can't he do that in private?'

'Sorry about him, Annis. But he's completely fucked up.'

'God!' she said. 'I hope this sort of thing doesn't happen in *France*. Goodbye, Doug.'

Spritz is on his second novel now. The publishers were persuaded to publish his first. His agent admired the way it seemed so real. A real story, he said, a real story that will appeal to the real reader – whatever a 'real' reader is. Knocked down to three hundred pages, over one hundred thousand words, his story encompassed the real events.

After realizing that he still had a cock, Spritz went straight out and started planning his terrible suicide. Terribly meticulously and terribly calmly, but terribly *badly*, he worked out a way to kill himself (it's all in his book, clearly autobiographical, but set in America as you would expect. It's called *The Sole Doctor* and will be published in time for Christmas). He loaded himself up with pills and drink and jumped off a bridge. He hoped to drown. Terribly he had marked the spot during the day and when he came back in the short span of night there was no tide. Off he jumped and landed in a sewage outlet whose pipe knocked him unconscious; he sank into the silt and shit. When he woke up he assumed he had successfully killed himself, but felt sure that he was now in *hell*. Everything was black, the shit had dried and covered his face. He said it smelt and tasted like hell. Well, if this is hell, he thought, I might as well try and make the best of it. So blind, and with a condom hanging over his bruised ear, he began exploring hell. In hell he discovered that it was very difficult to walk, there was no concrete or grass, just this deep sticky stuff, hell was the worst-smelling place he had ever tried to imagine. He decided that hell was a shithole. He regretted all the bad things he'd done when he was alive, he even started praying. He wanted to cry but his mouth wouldn't work in hell. In hell he fell. In hell he was attacked by flailing arms and kicking legs. In his hell he had tripped into a boat and landed on two gays doing their gay riverside-thing. Initially they beat him up, then they stopped: he smelt so badly of shit. Kindness then persuaded them to help him out, they guided him to the water, splashed it over him until he could see. When his vision returned he tried kissing them both, but he still stank so they didn't let him. Spritz describes meeting them as very romantic. He sees the younger one on regular basis now.

He put it all in his novel. His story is my story. I'm his Simon Sole, manipulated by his psychotherapist – who lost his heterosexual bias and, like Spritz, 'became' bisexual. Lucia de Londres, or Lucy, is there providing the retribution factor. Simon Sole sleeps with his best mate's girlfriend. Spritz put this in to provide the love interest – this is to keep the plot ticking over when the action is, as he describes in 'literary terms', on the 'back burner'. A slight exaggeration is in the novel though: the doctor's (now massive) penis gets completely severed at the base and the American surgeons sew it back on in their most successful penis-rebuild to date.

As he had said to me in the cold of late winter, 'The best novels reflect real life. I hope mine will be one of the best!' Spritz has turned my life into fiction. Or fiction gave me a real life.

★ ★ ★

Here she comes. Here comes Jenny in her summerweight clothes – loose white T-shirt, flapping shorts and sandals (from the Shoe Shop). Now, I've got to say – and don't think me unkind – that she is looking a little fatter, no, *plumper*, these days. I might be wrong about this though, and I'll freely admit it if I am. Maybe it's just that everyone else is losing weight. I don't know. However, she does seem a little out of breath, but perhaps that's the weather and the way that the sun has made the air virtually unbreathable by heating it into the boiling caustic gas that now circles the planet.

'Stand up and close your eyes,' she said. 'I've bought you a present.'

I stepped forward and stood on the pavement.

'Come on, shut your eyes . . . Right. Hold your arms out . . . Ready?'

I nodded. She placed something across my arms and I almost collapsed and dropped it to the floor. 'Christ! What the fuck's in here? A breeze block?'

'Open it.'

With the object still on the pavement (it proved impossible to lift), I removed the carrier bag and stared at it.

'Do you like it?'

'I don't know. What is it?'

'It's a book. Come on, pick it up.'

After a couple of attempts, and a dislocated fingernail, I had it in my arms. Fuck, no wonder she looked out of breath, this was the kind of thing they used to anchor aircraft carriers with. 'What am I supposed to do with it?'

'Read it.'

'Be serious, Jenny. It must be more than two thousand pages long.'

'It's only a *novel*.'

'I don't care what kind of book it is. If I can't even lift it, I don't see how I'm supposed to be able to read it.'

'I'll put it on a lectern for you. Come on, Doug. At least *try* to look pleased.'

I didn't see the van. I didn't hear the van. I *smelt* the van. Suddenly there was diesel and patchouli in the air. I looked round. The old hippie in the old gas van pulled up beside us. He wound his window down and poked his head through the smoke.

'I've been looking for you, Mr Down. Where've you been all this time? I need another one of your TVs, but you've gone and moved out of your flat, like the cunt that you are.'

'Don't speak to my Dougie like that!'

'Dougie?' said the hippie. 'Now that *is* a nice name. But I think I prefer Cunt.'

'Fuck off!' shouted Jenny.

'Ah, rest it, chops. I only want Dougie's TV.'

'I'll give you *chops*, Mr Hippie! Doug! Give me your present.' Jenny snatched the book from me, lifted it up high above her, allowed it to balance in one hand, pulled the hand behind her head and screamed.

Then she threw the book at him.

The old hippie fell sideways and on to the gear lever. The van started rolling forward, slowly at first. Then it accelerated down the street with its diesel roar and gearbox whine.

Through the exhaust smoke you could just make out the brake lights as the old gas van entered the busy intersection at an astonishing speed . . . And then the van couldn't stop. It had too much momentum – a product of its high velocity and the mass of that 2,000-page novel in there that had dented the hippie's head. It couldn't stop until the bulk of an obese beer truck halted it with massive deceleration.

But the old hippie didn't stop; he went on – through laminated glass and contaminated air. He went on and hit London blacktop with its scorched rubber, its fuel and oil loss, and its human-stained farewells. He met London blacktop and its many sad farewells.

A selection of quality fiction from Headline

THE POSSESSION OF DELIA SUTHERLAND	Barbara Neil	£5.99	☐
MANROOT	A N Steinberg	£5.99	☐
CARRY ME LIKE WATER	Benjamin Alire Sáenz	£6.99	☐
KEEPING UP WITH MAGDA	Isla Dewar	£5.99	☐
AN IMPERFECT MARRIAGE	Tim Waterstone	£5.99	☐
NEVER FAR FROM NOWHERE	Andrea Levy	£5.99	☐
SEASON OF INNOCENTS	Carolyn Haines	£5.99	☐
OTHER WOMEN	Margaret Bacon	£5.99	☐
THE JOURNEY IN	Joss Kingsnorth	£5.99	☐
FIFTY WAYS OF SAYING FABULOUS	Graeme Aitken	£5.99	☐

All Headline books are available at your local bookshop or newsagent, or can be ordered direct from the publisher. Just tick the titles you want and fill in the form below. Prices and availability subject to change without notice.

Headline Book Publishing, Cash Sales Department, Bookpoint, 39 Milton Park, Abingdon, OXON, OX14 4TD, UK. If you have a credit card you may order by telephone – 01235 400400.

Please enclose a cheque or postal order made payable to Bookpoint Ltd to the value of the cover price and allow the following for postage and packing:

UK & BFPO: £1.00 for the first book, 50p for the second book and 30p for each additional book ordered up to a maximum charge of £3.00.

OVERSEAS & EIRE: £2.00 for the first book, £1.00 for the second book and 50p for each additional book.

Name ....

Address ....

....

....

If you would prefer to pay by credit card, please complete:
Please debit my Visa/Access/Diner's Card/American Express (delete as applicable) card no:

Signature .... Expiry Date ....